D1521111

CHEAT RIVER THREE

SCOTT BAKER SWEENEY

Cover Illustration by Kelly Barrow

AuthorHouse™
1663 Liberty Drive
Bloomington, IN 47403
www.authorhouse.com
Phone: 1-800-839-8640

Published by AuthorHouse 2/6/2012

ISBN: 978-1-4685-4388-9 (e)
ISBN: 978-1-4685-4390-2 (hc)
ISBN: 978-1-4685-4389-6 (sc)

Library of Congress Control Number: 2012901055

Notes from the author -
Even though many of the adventures in this novel were based on actual events from my father's infamous youth, all the names of the main characters appearing in this book are fictional. Mentioning of public figures was done with the highest respect and may or may not coincide with the actual event. Any resemblance to real persons, living or deceased or past historical events may be purely coincidental.

CHAPTER 1

The morning sunlight flickered through the leaves of trees creating a natural kaleidoscope. It was enhanced ever so slightly by the southern Pennsylvanian breeze moving the porous canopies of green; just enough to provide access for the solar rays to meet the ground below. The beauty of this spring morning was not to be upstaged by the symphonic sounds of chirping birds, along with the muffled roar of the Monongahela River as it introduced itself to the mouth of the Cheat River.

Sunday morning, "the day of rest," was the only day of the week in which the sounds of nature were not squelched out by the heavy, metallic noise of rail cars heaped with coal grinding and clanging their hitches or the roar of the beehive coke ovens in the side of the Cheat Mountain. Yes, it was a peaceful, tranquil morning, indeed. Free of all artificial manmade noise pollution trespassing on one's senses. Well, not completely. This particular Sunday morning shutdown of the coal and coke operations was no different than many of the Sunday mornings that preceded it, but for one exception. If you listened closely, there was still one manmade noise disturbing this wooded high ground overlooking the river valley. For six consecutive mornings a peculiar noise of scraping—a sound of metal carving earth to be more exact—came filtering through the trees.

Near a tall spruce was the source of this grating noise: a young boy diligently churning up dirt with a silver serving spoon, which he had secretly commandeered from his mother's silver chest. Surrounding the boy as far out as perhaps thirty feet or so, was the evidence of his past excavations. There were piles of dirt twelve to fifteen inches high, and accompanying the piles were the numerous holes in which the same earth had originated. It looked as if a convention of gophers had just adjourned from a busy week of work.

The lad's freshly ironed white shirt was quickly becoming soiled, even before the church bell of the Point Marion Methodist Church had a chance to warn its parishioners of the start of Sunday school. Church, however, was the last thing on the boy's mind. A few weeks earlier, he had learned of an historical fact about the region in which he lived that would change the boy's daily routine.

Monongahela Indians, commonly known as "mound dwellers," had once inhabited the western and southern region of Pennsylvania. These particular tribes were believed to be the earliest inhabitants of the area. They migrated from Asia across a long, theoretical land bridge from Siberia to Alaska. How they arrived to Pennsylvania from Alaska, or even why they were drawn so far from their home in Asia to this inconvenient destination is still a mystery. More mysterious than their arrival was their departure. After enduring years of inherent dangers—nature, starvation, and the extreme weather conditions that accompanied a brutal journey of thousands of miles—the Monongahela tribe seemed to have vanished overnight in the early sixteen hundreds.

Leaving little evidence in the pages of our history books, this less-than-flamboyant people's only clue to their existence was the humble remains of the burial mounds they constructed.

The chronicle of the Monongahela tribe is based on years of scientific archeological studies by several universities, but this particular version of historical facts was absent some very important details of greater significance. That is, at least in the mind of this ten year old boy. *His* version came from more impressive authorities than mere doctors of science at local universities: the wisdom and knowledge of the "locals"—well, at least the local boys.

The year was 1946; the "local boys" were the rough and rowdy gang of males ranging in age from nine to twelve years. They were friends to the apprentice archeologist digging solo in the woods.

Who generated the local tale no one knows, but for years, it had been the most popular version for the youngsters in the town of Point Marion. Their account of the Mound Dwellers, based on pure myth, differed in the fact that the Monongahela's did not originate from Asia, but rather from South America. They were actually a group of several Inca tribesmen who stole tons of gold from the Incan empire, and then defected with their spoils to Pennsylvania, where they eventually buried their treasure, hidden safely under the mounds of earth. This tale was absolutely nonsensical, but to the enthusiastic minds of young boys, this tale bore plenty of plausibility.

There was gold to be had, and this morning was the morning this young treasure hunter was going to strike the "mother lode." Well, that's at least what he kept telling himself as he started clearing away the debris of old pine needles and decaying leaves to start a fresh excavation.

So this morn, the woods on the outskirts of Point Marion would have to share the sounds of nature with the grating noise of a silver serving spoon carving scopes of dirt and gravel. Suddenly another sound reverberated sonorously amongst the harmonious birds, river rapids, and of course, "silver spoon." A distant, faint, soprano sound; a voice sternly calling, "Eugene, Eugene," came searching through the trees seeking out its intended target. The method of the repetitive sounds was somewhat similar to a bell on an ocean buoy, used effectively when visual senses were impaired by the dark of night or thick shroud of fog—or in this case, a wooded forest. The constant clanging noise alerted ships or sailing vessels to the approaching land or jagged rocks. The warning in this case was not from a buoy, but from a mother, and it was not intended for sailors in peril, but rather to alert her to the location of her delinquent offspring and to summon him home immediately.

The boy had to be conscious of his mother's calling; however he kept to his business unfazed. He, in fact, increased the haste of his work. Faster and faster he dug, beads of sweat forming just under his hair line, then running down his forehead into his eyes.

The sting of a salty droplet meeting his eye broke his momentum just long enough for a quick swipe from his white shirt sleeve, and then activities were underway again.

"Eugene, Eugene!" His mother's vocal tone sounded slightly closer and more urgent with each announcement. The boy dug faster and faster.

Suddenly, without warning, the boy felt a hand grip the back of his shoulder, grasping a fistful of his cotton shirt. This dramatic intrusion incited a startled reaction from the young man, causing him to gasp as he arose to his feet, hurling the silver spoon several feet. The momentum did free the boy from his captor and allowed him to spin around to meet his unexpected guest. Surprisingly, it wasn't his mother.

A tall, skinny boy in his early teens stood before him, wearing a similar Sunday morning uniform consisting of a white cotton shirt and khaki pants. "It's time for church!" he said. The younger sibling stood in shock, a few feet away.

"You scared the hell out of me!" barked the young boy.

"Why didn't you answer Mother?" The tall brother retorted. He was not empathetic to his startled younger kin, not in the least. He stood smugly gazing over his brother's excavating accomplishments, thinking to himself what a foolish waste of time and energy. Then the elder brother remembered that his mission was only halfway completed. Find Eugene and deliver him home immediately was the direct order given by his mother, who was pacing the front porch of their company-built duplex house holding his baby sister in one arm.

"Come on, if we miss church you will be in big trouble." Begrudgingly, Eugene followed his brother out of the woods and towards home. The elder took satisfaction in the fact that his frequently in trouble brother was once again likely to receive punishment from not only his mother but also his father for disobeying an ongoing rule of wandering away and getting dirty before church.

The Briggs were not unlike most other families of Point Marion, or for that matter any other small coal community in Pennsylvania or West Virginia. The coal industry had been a part of their family's heritage since their ancestors' arrival from Germany in the late seventeen hundreds. They were hard working, conservative country folk. The world to them was only as large as their education. They were also survivors. This community suffered through the "Redneck Wars" over two decades earlier; next to the Civil War, this was the bloodiest time in history for Pennsylvania and West Virginia. Gun battles and assassinations between the union thugs trying to organize the local non-union mines—and the hired guns of the owners of the mines—left many children fatherless and wives widowed. More good men were lost by bullets than by actual mine-related accidents during this period of time. Life indeed was tough and so were they; excitement, adventure, or even mere relaxation, were not words familiar to their vocabulary.

Eugene Briggs was the exception. From his first steps as a toddler, it was apparent that he was not content with being the normal conformist. Eugene was the middle child; he had two siblings, Delbert, the elder and the baby, Mary Lou.

Eugene's mother, Ertta, handed Mary Lou off to Delbert like a quarterback handing off on a third and one to an awaiting halfback. She wheeled around and grabbed Eugene by the nape of his neck, marching him into the house. In the kitchen, she quickly wiped off his soiled shirt with a washcloth while her rebellious offspring washed off his hands and face under the flowing spigot. Ertta was used to this little setback, for it seemed to never fail that whenever the family had to be somewhere, and especially when her husband was out of town, Eugene would always come up missing. Then, when he was eventually recovered, he always needed some quick repair work before presenting him to the public.

Pacing back and forth outside, only stopping occasionally to kick a clod of dirt, Delbert and baby sis waited patiently for mother and brother to reappear. Ertta was a quiet lady of very few words, but when it was time to express herself or make her views known she had no problem articulating her point.

Suddenly, the screen door flew open. Out marched Mother with Eugene in tow.

"Come on, we're late! Thanks again to your brother!" Delbert nodded at his mother's response, then handed back his sister, and they were off. The church was only about a half mile away; still, they provided their normal grandiose entrance while the congregation was well into the first hymn. Settled in, Eugene began surveying the room for his mate, or should I say his usual partner in crime, James "Jimmy" Wilson. There he was two rows back and to the right. Of course, Jimmy knew exactly where the Briggs were sitting, watching them pass his pew only moments earlier. Jimmy was waiting for Eugene's eyes to make contact with his, and as soon as they did, both simultaneously gave an acknowledging partial grin and nod.

Mr. Briggs seldom accompanied his family to church, unless it was Easter or Christmas. This time he had a valid excuse. Fred was away on business in Pittsburg. He was taking an exam for a supervisory position from his employer, Sun Devil Coal & Coke Works. Fred was one of four brothers who were all employed by the local coal mining and coke company, which also had employed Fred's father, grandfather, cousins, and 85 percent of Point Marion and the surrounding county.

The minister's sermon was a blur to Eugene. His mind was still back at his archeological dig, along with the silver spoon he had tossed when his brother greeted him from behind. One of the things about Eugene was that he was stubborn. Very stubborn! Even though his excavations so far had been a complete waste of effort and had not yielded as much as a chicken bone let alone an artifact, he was now ready to ratchet it up, move into overdrive, and send his operations to the next level. He was going to strike it rich, at least that was what he kept telling himself. He had been thinking long and hard about this (well, at least through the Sunday morning sermon). He needed a partner. Someone he could trust. So at that moment, he made up his mind that there was no other choice but to commandeer Jimmy.

So what if he had to split the loot? There had to be more than enough for the both of them.

CHAPTER 2

Point Marion was a company town. Half of the townsfolk were employed by the local coal mine and coke producing company, Sun Devil. The company compensated their employees by building their homes and paying them with vouchers that they could exchange for food and other sundries at the town's grocery and small goods store, which was also owned by Sun Devil.

Obviously, this employer/employee relationship worked out well for the owner, creating an environment eerily similar to colonialism. For the men and their families, the system basically meant they were indentured servants. The fear that they would lose their jobs, which meant losing their homes, kept them totally committed to Sun Devil. This fear was about to become reality—not due to lack of effort from the workers—but because of the evolution of technology. There were growing rumors amidst this community regarding the introduction of new technology that would change the way coke was currently derived from coal. Coke was the main ingredient that revolutionized the world when it was introduced to iron. This was the molten cocktail which created steel. The established beehive cooking method, which for years had been used for converting coal to coke, was becoming obsolete. This method was the lifeblood of this community, and shutting down the ovens would devastate this town. If only Eugene were paying attention to the sermon, he would have heard the pastor's attempt to soothe and calm the anxious souls.

Soothe and calm the anxious souls, indeed! Eugene's soul had no time to be calm. It was purposeful and deliberate. Just as soon—and I mean *just* as soon—as Pastor Michael Browne's closing prayer concluded, Gene took a beeline path straight toward Jimmy. Jimmy was alert to his youthful colleague's accelerated approach; he had seen that look on Eugene's face before.

It was a look that was usually the precursor of some scheme that would ultimately end with the both of them in trouble.

"This is you're lucky day, Wilson!" Eugene beamed. "Gonna let you in on a chance to become rich and famous!" Jimmy shook his head as Eugene put his arm around his friend's shoulder, slowly spinning Jimmy around and escorting him out the door of the church.

"Whatever it is, Briggs, I'm not interested."

Jimmy Wilson was fair-haired and blue-eyed and always well-groomed. His attributes afforded him above-average intelligence. He often vented dry, sharp, and quick-witted sarcasm, which was mostly unappreciated by his youthful cronies. However, Jimmy's wisdom seldom separated him from his counterparts. Always apprehensive and somewhat reluctant, he very seldom turned down an opportunity to go along with Eugene's wild adventures. For Jimmy, Eugene provided an almost constant source of entertainment and excitement in this normally uneventful community. Boredom provided a pathway for curiosity, and true entertainment was rare in Point Marian.

Waiting outside of the church until the sidewalk vacated, Eugene proceeded to explain his archeological aspirations to Jimmy. Jimmy was unimpressed.

"Briggs, you're an idiot!" Jimmy gave Eugene a momentary cold stare, as if to say, "you wasted my time to tell me this nonsense", then spun around and ran off to catch up to his family.

"You'll be sorry, Wilson!" Eugene scowled. "Creep," he muttered, before running off in the opposite direction toward his own house. Eugene could not believe that his friend and longtime cohort was not just as excited as he was at the prospect of becoming rich and famous.

Eugene could not get home fast enough. In his mind, while he ran, he was planning a quick change of clothing and a bite of lunch. Then it was back to the big dig. Passing his mother, brother, and baby sister just before turning the corner to head for the home stretch, Eugene spotted something unexpected in his driveway. Behind him rang out the announcement from his brother, "Dad's home!"

The family's cadence instantly increased, heading with purpose now toward their house, excitably anticipating the homecoming of husband and father. Across the porch and through the screen door Eugene flew, followed closely by Delbert, then Ertta with sis.

"What's up, Daddy-O?" Eugene called out as he bolted past the kitchen, heading for the stairs leading toward his room.

"Hold on there, hot shot!" Mr. Briggs command froze the ten-year-old in his tracks. Crushing out his cigarette, then taking a gulp of coffee, Eugene's father pushed back his chair from the kitchen table, stood up, and opened his arms to receive his ration of hugs and kisses.

"You are home early!" Ertta stated in an inquisitive voice as she gave her husband a peck on the cheek.

"I have got some good news to share with you, and to celebrate we're going to load up the Ford and head for Morgantown for Sunday dinner."

"What's the news?" both boys asked in unison.

Staring directly at Ertta, but talking to the boys, Fred replied, "Boys, your dad has been offered an important supervisory position. A brand new job that was created to oversee safety at all Sun Devil mine locations. Seems the government has insisted by law that all commercial mining and coke operations now in the United States have someone in charge of safety, and they felt that your father was the best man for that job. We can talk over the details once we get to the restaurant in Morgantown. I'm starved!"

Going out to eat, even to a modest restaurant, was such a rare occurrence for most coal community families, and the Briggs were no exception. This event was usually reserved for very special occasions like holidays or visits from out of town relatives.

There were few things that would change the stubborn mindset of Eugene, and continuing his digging to this point had been the only thing on his agenda. But exploring for buried treasure paled in comparison to the rare opportunity of going to a restaurant in Morgantown.

As the family found out over dinner, the employment opportunity for Fred didn't come without a hitch, however. It did mean more money for the Briggs family, but he would also have to travel a great deal.

Monday morning, Eugene awoke to the sounds of his mother preparing breakfast downstairs for his dad. Eugene wanted to get a head start on his busy day, so getting out to the dig site at the break of dawn was imperative. If only he could sneak unnoticed past his dad, he would be home free. He knew if he waited until his father left for work, his mother would immediately head upstairs for her morning ritual of reveille to wake her brood for breakfast. The potential of chores always came after that. These delays were not an option for Eugene. So the choice was clear—leave now while hopefully both mother and father were preoccupied with each other. So down the staircase Eugene crept, slowly transferring his weight from step to step to minimize the sounds of creaking, hopefully just enough to be drowned out by the frying bacon and hum of the morning news coming from the transistor radio permanently stationed on the kitchen windowsill. Like a cat, young Mr. Briggs masterfully negotiated the staircase with minimal noise, thinking to himself, "just one more rung, then the floor, and out the door." One more rung, indeed. When Eugene's shoe finally met the flat surface of the floor, followed by his one hundred pounds of ten-year-old girth, a loud *SQUEEEEK* announced his arrival.

"Where are you going young man?"

Eugene slowly turned his head to see both his mother and father staring at him from the kitchen.

"Uh, going to help Jimmy!"

"Help Jimmy with what?"

Ertta responded with a suspicious tone.

"Oh, let him go, Mother, he looks like a boy on a mission!"

Ertta gave Fred a glare before yelling to Eugene as he fired threw the screen door, "One hour! Be back in one hour, young man! You and your brother have a garden to weed!"

"Thanks, Mom and Dad! One hour it is!"

Eugene ran towards town (the direction of Jimmy's house) just long enough to make sure he wasn't being watched, then doubled back, heading toward his dig site.

The beehive ovens were roaring, and the rail cars were heaped with coal. This, along with the distant industrial horns and crashing rail car hitches, replaced the sounds of singing birds and windblown spruce bows from a day earlier. Monday morning in Point Marion once again had returned to its normal bustle.

Eugene trotted along the wooded ridge line weaving between the pines, taking the least impeded path directly to his destination. Upon arriving at a familiar landmark, he then took a ninety degree turn and darted without hesitance into the dense woods. Stumbling through the thick bramble, he arrived at his desired clearing in the woods only to be frozen in shock. With fists clinched and jaws wide open, Eugene surveyed his dig site. His claim had been compromised. Over half of the holes which he had diligently excavated for days were filled in and smoothed over.

"Who could have done this?" The lad spoke as if he were expecting the trees to reply. "The only one who knew of this secret location was Delbert, and he was with me all day yesterday. And where is my digger?" Eugene asked, looking around for his mother's silver spoon.

For the next several minutes he shuffled around the area kicking dirt and looking for his spoon. Eugene was too befuddled to start any new excavations. He just shook his head and started back for home.

Eugene spent the remainder of the day attempting to interrogate his elder brother while helping him weed the garden. Even though he was pretty certain there was no way that Delbert could have snuck out and defiled his archeological dig without him knowing, Eugene had to be sure. He had to return in the morning and look for more clues.

The next morning, unlike the; previous one, Eugene awoke to the verbal request of his mother standing from the bottom of the steps.

"Eugene, time to get up, your breakfast is getting cold!"

In the background, he heard his father's car pull away from their driveway. He jumped out of bed and with one swooping motion, he grabbed his trousers from the bed post and slid in one leg. Amazingly, while hopping across his room, he was able to push the other leg through in time to grab the rest of his ensemble:

shirt, socks, and shoes before exiting. After finishing breakfast and taking care of a few requested chores, he was on his way. As many times as Eugene had made the trip from his front door steps to his pseudo excavation site, he could navigate it blindfolded. In fact, there was probably a path grooved out of the earth from the boy's numerous devoted jaunts.

Eugene cautiously poked his head through the thick bramble and studied the landscape before allowing the rest of his boyish frame to enter the clearing. Stunned even more then by what he saw yesterday morning Eugene trumpeted,

"What's going on here?"

To his amazement the remaining holes were now completely filled in, and staring at him like a shrine was his mother's silver spoon, tied to a tree with a bow of bright red ribbon. Eugene reached up and pulled a loose strand of the bow, releasing the spoon and allowing it to fall to the ground. Bending over, he picked up the shiny silver utensil and stared at his reflection.

"It must be an Inca ghost!"

This was the start of a ritual that went on for a few days. Eugene would dig his holes, leave the spoon, and come back the next day to find his work reclaimed.

Eugene realized that this phenomenon was too big to keep to himself. He must be getting real close to uncovering the Inca treasure. That was why the Incan ghost or ghosts were becoming nervous, backfilling his holes. He must show someone this now. "Who, though?" he wondered.

"Jimmy! He thinks I've been wasting my time, but when he

sees for himself what has been happening, he will practically beg me to let him in on the action."

As can be imagined, Jimmy did not believe the story of Eugene's excavated holes. Heck, he was one of the few boys his age that thought the whole story about Inca mound dwellers was a hoax. He even laughed at Eugene for suggesting that Incan spirits that guarded the mound site were responsible for magically filling up the holes. However, to put this nonsense to rest, Jimmy did finally agree (after hours of prodding) to go with Eugene to view the crime scene, so to speak, then hide and wait for the ghost to perform his little tricks.

The reluctant young Mr. Wilson leaned against a tree watching his compatriot, the young Mr. Briggs, feverishly dig out a new spot in the corner of a larger area. It was certainly apparent to Jimmy that his friend had been spending a large amount of his time there. Most of the forest floor was covered in pine needles, decaying sticks, and logs, except in this sparsely wooded opening which measured a little over half the size of a football field. This opening, in the middle of a larger wood, was at the peak of a significant hill overlooking the beehive coke ovens and, even further, the Cheat River. All in total, about two hundred yards in elevation. The blanket of pine needles covering the floor in this area was now disturbed by 50 percent and was replaced with what now looked like a freshly backfilled grave.

Today, Eugene advanced his excavating operations to include heavy equipment (a garden spade from his father's shed). This allowed him to dig his four by four, two feet deep hole in about one third of his normal time.

After sifting through enough disturbed soil to satisfy himself that there were no artifacts, Eugene stood up, dusted off his knees, and wiped his forehead with the bottom of his undershirt.

"Alright, Jimmy, the hard part is done. Now all we do is hide and wait for the ghost."

Eugene bent over and stuck the spoon in the pile of dirt, then walked over to the tree where Jimmy stood, reached down, grabbed the ribbon from the ground, and shoved it in his pocket.

"Listen, Briggs, all this is very impressive, and you have even managed to capture my attention, but I have already missed lunch and my mom will kill me if I'm not home by six for supper."

Ignoring his friend, Eugene spotted a lone oak tree just outside of the clearing and pointed to it.

"There she blows! A fantastic lookout. We can climb up and have a great vantage. Let's go, Wilson!"

So the boys crawled about ten feet up into the oak and waited and watched. It was a great location. They had a panoramic view of all fronts leading into the clearing. There would be no way any ghost could slip past them.

"Staking out" was hard and boring. The worst part for the boys was that there was no talking. One hour went by, then two, then three. At four o'clock, the coke ovens shut down, as they did each day. The ovens were not unlike an obtrusive fan. One became used to the constant dull hum of the motor, becoming oblivious to the obnoxious sound, until it shut off.

"All right, Briggs, I've had enough! I can't believe I let you talk me into this. I'm going home. I've been up here like a monkey for three hours and—"

"Shut up! Shush, did you hear that?" Eugene whispered his command while raising his hand to signal Jimmy to be quiet. Before Jimmy had a chance to respond, he heard the same rustling noise as Eugene. Something or someone was moving through the brambles and heading toward them in the clearing.

Both boys rose up from the six inch diameter branch that had supported them for the past three hours to take a better look. The footsteps stopped. There was dead silence. For whatever reason, at that moment not even the normal afternoon industrial sounds resonated up from the ovens below. Suddenly, the boys became paralyzed with fear. They swallowed hard, both straining to focus and listen for the next sound, or perhaps a vision.

Eugene's muffled voice quivered as he spoke into Jimmy's ear. "What if the Incan ghost is angry at me for me plowing up his burial ground? What if he wants revenge?"

Just then, from the edge of the thick overgrowth, their Incan tribal ghost appeared, dressed in a dingy yellow dress and standing about four feet tall. Instead of brandishing a metallic sword, she was swinging a wooden broomstick that she used to clear her path through the briars. The boys simultaneously let out a gasp of air in relief, but then their shoulders sank in disbelief.

"It's a girl!" Eugene muttered in disappointment.

She took a moment to look around, and then spotted Eugene's

work. Without hesitation, she walked over to the hole, grabbed the spoon, and then began filling in the small pit.

The boys were barely down from their tree when Jimmy burst out in laughter. Their anonymity was over. The girl jumped up, then stumbled over the pile of dirt, and fell back on her rear.

"Briggs, this beats all! Look at your scary Incan warrior now, sitting on her fanny in your hole! Ha, ha! You moron! You've been duped by a stupid girl!"

The unsuspecting child was terribly frightened by the loud, boisterous approach of the boys. Silver spoon still clutched in her trembling hands, she pushed herself to the far side of the crater, as if the additional two feet or so would provide some refuge. Jimmy approached the terrified girl, sheepishly followed a few steps back by his embarrassed counterpart. The girl raised herself as if she were about to run, when Jimmy spoke.

"You're that girl," Jimmy said, "who lives on Pearl Street with your grandma, aren't you?"

"Leave her alone, Jimmy." Eugene pushed his ill-mannered friend aside and presented his open hand to the girl, inviting her to take hold. After a second or two, she cautiously grabbed his hand and was pulled to her feet.

"I'm Eugene Briggs and he's Jimmy Wilson. We didn't mean to scare you. I guess we were expecting someone else."

"Right! Briggs here thought you were a ghost!"

"An Incan warrior, right?" This quick response from the girl made Jimmy once again laugh out loud.

"My name is Katrina, Katrina Garretson, but if you want you

can call me Kat, that's what my Grammy calls me. I didn't mean no harm. You see, I always come to the woods to talk to my mama and papa. Ever since I was a little girl. One day while I was sittin' on a rock, I heard this strange noise. I followed that noise right to you diggin' in the dirt with a spoon. So I just hid and watched you dig. I didn't know what you were lookin' for, but figured it must be real important."

"Wait a minute. Wasn't your mama and daddy killed?" Jimmy sarcastically inquired.

"Oh no, they just live out here in the woods. That is, their spirits do. They don't mind you diggin' around as long as you return the ground to where you found it. You don't do so good at that, so I help. Every day I hide and wait for you to come out. Sometimes you do and sometimes you don't. I reckon it's kind of funny that this time you hid from me." She looked at Eugene and smiled.

CHAPTER 3

Eugene was mesmerized by this sweet little gal. It may have been her innocent persona or perhaps it was her shoulder-length, silky brown hair and big brown eyes the size of coal. And now with every word Gene spoke, Kat's eyes increased their sparkle, glistening like the stars in a clear Pennsylvanian night sky.

"Well, I better get that hole filled back in, I don't want to go against the wishes of your mama and papa." Eugene picked up the spade and began to go to work.

"You have got to be kidding me, Briggs. You're as loony as she is. Talking to spirits! I've now heard it all." Jimmy spun around, threw his hands up, and walked away.

"Hold up, Wilson, I'm coming. See ya later, Kat!" Eugene, still too timid to be left alone with a girl, especially a girl he was smitten with, abruptly ended his conversation and ran to catch up with Jimmy.

This encounter cemented the beginning of an endearing friendship that would endure for years between the three. Even Jimmy who was reluctant at first to accept this girl into his exclusively male world was now beginning to warm up to her charm. She was not a girl to him any longer, she was a friend. Over time, he even developed patience for both Eugene and Katrina's quirky and sometimes eccentric ideas, bringing them back down to earth, or if the situation allowed, being a good sport and joining in the adventure. He soon developed a knack for keeping the two free spirits grounded to this world.

For several weeks after their introduction, Eugene made his routine trek to the woods. Only now, he would be joined by his compatriots. He would do his excavations, while Katrina would go off by herself to "talk with her parents."

She would return later to help Eugene sift through the soil and, of course, backfill the hole. Even Jimmy showed up from time to time to help out. Eventually, they gave up on the prospect of ever finding any artifacts and stopped with the excavations, but the boys never stopped accompanying Katrina. They would walk a ways with her, then usually sit on the same large rock overlooking Cheat River far below and wait, allowing her to have plenty of time with her parents.

Katrina's father had worked the coke ovens as a foreman for Sun Devil, one of the last mining and coke operations in the Appalachians to go union. Even though the Redneck Wars took place over a decade before Katrina was born, the anger and passion with many a family still ran deep. Because of the Redneck Wars, the owners of some of the remaining non-organized operations like Sun Devil were, at the very least, softened up. There was very little suppression of the workers. Every year since the late 1930s, their employees voted whether or not to become signatory with the United Mine Workers, but for whatever reason, every year they voted internally against it. Because of this, the unions shifted their strategy from intimidation of ownership to attempting to influence the labor holdouts. Mr. Garretson, Kat's father, was a company man. He was proud and stubborn and that was probably why he was targeted by the thugs.

The details are sketchy, but it is believed that on a cold, rainy Sunday night in December, thugs broke into the home of the Garretson's and, at gunpoint, kidnapped Mr. and Mrs. Garretson, leaving the baby behind. They drove Kat's parents to the beehive ovens where they ended the Garretson's lives execution style, with a bullet in the back of their heads. Then they dragged their bodies into the ovens to be destroyed the next morning by unsuspecting workers when firing up the ovens.

No one was ever convicted for this heinous crime. The only thing that supported this theory of the disappearances was the reports of gunshots late that Sunday night and a wedding ring that was found by a worker weeks later while cleaning out the oven. The ring was confirmed to be that of Mrs. Garretson.

Katrina's widowed grandmother moved in immediately to assume the role of guardian. The boys never knew the woman's real name. They really didn't even know her name was Garretson, but because Kat always referred to her as "Grammy," they called her "Grammy Garretson." Grammy came to America with her family from Germany as a teenager. She had dropped out of school at an early age to help with her immigrant family's candy business.

At the age of nineteen, she married a young Pennsylvanian farm boy who later died of polio. Grammy continued making and selling candy, but mostly depended on state money to support Kat and herself. As the months went by, Kat became a fixture at the Briggs house. Even when Eugene was not home she would come by just to hang out with Ertta or help watch Mary Lou.

Katrina was a tomboy through and through, but as she got older, it was apparent she had another side that wanted to seek out female companionship. Unlike most of the residents of Point Marion, Kat and her grandmother never went to church. It wasn't that Grammy was not religious, quite the contrary. Symbols of Christian faith adorned their humble home, meals would never begin without a prayer, and before bed each night, Katrina and her grandmother would get on their knees together and thank God for all their blessings. Many reasons could explain their absence on Sundays from the only church in Point Marion; it may have been as simple as no one had ever invited them to attend. . .that is, until Ertta Briggs did.

It took a while for Grammy Garretson to accept Ertta's invitation for herself, but encouraged Katrina immediately to attend, and of course, Kat was excited to accept. Sundays became a routine with the Briggs—meeting Katrina and sometimes Grammy at the front steps of the church before going inside for the service.

This introduction to church started an amazing transformation of social acceptance in the timid, somewhat introverted young girl. Soon, everyone knew Katrina, not as the unfortunate, orphaned girl, but as a vibrant and charming young lady that was an absolute pleasure to be around. This bud began to bloom into a beautiful flower. As pretty as she was, it was her enchanting, unpretentious charisma that captured the hearts of the parishioners. One in particular was the young wife of the pastor.

Lisa Browne was not only the preacher's wife, she was also a sixth grade teacher at Point Marion Elementary. There was an immediate bond between the two, even more than between Ertta and Kat. Lisa, having no children of her own, could devote more of her time to Katrina. And she did. Mrs. Browne, as most of the town's children knew her, helped Kat with homework. They made dresses together and Lisa even invited Katrina on special occasions to accompany her to Morgantown. There were often days when Kat's buddies, Jimmy and Eugene, felt left out and jealous, but Kat sensed this and always made up her lost time with them, usually by planning a surprise picnic.

CHAPTER 4

"A Snowy January Morning in Coal Country!" A copy of the Sunday, January 15, 1949, *Morgantown News* brandishing this headline lay at the doorstep of the Wilson home. In the snow-covered yard, a group of teenagers were tossing around a football, laughing and acting carefree. In the homes of these youth, things were not so jovial. Even though World War II was over, and most of the country was flourishing, the economy in Point Marion wasn't following suit. It was drastically going the opposite direction. Sun Devil had regretfully announced to its employees the previous Friday that they would be laying off half of the workforce for the beehive operation and sending 50 percent of the coal from their mines to a plant near Pittsburg. Technology had finally caught up with this small community.

Beehive ovens in the sides of mountains several miles from steel foundries were not the most efficient way to produce and ship coke. The evolutionary change of how coke could be derived from coal by plants with electric ovens constructed near the steel foundries was driving the beehive ovens into extinction. The final puffs of smoke from these fire-breathing dragons were becoming more imminent and in the months or years to follow would appear as abandoned corpses lining the sides of mountains throughout Pennsylvania and West Virginia. Some of the oven workers would find new positions within Sun Devil at their machine or carpenter shops or in the actual mines, but many would need to relocate to find employment in cities such as Pittsburg, Wheeling, or even Morgantown.

Jimmy's father was completely untouched by the demise of Sun Devil. He was employed by the local glass company, Houze Glass. The irony is that Houze Glass was once thought of as a second-rate employer. Only men who couldn't cut the tough conditions at Sun Devil worked there. Now it was a thriving company and soon to be the only company in Point Marion.

Fred Briggs position was secure, of course. He would equally spread his time between Sun Devil's six mining operations in Pennsylvania and West Virginia.

Because of its central location in town, Jimmy's yard was the gathering place for the local boys and of course, one gal. The game du jour, so to speak, for the last several weeks was football. It was always the "Cheat River Three" against any other group of boys who dared compete. The name "Cheat River Three" was Jimmy and Katrina's brainstorm, but after that their contributions diminished. Jimmy was the strategist, while Kat was the diversionist, which left Eugene to do basically everything else. Many groups of boys of all ages conjoined at the Wilson's side yard on Sundays with every intention of upsetting the champs, but whatever or whoever was put together as a team to oppose them would go home as losers. Eugene was an athletic prodigy even at the age of thirteen. He had grown bigger than most boys his age, but his real aptitude was that he was fast. Once he secured the pigskin, his strength and speed kicked in and it was all over. He would run over, he would run around, he would drag tacklers. It didn't really matter. If he wanted to score a touchdown, he would.

This Sunday was no different, despite the new ten inches of snow that covered their field. Up by three touchdowns and working on their fourth, Katrina tossed the ball to Eugene and, as usual, he proceeded to make quick work of his defenders. But he suddenly stopped when he noticed Kat running off the field and toward her home.

"Hey, Kat, where are you going?" Eugene called out. She spun around backwards but kept running.

"I need to go check on Grammy; she hasn't been well and. . . ." She turned back around and disappeared down the street. Eugene, with someone's little brother around his ankle, regained his focus long enough to lumber across the goal line with the young boy in tow.

The game concluded with Kat's departure. It was true that most of the males who showed up on Sunday afternoons were there to try their skills at stopping Eugene, but there were also other motives, especially with the older, red-blooded American boys. It was also a chance to see Katrina, and since the main attraction had just left, well. . . .

"What's up with Kat, Eugene?"

"I'm not sure, I guess her Grammy's sick. It's weird, even for her, just to take off like that."

"It was like someone called for her. You don't suppose it was the voices in the woods, do yah?" Jimmy looked at Gene and they both smiled.

When the bell rang Monday morning at school, there was no Katrina. Her empty desk seemed an enigma, as she was never absent. Jimmy looked across the room to a worried Eugene staring back. Something was wrong and the boys knew it.

It seemed an eternity before three o'clock arrived, but when the afternoon bell rang, Eugene and Jimmy wasted no time getting out of there.

"Hey, Briggs, wait up!" Jimmy yelled. "Where are you headed?"

"I'm going by Kat's. The way she left so suddenly yesterday. . .and today, not showing up for school… It's probably nothing, but this weird feeling has been eating at me all day."

"I'm going too. It's been bothering me as well."

The boys briskly trudged through the fresh snow, saying nothing until they arrived in front of the Garretson's house. They paused for a moment, standing in the street, staring down the walk and up to the front door. This bit of apprehension was interrupted when Jimmy's hand touched Eugene's back, directing him to proceed.

"Come on Briggs, I'm sure everything's fine! Kat probably overslept, so we'll give her a hard time and then be on our way."

Gene knocked at the door and they waited, but no one came.

"Look in the window, Jimmy!" ordered Eugene as he continued knocking, this time a little harder.

"It's dark inside, man. Maybe they had a last minute emergency and had to leave town." Eugene gave Jimmy a look of disgust.

"Yes, Briggs, I know it was a dumb thing to say. I know they have no means or money to travel anywhere. Come on, let's check the back door." The boys walked around back, knocked on the weathered rear door, and waited.

"See if the door is unlocked." Gene reached out and pulled open the dilapidated screen, then with his other hand grabbed the knob of the door. The metallic doorknob, which had been absorbing Pennsylvania's January freeze for weeks, delivered its revenge with a burning sting to Eugene's naked palm. He immediately pulled back to examine his flesh. Instinctively, Jimmy who was wearing gloves, reached around, gripped the knob, and turned. The door creaked open, allowing the boys to walk unabated through to the Garretson kitchen. Their hearts were pounding like a bass drum as they both contemplated the wisdom of what they had just done.

"It's freezing in here!" whispered Jimmy.

By their visible breath it was apparent that no one had been attending the furnace for a while.

"Well, I know that they're not out of coal. We practically tripped over the pile next to the chute outside," Jimmy said nervously.

"Grammy Garretson! Katrina! Is there anyone home?" Besides being cold, the house was also dark. This was somewhat attributed to the overcast afternoon, but mostly to the drawn curtains. After their eyes adjusted, they noticed a faint glow coming from beyond the kitchen. Eugene slowly moved forward through a doorway and entered the hall.

The light was coming from a room halfway down the hall; Gene knew the room was Grammy's. The boys were familiar with the house—had been there on several occasions with Kat. However, their familiarity didn't dismiss the eeriness they felt. As Eugene cautiously walked down the hall and toward the door he became aware of a sweet sickly odor. He tasted the unavoidable stench with every breath.

"Kat!" Eugene bellowed.

"I'm in here, Gene."

Eugene pushed open the door to the bedroom.

Grammy was as white as a ghost, lying motionless under layers of quilts that were pulled to just below her chin. Surrounding her on the bed was a chaotic mess of clean and soiled towels. A blood-spackled bed pan was poised next to her pillow. Next to the bed sat Katrina, wrapped in a blanket and slumped forward in her chair. The despair in Kat's worried eyes was heartbreaking; she seemed full of emotion but too exhausted to cry.

"I don't know what to do! She started feeling bad a couple of weeks ago, with a cough and all. She just said it was nothing but a cold, but her cough kept getting worse. I tried to talk her into going to see the doc, but she said we had no money for wasting, especially on doctors. She got real bad yesterday. I felt that something was wrong that's why I ran home. I found her on the floor and got her into bed and that's where we've been ever since. If she hadn't spent all of this month's money on coal for the furnace. . . ." Katrina momentarily lowered her head. "Speakin' of the furnace, I've been afraid to leave her for a minute even to go to the basement to shovel that damn coal into it."

"First thing we gotta do is get your Grammy to a doctor! We will figure out how to pay for it later," Eugene said.

"What we need, Briggs, is a car and someone that knows how to drive it!" Eugene hadn't realized that Jimmy had been standing behind him instead of still in the kitchen. "Our dads have cars, but they are both at work."

"Wilson, you stay here, I'm going to get Mom. And go fire up that furnace! Get some heat back in this place." Eugene shouted and headed for the door.

"We could put a saddle on him and then all three of us could ride to the doctor!" Jimmy said and smiled at Kat.

Eugene bolted from the house and ran for home, and several minutes later returned with Ertta. Eugene was thrilled to see a familiar car on the way back to Kat's house, a car driven by Lisa Browne. Vehicles during the 1940s were not a luxury and usually limited to one per family, and during the middle of the day in Point Marion work-related trucks were usually the only vehicles on the streets. Cars were indeed scarce, and they were viewed as machines—controlled by men in a man's world and for the men who were still employed. Scarcer were women that could operate cars, but Lisa Browne was the one of the few exceptions.

Knowing Lisa's affection for Kat and their need for a vehicle, they immediately waved her down.

They loaded the half-conscious Grammy in the car, but to the disappointment of the boys, Ertta had different plans for them. "Sorry fellas, women only for this trip! Jimmy, you go home, and Eugene, go help your brother watch Mary Lou." Both boys gave Katrina a hug before she slipped into the backseat, but her departing words to Eugene remained with him all night. "I can't lose her; she's the only family I have!" Eugene shut the door and the boys solemnly watched as the car drove away.

It was nearly midnight when Mrs. Browne's car pulled in their drive. The Briggs men sat anxiously most of the night awaiting the return of Ertta, so when they heard the car pull up, Eugene and Delbert ran to the window. Fred and their sleepless three-year-old sister walked down the stairs and joined the boys at the door. Finally, the door swung open and Ertta entered, escorted by a blast of cold air.

"Mommy, where you been?" cried out Mary Lou.

"Mommy's been helping a friend, and why aren't you, young lady, not upstairs asleep in bed?" Ertta gave Fred a glare as she took off her coat.

"How's Grammy?" Eugene asked the obvious question which was foremost on everyone's mind, and by his mother's hesitance to answer, he knew the response wasn't good. Fred sensed this as well and picked up Mary and headed toward the stairs.

"Give Mama a kiss; I'm putting you back where you belong." Fred gave Ertta a concerned look with a nod and proceeded with their daughter up the steps. Mother Briggs put her arms around her sons and walked them over to the couch and set them down.

"Boys, Grammy passed away. She died in Katrina's arms in the hospital."

"Couldn't the doctors save her?"

"They tried their best, Eugene, but there was nothing that they could do. They said that she had an advanced stage of lung cancer, as well as pneumonia. I think she was almost gone when we arrived at the hospital in Morgantown. After it was obvious that they couldn't do any more for her, they brought us into the room and Katrina held her until she passed."

"Where's Kat?" Eugene cried. "I need to go to her!"

"She is staying with the Browne's. Mrs. Browne, Lisa, will take good care of her. What Kat needs tonight, Eugene, is sleep. You can go be with her tomorrow after school."

The next morning on the way to school Eugene walked by the church's parsonage and left a note addressed to Kat in the door.

The note simply said, "You are not alone. We are your family too. Love, Eugene."

It goes without saying that the rest of the week was tough on Katrina as well as the Briggs, Wilsons, and Browne families. Katrina slept a lot; she didn't talk or eat much or even express much emotion. In fact there was more crying done by Lisa, and Ertta than by Kat. "Healing will come, it just takes time!" Pastor Browne kept assuring his wife.

CHAPTER 5

Eugene and Jimmy would come by regularly before and after school, sometimes together and sometimes separate. Kat would always see them, but she wasn't herself. Eugene was curious whether she had gotten his note and read it, but she never brought it up and he never asked. The funeral was set for Sunday. The church had some money set aside for such occasions and collected the rest from the good folks of the community to give Mrs. Carpenter a proper funeral and pay for her final expenses. Yes, Mrs. Carpenter. Mrs. Janice Carpenter, who was known throughout the community as "Grammy Garretson." Janice was, in fact, Katrina's grandmother, but on her mom's side. It was probably Grammy herself that allowed the incorrect last name to stick. She never tried to correct Kat's friends who would address her by Garretson; she was proud to assume the last name of her granddaughter. The symbolic name of a household was very important, especially to a household that had been brutally torn apart early in a child's life. This one simple gesture may have been the greatest gift of love this poor woman could have gave her granddaughter.

The funeral was held immediately after church. It was a simple ceremony starting at the church and concluding at the cemetery. The eulogy was given by Pastor Browne. Katrina sat sandwiched between Mrs. Browne and Mrs. Briggs, her eyes welling with tear but still never fully letting go of her emotions. A ham, along with various covered dishes, had been brought to the parsonage by the women of the church and awaited them upon their return from the cemetery. Katrina picked at her plate while listening to Gene and Jimmy's attempts to engage her in conversation, but it didn't work.

She politely smiled and would say a brief word or two, then slip back into solitude. Finally, she excused herself to the guest room that Lisa had made up for her, but not before thanking everyone for all they had done and giving Lisa and Ertta a hug. The awkward silence was broken by the sound of Kat's bedroom door closing, which was also a signal to the guests that it was the appropriate time to head home. Eugene and his family left as well.

Most Sunday nights at the Briggs were spent huddled around the radio listening to news and their favorite shows, and this Sunday was no different. That is until about nine o'clock when a knock came at the front door. It was a frantic Lisa Browne.

"Kat's missing! I went to her room to check on her and she was gone. Mike has gone to over to her house hoping that she maybe has gone home. I told him that I would meet him over there, after coming by here first."

"I'm going to look for her, Mom and Dad!"

"We're all going, Eugene," Mr. Briggs replied as he grabbed the car keys from the kitchen table. Seeing Father's quick reaction caused an immediate response from the rest of the clan. Ertta and the kids hastily grabbed their shoes and coats, while Fred started the car to warm.

"We'll meet you over at the Garretson house!" Fred said to Lisa as he escorted her to her car. Ertta, Mary Lou, Delbert, and Eugene came flying out of the house when suddenly Eugene stopped.

"You guys go ahead; I want to check somewhere else first. I'll catch up with you later." Eugene momentarily ran back in the house and grabbed a flashlight, then headed back outside to start walking toward the familiar haunt. The moon was full, and with the white snowy ground, there wasn't need for any additional illumination from the flashlight so Gene turned it off. Indeed it was a beautiful snow-lit night, ideal for a winter walk, but that was the last thing that entered Gene's mind as he trekked towards the opening in the woods.

Eugene had a hunch maybe Katrina had went to the woods to "talk to her parents". Besides Jimmy and himself, he was sure that no one else, including the Browne's, knew of her secret ritual and would ever think of searching for her in the woods.

Eugene trampled through the deep snow calling out her name. He went directly to the open area where his excavations were, then walked on to the thick wooded areas he had seen her walk to in the past, but no Katrina. Finally he made his way back to the clearing and to the rock where Jimmy and he would routinely sit and wait for Kat. Dejected and confused, he sat down.

"Where are you, Kat?" Gene's eyes were drawn to the entrancing beauty of the river below. The rapidly flowing dark blue water flashed and flickered from the reflecting moonlight. This scenic view, along with the pleasant sound of the wind sweeping the boughs of the spruce trees, was pure utopia. Eugene sat and stared for several minutes until the rustling wind intensified and brought him out of his mesmeric state. This was a wild goose chase, he thought. He needed to get back to town immediately and catch up to the others. Suddenly, as he was about to get up, he noticed something fluttering in the snow directly in front of him. "Where did this come from," he wondered. He walked over and bent down for a closer inspection.

"Red ribbon!" Gene spoke softly. "Kat always has tons of this stuff."

Just as he extended his hand to grasp the strand of fabric from the snow, a gust of wind whisked the crimson sash high in the air, swirling and twirling, as it soared out over the edge of the cliff. It seemed to dance perpetually through the crisp winter gales as if it were held by the fingertips of an angel. Then, without warning, it darted downward, descending toward the beehives and finally out of Eugene's sight.

"The ovens!" Eugene shouted as he jumped up and bolted into a run.

He recklessly ran along the ridge, dodging trees and jagged rocks, constantly looking over the edge toward the service road and rail below. He headed for a path several hundred yards away that would lead him down to the service road and, ultimately, to the ovens. When he arrived at the rows of ovens hollowed into the side of the mountain, he pulled out his flashlight and began shining the light in each. With quick inspection he moved from oven to oven, poking his head in and shining his light into the pitch black chamber. After several ovens, there she was, huddled inside, bundled in a blanket, sitting with her chin touching her knees. Her teary eyes looked up when Eugene shined his light on her, but she quickly looked away.

"Go away, Gene, leave me alone!"

Eugene pulled back, turned his flashlight off, and leaned against the brick arched doorway.

After a moment of uncomfortable silence, Katrina's words came firing out of the dark crypt.

"You're not going to leave, are you?"

"Not without you!"

"You know, Eugene, it should have been me that died along with my mother and father thirteen years ago. Why didn't God take me then? Why now has he taken the only family I had, the only one here on earth who loves me?"

Finally, with those heartbreaking words Katrina broke down.

"Please come out of there, Kat!" Eugene's request was answered with sobbing "no."

"Hey, Katrina, I can't answer why things happen in this world the way they do, but I'm as sure as the coal is black that both God and your parents didn't want you to die then or now! A few minutes ago I was sitting up there on our rock, with no idea where you were. . . that is until something strange happened. You left behind your red ribbon, and believe it or not, with the help of the wind it brought me to you."

Her crying had stopped, but there was no reply, so Eugene decided to take a different angle to try and coax her out.

"Well, stop thinking about yourself and start thinking about the team. If you're gone, we will have to dismantle the team. There can't be the 'Cheat River Three' if there's only two! And leaving me with Wilson, you know he stinks at football!"

From the dark bowels of the brick beehive oven, the faint sound of a giggle—and then a few moments later, a grieving young girl—emerged. Eugene wrapped his arms around her and held her tight until she finished weeping. The healing process started that night, confirmed by the smile that appeared on Katrina's face when she looked up and into Eugene's eyes.

"You do realize, you dumb lug, that the oven I was in hadn't worked for months? It was one of the first ovens Sun Devil had shut down. I can't believe you thought I wanted to kill myself. I just needed to come here alone, and didn't want to explain to the Brownes where I was going, so I snuck out the window. I was planning on returning before morning. I didn't think they would check on me again. So much for avoiding trying to explain that I'm really not crazy for wanting to sit in a dark coal oven in the middle of the night."

"Well, it's worse than that Kat. I'm guessing that by now

everyone in Point Marion is looking for you, and they will all need an explanation."

"Great!" "! Okay, maybe I do want to kill myself now!" Eugene couldn't help laugh.

"Don't worry, you sitting in the oven is our little secret. I'll just tell them I found you at the big rock in the woods, crying your eyes out." Gene let go of Katrina to turn on his flashlight, then began surveying the ground.

"What are you looking for, Gene?"

"I was looking for that red ribbon."

"A ribbon! By the way, you're right. I was sitting on the rock earlier, but I wasn't wearing any ribbons. In fact I haven't worn any ribbons in my hair in weeks. Silly boy!"

Katrina wiped the tears from her eyes with her coat sleeve, then walked over to Gene and gave him a kiss. This was not just a kiss; it was a kiss right on the lips, his first female kiss from someone other than his mother or grandmother. Eugene was a mess. He totally wasn't expecting that.

"You are my hero, Eugene Briggs!" Katrina declared with a flirtatious tone in her voice. "Thank you for finding me. I knew you would. And I know that I'm way overdue, but thanks for the note you gave me a few days ago. I will keep it forever."

"Come on, let's go find everyone, and get out of this cold. Don't tell Wilson that you kissed me, okay!" Eugene put his arm around Kat and they walked arm and arm up the service road toward town.

The next few days, Katrina moved from grieving to worrying.

She never expressed it openly, but she was understandably very nervous over what would be her fate. She was under the age of eighteen, and this meant that if no one would step forward and accept the responsibility of legal guardianship over her, she would be sent to the state home. Unknown to her, the Brownes had been discussing and praying over this issue since the day after Kat's grandmother's passing. Even though both Mike and Lisa loved Katrina very much, this was still a big commitment, and they wanted to make sure that they were all three compatible.

Katrina did finally confide in Lisa the fact that she had, almost daily since she was a small child, ventured into the woods east of town. She told Lisa how she felt comforted just by walking and talking out loud to her parents; and that she felt their spirits were always close. Lisa was also comforted when Kat told her that she did all the talking, and that not once did she hear voices back from her parents. The Brownes' decision was, in the end, easily made.

It was a special day when Kat got home from school and Mike and Lisa were waiting at the door with a cake, which said, "Two's company and three's a family."

In a small community, it takes a while for things to return finally to normal, but life does go on, and with love, friends, and the support of the community, Katrina adapted to her new home. Katrina found closure to that sorrowful chapter of her life and never returned to oven row. She did however faithfully continue her routine visiting the woods along with her two accomplices. In fact, as it would turn out, most of their future memorable "life moments" would start and finish at that location.

CHAPTER 6

It was the spring of 1953, with only a few more weeks of school for the three high school juniors. Staying true to the custom they'd created, the boys sat patiently biding their time by carving their names with a chisel into their claimed limestone rock, waiting for their female compatriot. Smiles appeared simultaneously on the faces of Eugene and Jimmy as they heard the approach of Katrina singing the newly released hit song, "Unforgettable." She hopped up on the rock and stood over the boys, theatrically bellowing out the final words with a performance that would make Nat King Cole himself proud.

"How are my men today?" Katrina asked, leaning over to inspect their carved names, before playfully grabbing the chisel from Jimmy's hand.

"Can I try?" she asked. Burrowing between them, Katrina started carving. When she was done, below their scribed names was the added statement, "loves Kat." After the three admired the finished product, they turned over on their backs and stared at the sky.

"What are we going to do this summer?" asked Jimmy.

"Do what we always do, play football," replied Eugene.

"What we need is an adventure! Something unforgettable," stated Katrina.

Katrina sat up and gazed at the swollen Cheat River, its banks almost breaching from the heavy spring rains over the last several days. Both boys rose to join her, staring at the river below.

"What we need is a trip down the river!" Eugene suggested. Jimmy gave Eugene an unsettled look while Katrina nodded in agreement.

"Who do you think we are Gene, Huckleberry Finn and Tom Sawyer? And don't forget our side kick here, Pocahontas," Jimmy said, rolling his eyes. Katrina's giggle contagiously started the boys laughing.

"No, no, there is no way we are going down Cheat River!" Jimmy continued. "You two can forget that right this minute!"

"Doesn't your dad have a canoe, Wilson?" Eugene asked.

"What part of 'no' do you have trouble understanding, Briggs?" Jimmy asked. Katrina continued laughing hard at Jimmy's responses.

"Cooper's Rock! That can be our destination! That's way upstream from here."

"There is no way we can paddle against that kind of current, moron!" Jimmy said.

"Call me moron again and I'll stick a motor up your rear and Kat and I will drive you up the river. And who said anything about paddling up stream? I'm talking about starting south of Cooper's

Rock and shooting the canyon. We can load your canoe up with supplies. Shoot the rapids! Climb the rock! Camp all night, jump back in the canoe, and float home the next day."

"That sounds so exciting! Let's do it, guys." Katrina said, "Wait, the Brownes may have a problem with me camping overnight unchaperoned with you boys."

"Have you both lost your minds?" Jimmy asked. "Having a chaperone is the least of our problems. Cooper's Rock just happens to be right above the most treacherous part of Cheat River. Even though we don't have a vehicle to haul the canoe upstream, getting there is the easy part. If we survive the rapids without drowning and manage somehow to get the boat to shore in one piece, we then have to deal with scaling the two thousand foot vertical hike from the river up to the top. What are we going to do with the canoe while we are camping at the top? There is no way we can hoist it up there."

"Well, we have a few details to work out, but with your brains and my brawn, Wilson, it should be a cinch."

"What about me, what can I offer to this trip?" asked Katrina.

"There is not going to be a trip, Katrina! Your lame-brained friend here is not talking me into this one! No way! No how!" Jimmy crossed his arms in defiance. Gene looked at Katrina and smirked.

"Don't worry, he'll go. You know he always reacts this way at first." Kat put her arm around Jimmy, knowing she could manipulate his decision.

"Come on, Jimmy, it will be fun and exciting. We can't do this without you. You're part of the team, the 'Cheat River Three' and all." Jimmy turned red-faced with shame and shook his head. He didn't want to admit it, but he was just like Gene, powerless against Katrina's wishes. Like most of the female species, she knew exactly what buttons to push, especially on a young, hormone-crazed male, to make them conform to her wishes.

"I am leaving you two hillbillies to your fantasy suicidal river expedition alone." Jimmy jumped off the rock and headed for home. This concluded their social gathering for the day, but the basic foundation for their adventure was forged and their ideas were set in motion.

As predicted, Jimmy did eventually conform to his friend's wishes. After it was apparent that they were not going to forget about the trip, and they certainly were not going to leave him alone, he gave his conditional consent. If Jimmy was to go along and supply the mode of transportation, his father's canoe, he would also need to assume the role of strategist, navigator, and guide boss for the adventure. If this trip was to be successful and more importantly, safe, he knew that he would need to plan it and also go along to supervise. In the past, deciding whether or not to go along with the wild schemes of Eugene was always a double-edged sword for Jimmy. He knew that Eugene would attempt a particular stunt whether he was along or not. Now it was twice as bad. Gene had an accomplice, and she was just as much of a freelance, thrill-seeking maniac as he was. Together they raised the bar when it came to being footloose and fancy free. Jimmy was well aware of the inherent dangers that were associated with canoeing down a violent, rapidly flowing river such as Cheat, and so was Jimmy's father, who had mentored him on many occasions as to the safeties and cautions of such trips. He also knew his father would not willingly consent to his son attempting this trip without an experienced guide along such as himself.

Jimmy, without argument, got Eugene and Katrina to agree to his terms. He even got them to sign a handwritten contract he had architected. His written terms were simple. He would be in charge. He expected them to follow his plan to the tee. There were to be no side trips, no crazy dares, and most importantly, and at all costs, there needed to be secrecy. There must be total covertness, or it would blow the deal. Jimmy had to explain the word "covert" to Gene and Katrina, but they got the context. No way would the boys' parents, or especially Katrina's new guardians, allow this trip to happen. And if they ever found out later that they did something crazy like this behind their backs, they would be grounded for life. Not only did Jimmy need to devise a plan to navigate the river and scale Cooper's Rock, he needed to come up with an excuse or alibi for each one of them being gone overnight.

Memorial Day, the last day of school, was Jimmy's target date for execution of his plan. The holiday just happened to come on a Monday and this was Friday, and the plan was still missing some key elements. Coming up with a date for their event and finding an excuse for Kat's being out overnight were the most arduous tasks. He needed excuses for Katrina and was coming up with nothing. It was time for help. After school on Friday, they would need to meet, so he notified his mates and when the bell rang, off to the rock they went.

"What's the matter, Wilson, having trouble with your plan?" Eugene said with a smirk.

"I've figured out how to get the canoe upstream. I have also figured out where to launch and what to do with the canoe overnight. Also, how to scale the canyon and how to find our way back down the mountain, then back home. As far as our alibis go, I plan on telling my folks that Gene and I are going camping in the woods. We've already done that many times since we were fourteen. Dad would never miss the canoe from its resting spot under the tarpaulin in back of the shed. The problem is you, Kat. I don't have any idea how to have you out all night without the Brownes knowing."

"Well, maybe I can help, doll! In two weeks the Brownes plan on attending a three-day church conference in Wheeling and they already told me I didn't need to go. How's that? Any other problems I can solve? You have been racking your brain for days over this one, haven't you, James? By the way, I am not your 'problem,' as you so lovingly put it. Maybe dear, you need to be relying a little more on Eugene and me. We might surprise you at how capable we actually are, even on our own." It was apparent that Jimmy had struck a nerve with Kat. The more she spoke the sharper her tone became. She had been tolerant of his elitist, arrogant attitude since the day she'd met him in the woods seven years prior, but the days of her naivety were quickly coming to an end. She was not yet Jimmy's equal in the class room, but she made sure he knew that outside of that environment she was instinctively every bit his egalitarian.

On June 4, at seven o'clock that Thursday morning, Pastor Browne finished loading luggage into the new car provided to him by the church, while his wife Lisa gave final instructions to Katrina. Down the street at the Wilson's, Jimmy was packing his camping gear and rolling up his sleeping bag awaiting the arrival of Eugene with his gear. A key component to this operation was a vehicle, and soon Eugene would be driving up in that component. Eugene had been working summers for the past couple of years on his Uncle Mendel's farm. With Jimmy's encouragement, Gene asked to borrow his uncle's old farm truck. The plan was, once Gene arrived he would park the truck on the street behind the Wilson's house, just out of view. Then discreetly, the boys would carry the canoe down the alley to the truck and load it. Jimmy would return to his house, grab his camping gear, kiss his mother goodbye, and walk off toward Eugene's house, only to be picked up by Gene waiting a few blocks away. From there they would drive about fifteen miles south of Point Marion then another three miles south to Ices Ferry Bridge (the closest crossing of Cheat to Cooper's Rock). Then they would drop the canoe and Jimmy at the river.

Eugene then would drive the truck back, just south of Point Marion at Lake Lynn Dam. Eugene would park the truck and wait for Katrina, driving the Browne's other car. Kat would pick up Gene and they would both return to the waiting Jimmy to begin their voyage.

This was the plan that Jimmy had been working on for weeks, and rehearsing for the last few with Eugene and Katrina. There was no reason why it shouldn't be carried out flawlessly. Well, that mindset of Jimmy's was a kiss of death. Operation "Grand Rapids" was the corny moniker that the overconfident and smug James Wilson had dubbed his deceptive adventure.

POW! The loud backfire of the rickety old farm truck Gene drove could be heard for blocks as it sputtered and spit its way down the street. This was not the stealthy beginning of the operation Jimmy had hoped for. Even Jimmy's mother, who was in the middle of household chores, stopped what she was doing to comment, "What in the world!"

"It's just an old truck, Mom!" Jimmy dropped his rolled sleeping bag and ran out the front door and down the side yard to the alley. From the alley he viewed the waiting rust red, iron monster pulled to the curb. Even from this distance, he could clearly see the huge grin on Eugene's face as he sat behind the enormous steering wheel. Gene waved at Jimmy and held up his index finger as if to indicate the grand finale. Reaching to the dashboard, Gene turned off the ignition, which incited an ear-piercing screech followed by a horrific bang, and for the added dramatic visual effect, a puff of black smoke discharged from the tail pipe. Unphased and unamused, Jimmy wheeled around to return to his house, leaving Eugene rolling with laughter in the truck. Jimmy failed to see the humor and quickly ran inside to bundle his gear and announce his departure to his mother. As he embraced his mother and accepted her kiss, the silhouette of Eugene blacked out the morning sun and filled the space of the front screen door.

"Hello, Mrs. Wilson!" Talking through the screen, Eugene was still grinning from ear to ear like the proverbial Cheshire cat. "Is your son ready to go camping in the woods?" Jimmy gave Eugene a piercing glare for his sappy introduction as he escorted his mother through the door to join him on the front porch.

"And good morning to you, too, Eugene!" Mrs. Wilson gave Gene a kiss on the check. "You boys take care. I have made enough sandwiches for both you boys, and if you get cold…"

"Mom, we'll be alright!"

"Don't worry, Mrs. Wilson, I won't let anything happen to your little Jimmy."

With that comment, Jimmy pushed Gene off the porch, but quickly grabbed him, changing his direction as Gene mistakenly started walking toward the parked truck. Both boys smiled and waved as they went walking down the street in the direction of the big woods. Once out of eye sight, they circled back around the block and toward the truck.

"Wilson, we are going to have the time of our life!"

"Yeah, let's just hope that it's not the final time of our life! You probably didn't notice, but with all the rain that we got the last few days, the river is really flowing hard."

"Such a worrywart you are, Wilson!"

The boys tossed Jimmy's sleeping bag in the back and headed toward his shed to retrieve the very important canoe. The thirteen-foot wooden vessel was heavy. After peeling back the canvas tarp both boys strained to lift its weight and carry it to the truck. It was unquestionably apparent to Jimmy that even with Kat's help they would have their hands full lowering this heavy canoe filled with camping gear into the water. But it was too late to change plans now and it was pointless to discuss this problem with Gene. He was in full speed ahead mode and to hell be damned. Once the boat was loaded in the truck, the solution came to Jimmy. He ran back to his father's shed and returned with an armload of rope and a pair of wooden pulleys.

He threw them in the back along with the rest of their gear and jumped in the cab with Eugene.

"What the heck is wrong with this truck, Briggs? It screams like a stuck pig."

"Ain't it great, and then it farts!" Jimmy just shook his head. "You don't think he just unconditionally loaned it to us do you, Wilson?

We are supposed to work on it, installing new plugs and changing the oil." Gene pointed to a box on the floor with quarts of oil and spark plugs.

"When do you think we will have time to do that, Briggs?"

Gene turned the key and fired up the noisy monstrosity, then pulled the gear stick back, grinding it into first gear. He then released the clutch and depressed the gas pedal, which announced to the world the beast had awakened. Eugene finally answered Jimmy in the form of a quote from the wicked witch in the Wizard of Oz. To be heard over the buzz of the engine, Gene needed to amplify his reply.

"All in good time, my dear! All in good time!"

The mission was underway and within thirty minutes the boys were just about to their launching spot. Buzzard Run was a fitting name for the desolate gravel road that paralleled the river. A buzzard would have to walk. It certainly would be a challenge for a high flying bird like that to soar down the road. It was like driving through a tunnel of foliage. Trees lined the sides, creating a natural wall, and their limbs extended over the road, becoming the canopy. The road was so narrow and there were so many trees it virtually blocked out the sunlight. As far as paralleling the river, the only way they knew this was to stop the truck and walk through the woods until they could physically view the water below. Jimmy was somewhat familiar with the river, so when Gene would stop the truck, Jimmy would disappear into the trees to look for a landmark he could he could identify. The landmark he was searching for was not down at the river but high across the other side. He was looking for a bald spot on a mostly wooded mountain. The bald spot was Cooper's Rock. This limestone protrusion was easy to spot. It stood out like a sore thumb.

Cooper's Rock was a well know scenic overlook named after a fugitive in the eighteen hundreds who avoided capture by having the unfair advantage of being able to see his adversaries well in advance. From the gorgeous panoramic vantage one could see miles of trees, mountain laurel, and, of course, the rock cliff river gorge. After several repetitions of this navigational technique, Jimmy came euphorically running out of the woods waving and yelling.

"There it is! We are almost straight across. We need only to go another mile or so and find the best place to unload and launch." Just a little over a mile later, the boys came across a place in the road and they were able to pull over. After inspecting the surroundings they decided that this spot would have to do. There appeared to be an already beaten path down to the river and even a rare, small sand bank. Even though the grade was not as severe as most places up or downstream along Cheat Canyon, they would still need to hoist the loaded canoe down the bank.

"Come on, Wilson, let's check it out." The two scouts cautiously shuffled their way down to the river's edge.

"Looks rough, Briggs!" The two boys stood in the damp sand overlooking the alacritous rush of the rapids. The mighty, perpetual display of force and energy of the river held them momentarily captive.

"Maybe by the time Kat and I get back it will have calmed down some. Come on. Time's a wasting!"

Gene and Jimmy returned to the truck, pulled the canoe back across the steel bed of the truck, and then lifted it cautiously to the ground. After securing their gear, they lugged the wood boat through the trees until the path became too steep. Jimmy then ran back to the truck and grabbed the rope and wood pulleys. By tying the pulley to a stout tree, then running the rope through it and securing the end to the canoe, the boys were able to lower it safely and without incident down the steep rock bank. Proud of their accomplishment after unleashing the canoe, they gave each other a hardy handshake and headed again back up the incline.

Gene jumped behind the wheel and pulled away, leaving Jimmy in a cloud of black smoke.

It was close to noon when Eugene arrived at the dam. He pulled the truck as far as he could off to the side of the steep service road and shut it off. He waited, but not for long. Over the crest of the hill she came, blowing her horn to alert her arrival. When she pulled alongside Gene she locked up the brakes and squealed to a stop. Eugene jumped from the truck and slammed the door. He then opened the door of the awaiting chariot and slid beside his female counterpart.

"Need a ride, Clyde?"

"Only if you're ready for adventure, Bonnie!" They both laughed, and then Katrina did a U-turn and headed back up the hill.

As the two gleeful teens drove back over the top of the hill, they were oblivious to the fact that Uncle Mendel's truck wasn't about to stay put. Apparently it wasn't fully in gear when Gene shut off the engine, and the jar when he slammed the door was just enough to totally disengage it. At first it began rolling slowly, but with each steep grade of yard it traveled, the truck picked up speed as Newton's law began to apply. By the time it hit the water, it must have been traveling a good twenty-five miles an hour, more than enough to cause a tremendous splash and send the large vehicle completely into the rushing river. It rolled a few more feet before stopping, luckily, just before the really deep water. There it sat, halfway submerged and creating its own pitiful eddy.

When Bonnie and Clyde arrived at the launching site, they

wasted no time in the parked car. Kat grabbed a bag from the backseat and they started their walk to rendezvous with the awaiting Jimmy. When the pair arrived at the canoe, they found Jimmy asleep inside. They couldn't resist the temptation and splashed water on his face to wake him. Jimmy sat up and looked at his watch. "Damn!"

"We need to get going if we are to get to the top of Cooper's Rock before dark."

All three grabbed ahold and dragged the wooden vessel till its bow was well in the water. Letting go of their grips, they stood up and looked into the eye of the beast which was the river, surveying the daunting task which lay before them.

"It hadn't slowed much has it, Wilson?" The boys looked at each other with a bit of reservation.

"Alright, you two, we have about a mile to get from this side of the river to that side. It's all about steering, so whatever you do, do not let go of the oar." Jimmy barked. The boys continued, staring at the forceful display of God's aquatic wonder, while Katrina was poised with hands on her thrusted hips, staring open-mouthed at the two males.

"Well, what do you think, Briggs, should we do this?" asked Jimmy.

"Are you two wimping out on me? Come on, boys, this could be the most exciting thing we may ever do!" Katrina reached down and took a hold of the rung, shaking the boat. "Let's do this!"

Eugene looked at her and smiled, then turned to Jimmy. "You heard the lady, Wilson, let's do this!" Whether it was calling the boys on a dare or simply rallying the troops, Katrina's motivation reenergized them. They were able to face their fears, perhaps throwing simple wisdom to the wind and succumbing to foolishness.

Jimmy instructed Gene and Kat where to sit and what to do. He quickly showed Gene how to hold and use his oar to steer and paddle the canoe. Jimmy and Kat were on one side of the canoe and Gene was on the other. Once the boat was completely floating in the water, Kat, as instructed, hopped in the middle first, then Gene moved up front, followed by the more experienced Jimmy in the rear to steer. Once the current grabbed the canoe, they were off like a shot. With the exception of the whitecaps, the water was a dark green and it was cold, as the three quickly found out every time the water would break over the sides and bow. They also quickly discovered how insignificant they really were. Jimmy barked out orders and Gene responded, but they were at the total mercy of Mother Nature.

The three friends were just along for the ride, and only when the mighty river decided they had enough would she spit them out. This reality was burning the back of Jimmy's brain. It was all they could do just to keep the canoe straight. Using their oars as rudders Jimmy and Gene were trying to direct the craft from west to east but the canoe would overreact and pitch sideways. Adrenalin flowed through the boys' veins as fast as the rapids they rode. Being scared to death may have been an understatement for the boys. However, this rush of life and death excitement inspired the opposite response from Kat. This white water rocket ride had just delivered her to the pinnacle of life. She was laughing and yelling at the top of her lungs. She loved it.

They all three were soaked to the bone and working desperately just to stay upright. Jimmy knew they must be able to somehow gain control of the canoe well enough to steer it to shore or they would miss their intended target, the spot directly below the rock. He was also beginning to think that the middle of the river was the safest place to be. Traveling at that high speed, then coming to an abrupt stop on the rocky shore could be suicidal. The time to make a decision about whether or not to try to go to shore was fast approaching.

Jimmy believed they had traveled a mile and it was either now or never. The water for that moment seemed somewhat less hostile, and because of that, his split second decision was made. Yelling his order forward to Gene, they simultaneously drove their oars hard to the starboard side. But the rapids didn't agree to their terms and the canoe spun sideways, then completely around. They were disastrously out of control and heading backward. The boys were frantic. Jimmy was yelling orders and jamming his oar repeatedly in the river, looking as if he were wheedling a sword deep into the heart of a beast. Eugene was desperately paddling from side to side but to no avail. With all this chaotic activity, Katrina remained blissfully content.

"Take me to shore! Please take me to shore now!" Katrina shouted loudly enough to be heard over the roar of the river, yet she still remained calm.

"What do you think we are trying to do Kat?" a frustrated Jimmy bellowed.

Things looked dire for the three. The canoe was now half full of water and still pointing in the wrong direction. Eugene and Jimmy looked over their shoulders trying to anticipate their fate, but had little to no result in changing the outcome. Katrina was still requesting to be brought to shore, but it was as if she were talking to someone other than her two counterparts on the boat.

"Please take us to shore!"

Suddenly and without provocation, the canoe did a one hundred and eighty degree turn, and miraculously they ended up within an oars length of the east shore line. Before the boys could even react they came to a smooth stop next to the bank. Eugene moved his oar to the outside of the canoe and pushed it into the water, wedging it down with his weight into the rocky bottom. This stabilized the boat against the shore and allowed the others to exit to land. Out of the corner of his eye, Eugene caught a glimpse of something red tangled on his oar. The oar had snagged a crimson red ribbon from the river. This resulted in instant déjà vu. The ribbon was similar to the one that he saw four years earlier that allowed him to find Katrina hiding in the ovens.

"Kat!" Gene cried out.

He momentarily took his eyes off of his capture to turn to Katrina. She was now standing onshore attending to her bag. Gene quickly turned back, and as he did, the oar moved a few inches, freeing the strand of cloth just enough that the current took it. Before Gene could react, it was gone.

"What, Gene?"

"Nothin'. Were you wearing one of your. . .oh, ."

Gene hopped out of the boat and joined his friends on the narrow strip of security called land. Grabbing the front while Jimmy grasped the back, the boys pulled the canoe as far as they could up on the four foot wide rocky shore. They unloaded their soaked backpacks and sleeping bags from the belly of the canoe and turned the boat on its side to drain out the water. When finished, they collapsed to the ground in complete exhaustion. As uncomfortable as it must have been, both boys lay on their backs across the uneven rocks and gravel staring straight up at the sky. Jimmy was nearly in tears from this terrifying ordeal. Gene's chest was still pounding from the adrenalin rush, and Katrina was retaining her natural high, radiating a glow of life.

"It's great to be alive!" Screamed Katrina as she tossed her head back and opened her arms wide. "Come on you two, get off your bums, we got a mountain to climb."

Eugene sluggishly rose to her command but quickly came to life when Kat jumped in his arms and gave him a vivacious kiss. This spontaneous reaction from Katrina quickly returned the blood to Gene's fear-flushed face. It even caught the attention of Jimmy, still sprawled on the ground.

Looking like a koala bear clinging to a eucalyptus tree, Kat looked down at Jimmy and winked.

"Sorry, guys, I just got carried away. That river was so much fun!"

Jimmy stood up shaking his head in disbelief at Kat, and began sarcastically formulating his first words since their arrival ashore. "What do you think, Briggs, wasn't that river a hoot? Not quite as scary as that smooch she gave you, was it lover boy?" Still dazed and embarrassed from Kat's kiss, Eugene had no comeback.

"Well, I guess this concludes Operation Grand Rapids!" Jimmy continued. "Okay, we need to tie off the canoe. Gene, take the rope and winch and climb up the bank and tie off to a tree. We will winch the canoe up to the tree and chain it off."

From the back of the narrow shore there was a nearly vertical, eight-foot jagged limestone bank that was a challenge to scale. Jimmy knew that once over that wall, the terrain slightly flattened, allowing a still-treacherous, but manageable assent. The solid rock ground eventually changed to soil just enough to nurture the heavy growth of white oak, hemlock, and poplar trees that clustered the slope all the way to the summit. Not unlike most of the forests in West Virginia, the trees up Cheat Mountain were so numerous it was easy to get disorientated and lost. So dense were the trees that a person couldn't even pick out a navigational reference point. Once you delve just a few yards into the vertical forest, your only true reference was up or down.

Gene managed his way up the eight-foot rock face and secured the pulley to a stout tree, then ran the rope through the small wheel. Below, Jimmy attached his line to the canoe and he and Kat tossed their bags and gear back into the boat and climbed up the cliff to join Gene. Jimmy tied an additional pulley to another tree to create a double pulley system for more leverage, and they began to hoist. The canoe made an awful scratching sound as the wood scraped over the hard rock with each tug the three exerted. Finally, the bow peeked its way over the crest to the cheers of the hoisters. They dragged it close to the tree and Jimmy secured it with a chain and padlock.

"Who do you think would possibly steal your canoe here, Wilson?" Gene asked. "The ghost of fugitive Cooper!"

"No, your Incan ghost!" Jimmy said. Katrina laughed at the quick response.

"Just covering my bases, Briggs." Jimmy pulled out a silver, cylinder-shaped canister from his backpack.

"What you got there, Wilson?" Gene asked.

"This is what you call an aerosol can of paint. You just shake it up, point, and spray. I am surprised, Briggs, as worldly as you are, that you haven't seen one of these before." Jimmy demonstrated to his captive audience by shaking the can until the steel ball rattled inside, and then he sprayed a yellow spot on the tree over the canoe. Eugene and Katrina were amazed by this revolutionary invention recently introduced to the world.

Jimmy recognized their astonishment and responded accordingly. He was like a street performer in Paris showing off magic tricks or Paleolithic man introducing fire to his fellow cave people.

"Enough of the demonstration. Briggs, you'll be bringing up the rear and in charge of this spray can. Mark our trail by spraying yellow spots on the trees so on our return trip in the morning all we need do is follow the paint, which will lead us back to the canoe."

They grabbed their damp bags and started their ascent. Up the mountain they trudged in and around trees and over rocks. Gene marked trees as they went. The hike was tremendously grueling both physically and mentally. They needed to stop every one hundred yards or so to rest and rehydrate. Jimmy kept pushing them to continue to keep on schedule. He constantly had to remind them to conserve their water, but the thin air and high humidity made their thirst unquenchable. Every tree and rock looked the same. There were no significant landmarks and no way to judge distance, so it felt as if they were going nowhere. Katrina began to sing to keep her mind off the monotony, as well as the burning sensation in her calves. Her voice would fluctuate in octaves depending on her intake or exhalation of air. Some words trailed off to whispers, while others failed to even resonate past her lips. But there was enough lyrical melody to keep up the group's morale.

"I think I see it!" Jimmy's words were so pleasing to hear. The excitement reenergized the trio and they picked up their pace. Finally they were at their destination—a bit weary, but with no real complaints. Celebrating their accomplishment, the three gave a sweaty group hug. The afternoon was almost gone. The three adventurers were wet with river water and sweat. They were tired and hungry, but their objective had been met and they now stood upon it. Cooper's Rock was just that: a large, flat rock. But it was also a popular overlook for tourists, the kind of tourists which normally arrived by automobiles. But it was five o'clock and there were only a couple of stragglers left. The parks department did not allow overnight camping in the spot, so they waited patiently until everyone else had left before setting up camp.

"First thing we need to do is make a fire and try to dry out everything, especially our sleeping bags," Jimmy said. "Briggs, you go gather wood. Kat, we need more water. There is an old hand pump well about a hundred yards or so from here. The Civilian Conservation Corps ran a waterline up the mountain during the Depression." Jimmy handed Kat his and Gene's canteens. "Fill both of these along with yours. And Kat, try not to get spotted by a park ranger!" Katrina gave Jimmy a salute, grabbed the canteens, and went skipping down the trail. He started unpacking his duffel bag and backpack, and unrolled all three sleeping bags on the smooth, grey limestone. Eugene made several trips back and forth from the woods, dropping arm loads of sticks and logs. When he felt he had enough, Gene began gathering rocks and circling them for a fire pit. Luckily, Jimmy's matches had stayed dry and Gene was able to ignite some tinder and before long had a nice fire. The boys found three branches equal in length, and by using some rope they made a tripod which they then placed over the fire. This contraption would serve as a way to dry out their sleeping bags, as well as socks and other damp clothing. The sun was setting and the boys were hungry, and Katrina had not yet returned with the water.

"Hey, Wilson, were you scared earlier on the river?" asked Gene. "I thought for sure we weren't going to make it!"

"Scared? I was terrified. Things were happening so quick I didn't have time to react. I really don't know what kept the canoe from turning over. I couldn't believe how stupid I was for not packing life jackets. If we were dumped in the water, the undertow and current would have…" Jimmy didn't finish the sentence, he realized that he conveyed enough of his feelings regarding the earlier events. He took a deep breath, exhaled, and then moved on.

"Did you hear Kat carrying on? Is she crazy or what? Who was she talking to, Briggs? It sure wasn't me or you!"

Eugene just sat quietly, staring off at the sunset, while Jimmy looked at him, waiting for his response. Finally, Gene spoke, but not the confirmation that Jimmy was expecting.

"Where is that girl anyway?" The words had no sooner left Gene's mouth when down the path she came. Her hair was wet and combed. She was wearing a clean pair of denim shorts and a cotton blouse. In her hand was her bag and around her neck were all three canteens.

"Are you boys cooking the sleeping bags?" Smiling, she pointed to the steam rolling off of the bags that hung over the fire on the makeshift pyramid.

"Oh crap! Briggs, pull them off before they catch on fire!" They quickly grabbed them and spread them out on the limestone ground.

"We should have let them finish cooking," Gene said. "I am so hungry I could have eaten all three sleeping bags!"

"Well, don't just stand there complaining, Briggs. If you're hungry, let's see what we got." Jimmy pulled out a pot from his pack and filled it with water.

"I've got beef bouillon cubes. As soon as the water boils we'll toss in a couple to make broth. Mom also packed some braunschweiger sandwiches. They're a little soggy, but the bread will dry out next to the fire and they'll be fine." Eugene contributed peanut butter and saltine crackers, and the dessert du jour was provided by Katrina. She surprised her male counterparts with black walnut brownies which she had baked the night before.

Some of life's most enjoyable pleasures are the most simplistic things. Our senses intensify after triumph, especially if overcoming extreme difficulties when achieving such victory. To the three young adventurers, the taste of peanut butter and braunschweiger was as scintillating to their taste buds as lobster and crème brûlée. That night on the rock they celebrated their victory even though their journey was only half over.

After they'd devoured their feast ("they" referring mostly to Gene), they lay flat on their backs with the top of their heads touching and each of their torsos and legs pointing a different direction. Katrina said they were, *making a star to look at the stars.* The night sky was spackled with millions of sparkling stars, with a three quarter moon setting the table. When they were looking straight up there were no obstructions between them and the stars and planets. There was an illusion of being so close to the celestial masses that each felt they were floating in space. Before long their conversations faded to silence and the exhaustion of the day finally caught up to them. They quickly slipped off into slumber.

Jimmy's eyelids flew open and he quickly sat up. "Wake up!" His alarming tone interrupted the two sound sleepers as they unconsciously huddled next to each other for warmth. "We gotta get going! People will soon be arriving! And the rangers! We cannot get caught here by the park rangers!" Both Kat and Gene, still somewhat embarrassed by their unsuspected, intimate situation and feeling very vulnerable to the opposite sex, did a quick personal hygiene inspection. After regaining their composure, all three jumped up and ran off in different directions into the woods to pee. Because of the bright morning sun, Jimmy assumed that it was later than it was, but once he examined his watch, his urgency subsided.

Morning on Cooper's Rock was a spectacular experience. The three had awoken emerged in nature. Chirping birds, spring flowers, and the gorgeous, clear blue sky that allowed the viewer to see out over the tree tops for miles, made this place truly heaven on earth. After returning from the woods, they immediately began to breakdown camp.

"When you guys are ready we'll start the hike back down to the river," Jimmy said. "The way I see it, we have two ways to manage the rapids. We can jump back in the canoe and take our chances, mindful that the river will be widening soon and the rapids will calm down.

"Or we can walk along the shore with a rope tethered to the canoe out in the water, hoping the three of us can hold on. It will be kind of like walking an aggressive, big dog on a leash."

"Boys, we'll be fine!" Kat said. "The canoeing was the best part of the trip yesterday, and besides, don't you feel we'll be shorting ourselves on the adventure if we don't do exactly what we planned?"

"She's right, Wilson. It would seem like we cheated ourselves. Anyone can walk along the shore. And you did say the rapids would be calming. I say we get back in the canoe and finish this trip!"

"All right, so canoeing it is! Let's go! All we need to do is follow the trail of yellow paint and it will lead us back to the boat." Energetically, they grabbed their gear and disappeared in the trees. Down the steep slope they went. All were carefully minding each step and using trees when needed for balance and support. At first there wasn't the obvious need for navigation. They knew where they had exited from the woods onto the rock, so they knew exactly where to enter to go back down. But as soon as the trees had closed in, they started looking for the yellow splotches of paint.

"Briggs, I don't see any paint! Are you sure you kept spraying all the way to the top?"

"Heck, yes! Both of you saw me!"

Gravity pulled the three at a quickened pace as they descended the mountain. Their heads swiveled from side to side looking for the painted trail markers, but none could be seen.

"Well, don't this beat all!" muttered Eugene. He finally grabbed a large tree with one arm to stop his momentum and with the other arm grabbed the trailing Katrina, who in turn grabbed Jimmy. Loaded down with camping gear, they plowed into each other like an accordion. "This is crazy!" said Gene. "What happened to the paint, Wilson? I knew that your newfangled spray paint was too good to be true. It probably washed off with the overnight dew."

"There was nothing wrong with the spray paint, only the one using the spray paint. I knew you would somehow screw it up, Briggs."

"I'll screw you up, you little—"

"Boys! Stop it! This is not the end of the world. It's not like we're lost or anything. Down there is the river and that's where we will head." They collectively agreed but took a moment to survey their surroundings one more time in search of the mysterious, missing yellow paint before resuming their hike.

Even though it was more treacherous going down the mountain, it was a whole lot easier and quicker than going up. And before they knew it, they could hear the insidious sound of the river.

"Where are we?" When they finally broke through the clearing and toed up to the cliff overlooking the river, they were surprised to see that it wasn't where they had come ashore. And of course there was no canoe chained to a tree near where they stood either.

"I don't know exactly, Briggs, but we are either upstream or downstream from where we need to be." Jimmy rolled his eyes as he knew how dumb his statement sounded. "And you can save your sarcastic response, Eugene, I know that's obvious! In a dense forest where you can't see past the trees to give yourself reference points to judge distance, it's so easy to get lost. It's been known to happen on several occasions. Hikers without a compass may think they are going in a straight line and end up making a complete circle. I guess maybe we should have brought a compass instead of yellow paint."

"Hey, James," Kat said, "you're right. It's either upstream or downstream from here. We can't be too far away. It's probably just a short hike from here. We have a 50 percent chance of going the right way the first time." Katrina picked up her long-strapped bag and tossed it over her shoulders. She took a look left, then right, and then started walking downstream. Eugene and Jimmy followed her lead and fell in behind. After less than fifteen minutes of walking north, they arrived at the canoe. Jimmy started immediately unchaining the boat and Gene began preparing the winch and pulley lines to the trees to lower it back over the side of the rock face.

"Would you look at that, fellas!" Jimmy and Gene looked at Kat who was pointing up the steep incline. Starting fifty feet or so from the canoe, and running straight up the mountain as far as the foliage would let them see, were yellow spots.

"I knew it!" shouted Gene. The three went sprinting to the first tree, then the second, then third. The yellow spots were as clear as an airport runway, marking a trail, straight and true.

Jimmy put his hands on his hips, walked about thirty feet up to the next marked tree, and turned around, looking down at his friends. "Look at all of those spots! How come we couldn't find the yellow marks when we started down?" After a moment, Jimmy yelled down again. "Come up here you two, I've just figured out our little mystery." Kat and Gene quickly joined him. "Look up the mountain and tell me what you see on the trees."

"Yellow spots!" answered Katrina, with the nodding approval of Eugene.

"Of course, yellow spots. Now turn around and look at the trees below us, specifically the four ones that were marked and tell me what you see." There was a second or two of silence.

"I see nothing, no yellow marks." Katrina sounded confused.

"The reason you don't see anything is that Briggs here marked all the trees from the lower side. This is okay for the next set of hikers who want to climb to Cooper's Rock from the river. It's not until they start their descent back down the mountain that they will have trouble. That is unless they have x-ray vision and can see through the wood of the trees to the yellow marks on the other side."

Eugene lowered his head in embarrassment, turned and walked back down to the canoe.

"I hope you are happy, James Wilson! You know that anyone including me would have done the same thing. Hell, if you're so smart why did it take you this long to figure it out?"

Katrina was steaming. This was a side of her that neither Jimmy nor Eugene had ever seen before.

She walked over to within a few inches of Jimmy and gave him a scolding glare before spinning around herself, then heading down to join Eugene.

"I didn't mean anything by it, Kat. We always give each other a hard time. I'm sorry!" Jimmy's shout was directed toward the departing, highly agitated female, causing her to stop in her tracks.

Kat turned around, marched back, and got right in Jimmy's face.

"Why are you apologizing to me? I am not the one who has been hurt by your insensitivity." Kat reached out and grabbed Jimmy's hand, pulling him along like he was her defiant child.

"Come on, you're going to tell Eugene that you are sorry. And I want you two to stop with your petty, disrespectful comments toward each other." When they approached Gene, he was facing away from them so they were unable to see his face.

"Eugene, James has something he wants to tell you. Well, Jimmy?"

"I'm sorry, Briggs. It wasn't your fault. The paint thing was a bad idea. And well, the thing is, I probably would have painted on the wrong side of the trees too." For a moment, Eugene said nothing. He just stared down at the canoe while his two friends stood behind him feeling awful and awaiting any type of response. Finally, Eugene slowly turned around, and to the surprise of his friends, was sporting his patented grin from ear to ear.

"You know, it is kind of funny. I spent all that time painting the trees, marking them so we could find our way back and it was on the wrong side." Gene couldn't even get through the sentence without breaking out in total hysterical laughter. "X-ray vision!" Within seconds all three were in tears from laughing so hard.

"Okay, you boys, I give up! You win! I know now that there is no way I will be able to change your constant verbal sparring. All I ask is for you to have a little more respect for each other's feelings. Please!"

"Well, if Mrs. Sensitivity is done with her little lecture, we need to get this canoe in the water." Kat gave Jimmy a playful shove and the break was over and the journey resumed.

They lowered the canoe by winch back down the eight-foot cliff from which it was pulled up fourteen hours earlier. Then Jimmy and Katrina shimmied down the rope and waited for Gene to toss over the freed lines and wood blocks. Gene joined them momentarily after climbing the long way down. Once again Katrina's demeanor was the complete opposite of the boys'. She was bursting with enthusiasm and energy while Jimmy and Eugene were understandably nervous and apprehensive. She could not wait to get started. In fact she hurried Jimmy through his pre-voyage ritual of specific instructions on what to expect and how to react.

"Jimmy, dear, you went through these instructions yesterday."

"Yeah, Wilson, and we found out they don't work!" Gene said.

With some signs of trepidation in the tone of his voice Jimmy took in a deep breath, looked down the river, and then spoke.

"All we need to do is get the canoe in the middle of the river and keep it straight. This time we don't need to worry about getting the canoe to shore in the most violent part of the river. We just ride the rapids out until the river gets wider and the water settles down. Well, if we're going to do this, let's go."

"It's about time!" responded Katrina. Gene and Kat assumed their positions with Gene at the bow and Kat in the middle.

Jimmy exerted little effort casting off from shore. There was no need; the river reacted to the canoe as an electromagnet reacts to a hunk of iron. In a millisecond they were sucked in, and before they could exhale and draw their second breaths they were once more part of the wild ride. Bobbing up and down in the swells of the river, they sped north.

Whitewater spray was constantly crashing over the twelve-inch sides of the canoe, soaking them to the bone. The expressions of angst on Eugene and Jimmy's faces and their saucer-sized eyes were a stark contrast to the laughs and cheers of gleeful excitement coming from Katrina.

What seemed to be an eternity of intense excitement was soon coming to a close. As Jimmy had forecasted, the narrow gorge, which intensified the ferocious river, suddenly ended about a mile and a half downstream. Cheat River finally lost its sadistic control over the three adventurers and their canoe and spit them out like a cherry pit. They had successfully made it to Ices Ferry where the river substantially widened and the whitewater disappeared. Cheers of victory erupted from all three. They had slain the beast. From here to the dam, they knew it would be a relatively easy and relaxing ride. Cheat River technically became Cheat Lake, a four-mile winding body of water from this point on to the dam. Even though it was a reservoir, there was still a pretty strong current doing most of the work, propelling the watercraft so that Eugene and Jimmy had only minimal rowing. Four miles took four hours, so making their way around the last sweeping curve in the lake and heading for the home stretch was like a marathon runner catching a distant peek at the finish line.

"Half a mile to go!" Jimmy's statement of encouragement converted to energy and caused them to row harder.

"Don't forget, boys, we need to pick up the Browne's car!"

"Yes, and we also need to change the oil in Uncle Mendel's truck and return the canoe." Eugene responded

In the distance, and drawing closer, was their finish line, the dam. But there was something else that caught their attention. Something that looked like a red hump was protruding out of the water about twenty-five feet from shore, and a small boat was circling the object. As they got closer, they noticed a crowd of people at the shore.

"It looks like we have a welcoming committee!"

"That's not exactly what we wanted, Briggs. By the way, where's the truck?"

"I parked it up the hill a ways." Gene pointed past the crowd of people and other vehicles, but there was no truck.

"Oh no, boys, that red hump is the truck!" Katrina cried.

"We are in so much trouble!" said Jimmy. "Those aren't just people standing on shore, that's my parents. And standing beside them, Briggs, are your mom and Uncle Mendel. And please tell me that's not Sherriff Sullivan in the boat." The sheriff had now spotted the canoe and was heading his boat towards them.

"What are we going to tell them? My dad is going to kill me! At least yours is not home to kill you, Briggs."

"Don't sweat it, Wilson, we just went for a canoe ride. We don't know what happened to the truck!" The sheriff's boat idled down its motor as it approached the canoe.

"Where have you kids been? Your parents are worried sick."

"Hello, Sheriff Sullivan! What a lovely day it is. What's all the commotion?" Eugene's syrupy reply brought groans from Jimmy.

"Well, you better hurry on to shore; you've got a lot of explaining to do." The sheriff gave them a long stern look as he circled their canoe and then escorted them to shore. Both boats nosed their bows on to the sandy shore at approximately the same time. Within minutes, the emotion of the welcoming committee went from concern to anger. Apparently, an employee of the dam spotted the truck in the river and called the sheriff. He also told the sheriff that earlier he remembered seeing what he believed to be the same truck driven by the Briggs boy. So with that information the sheriff was able to conduct a quick investigation that brought all parties—with the exception of Fred Briggs and the Brownes, who were all out of town—to the river. Really the sheriff just wanted Mendel to go to the river to identify if indeed that was his truck. But of course, there was no way he would be able to keep the families away. Anxiously, they were awaiting the arrival of the wrecker to pull the truck from the river when they spotted the canoe.

"Where in hell have you three been?" cried Jimmy's parents simultaneously. "I don't remember you asking permission to use the canoe! Do the Brownes have any idea where you have been, young lady?"

"Eugene!" Ertta cried, "I have a strong suspicion that you are behind all of this. Why did you drive your uncle's truck into the river? You told me that you and Jimmy were going camping. You wait until your father gets home!" The questions were coming fast and furious, leaving the boys with no time to respond.

"Mom, I didn't drive Uncle Mendel's truck in the river, but we did go camping."

"You don't mean all of you, do you?" Ertta was shocked, and turned to look at Katrina just as Mrs. Wilson shrieked.

"Everyone, all of this is my fault!" To the boy's surprise, it was Katrina who spoke up. "It was my idea totally. I planned everything from the start. I had to beg Eugene and Jimmy to take me on this canoe trip. At first they said no, but I kept working on them until they gave in. You see, ever since I was very young, I would go to the woods near our house and look down at Cheat River and dream about floating down the rapids. My Grammy would tell me stories about my mother and father taking me on overnight camping trips on the river when I was just a baby. She promised me that someday I would get the chance to do it again. She would see to it." Kat went on and on, laying it down thicker and thicker as she went. Finally, she turned and looked at the red truck cab sticking out of the river. "I don't know how your truck ended up in the river, Mr. Briggs."

"Call me Uncle Mendel, missy."

"Uncle Mendel." Katrina gave Mendel a warm smile that blushed his cheeks. "Eugene parked your truck way up there on the hill. By the way, thank you so much for the use of your truck. The boys would have not been able to take me canoeing were it not for your truck. We were not trying to be deceitful. I will repay you for any damage to your truck, even if I have to work it out in labor all summer."

"Aw, shucks, lass. I'm just happy that you three are alright. Shoot! That old truck needed a bath anyway. I am sure once we drain the water from the engine and transmission it will run just as good as it used to."

Gene looked at Jimmy and rolled his eyes and muttered, "Run just as good as it used to!" Jimmy couldn't hold back his laugh, recalling how the truck whistled and backfired whenever it was shut off.

"You know," Uncle Mendel said, "now that I think about it, it was actually somewhat my fault that the truck ended up in the river. I forgot to tell my nephew not to park on any inclines. That darn transmission never stays in gear when you shut off the engine."

"Well, here comes the wrecker," said Sheriff Sullivan. "Since everyone's safe and sound, if you all don't mind, I will be on my way." Everyone thanked him including Gene, Jimmy, and Kat, who also apologized as well. "You need to apologize to your parents, not me. And the next time you go out camping or canoeing you best make sure they know exactly where you are and what you are doing. If I have to go looking for you three again, I won't be so nice."

The end of the world did not come as Jimmy had predicted. In fact, quite the contrary. Katrina's dramatic embellishment of the truth played on the heartstrings of the adults, and in turn, pulled her and the boys' rear ends out of the fire. Throughout Kat's performance—which, by the way, would rival any Oscar winning actress—Eugene and Jimmy had stood openmouthed and amazed, listening to her work her magic and watching her captive audience hang on every word or bat of her eye. By the time she was done, not only were the boys not in trouble, they were heroes for making this little orphan girl's dreams come true. It was at that moment that Jimmy realized that indeed, she was every bit as clever as him, quite possibly a bit more devious.

"Dad, we borrowed the Brownes' car to drive us up river," Jimmy said. "Can I borrow your car to take Gene and Kat to pick it up?"

"Absolutely not, son!" Jimmy's dad said. "Your mom and I will drive Miss Garretson to pick up the car. You and Gene will stay here with Mendel and help pull the truck out of the water.

"Then you will stay as long as it takes to drain the water out and change the oil and whatever else Mendel needs done to get the truck running. Then for the next two weeks, if this is okay with you, Ertta, and Mendel, you boys will show up at Mendel's farm every day to help with any chores he may have."

"I thought we weren't in trouble," protested Eugene.

"What about Katrina, isn't she going to help on the farm, too?" inquired Jimmy.

"I think we'll leave Katrina's discipline up to the Brownes when they return. Come on, Katrina, let's get the car."

Jimmy stood and stared at the backs of the heads of his mother, father and Katrina as they drove away in the forty-seven Ford.

Even though Kat had bought them a brief reprieve, Jimmy knew he was destined to be punished when his father found out the part of Cheat that they had actually canoed. And he certainly would find out when he dropped Kat off at the Brownes' car at the launch location. He knew he had committed a cardinal sin with his father by going whitewater canoeing without a proper guide, and most likely would have to suffer the consequences upon his return.

Well, Jimmy did get in additional trouble with his folks. But after the yelling and screaming stopped, and as soon Mrs. Wilson wasn't present, Mr. Wilson changed his tone. He told Jimmy that even though it was a boneheaded stunt which could have cost someone their life, he was proud of his courage. Katrina, without any persuasion from the Wilsons or the Briggs elders, fessed up to the Brownes. Because there was no need to protect her friends, her theatrics were somewhat less dramatic. Nevertheless, she was able to sway their emotions toward a light sentence of cleaning the church each Monday for a month. Eugene was sentenced to hard labor on the farm, which was, of course, Uncle Mendel's farm. His payless job was baling hay, which in the past he relished because he recognized the hard labor as a potential contributor to his strength and stamina. Even though this time he wasn't receiving any monetary payment for his services he was still getting benefit from the tough physical workout. Wisely, Eugene accepted his punishment and didn't complain.

CHAPTER 7

It was a typical Sunday in August, hot and dry. Eugene's brother, Delbert, who had been drafted into the army, was home on a brief leave before being deployed to Korea. As a going away party, Ertta was preparing a late afternoon barbeque. It was too hot for football so the "Cheat River Three" went for a swim after church, then up to their secret meeting spot in the clearing overlooking Cheat and the ovens. Eugene and Jimmy perched themselves on top of the large rock, drying off in the hot sun. As per protocol they were patiently waiting for Katrina to finish her walk. Gene had something he wanted to discuss with his friends and was a little nervous about how they would receive it. On cue, just as the boys began to look over their shoulders for their girl, she showed up.

"Mother and Father say hello!" Her bizarre, quirky greeting was received as the normal. Even Jimmy had no sarcastic reply. In fact, it was usually Eugene who responded with a quick "Hello, Mom and Dad G." But not today. Kat took her spot on the rock and drew her face up next to Gene.

"Oh, I'm sorry, Kat. How's Mom and Dad?" Eugene's hesitant response caught the attention of both Kat and Jimmy.

"A little preoccupied today, Briggs? You're not playing her little game."

"Is something bothering my big guy?" Kat playfully inquired.

"Ah, it's nothing really. It's just this friend of my dad's that wants me to finish high school over at Fairmont."

"What! Fairmont! You're kidding, right?" asked Jimmy.

"Please don't say that you're moving away," said Kat. "You're not, are you, Gene?" His friends stared at him in disbelief.

"No, Kat, the Briggs are staying put! Well, kinda. I guess I need to start from the beginning. There is this cat across state lines at Farmington. I think his name is Huff."

"Hey, I remember reading his name in the Morgantown paper last year. Football star, right?" remarked Jimmy.

"Well, as a junior last year he led their football team all the way to win the state championship in West Virginia. Apparently no one could block him. They say he eats quarterbacks and running backs like popcorn. I understand that almost every game last year they carted off at least one of their opponent's players on a stretcher. Well, this is where I come in. My dad's longtime friend and high school football teammate, Mike Shumaker, also happens to be the football coach at Fairmont. Fairmont and Farmington are fierce rivals. If I transfer across the state line to West Virginia and go to Fairmont, I gotta stay at their house. But only through the week. I will still be home on the weekends for your amusement and abuse.

"I guess Coach Shumaker and my dad have been secretly watching us play for a couple weeks. I must have impressed the coach. He told my dad that he thinks I will give the Huff boy a good dose of his own medicine."

"Are you sure he really wasn't looking at Kat or me?"

"Katrina, probably, but you, no!" Gene's wisecrack on Jimmy was wasted on Katrina. She was visibly saddened by the news, but gave Eugene a hug for support anyway.

"I guess we should get along to Delbert's party." Eugene announced. Kat slightly brushed up against the side of Gene as she hurriedly walked past. She didn't want the boys to see the tear rolling down her cheek. Kat was surprised and confused by her sudden emotions. She could see Eugene was excited and was happy for him. She also believed Gene's assurance that he would only be away during the week, and home on weekends. But that didn't subdue the cold, lonely pain that penetrated her heart.

As with most small towns in America, everyone in Point Marian knew everyone, and many folks were related. Needless to say, most of the town was over at the Briggs that day for Delbert's sendoff. Despite Kat's hopes, nothing more was mentioned that day regarding Gene's changing high schools.

While the boys were involved in a rowdy game of horseshoes, Kat was shadowing Ertta. She wanted to talk to her about Gene, and eagerly waited for someone other than herself to initiate him as the topic. But no one ever discussed the subject of Eugene finishing high school at Fairmont or anything remotely close. Katrina eventually gave up, realizing her conversation with Ertta could wait. She realized Mrs. Briggs had much bigger and more important worries to deal with in regards to her older son.

A clang from a cow bell signaled it was time to eat. Pastor Browne blessed the meal and the feast began. After a while Fred gathered the crowd, telling a couple of humorous stories about Delbert, then paused for a moment of silence. With a crack in his voice he proclaimed how proud he was of his son and thanked everyone for coming. The guests collected their covered dishes and belongings and formed a line to shake hands and dole out hugs to Delbert and the rest of the Briggs family.

A few days passed before Kat ventured back to the Briggs', but this time she was not there to visit Eugene. She picked a time when she knew Gene and Jimmy were fishing. Fishing was one of the few activities that Kat usually excused herself from and let the boy's go alone. Katrina admired Ertta for her wise maternal instincts and would respect whatever she had to say. She needed to hear Ertta's thoughts regarding Eugene going away to school, mainly to put her own mind at ease.

Ertta and little Mary Lou were baking pies when Kat arrived, so naturally she was excited to accept the offer to lend a hand.

"I figured you would be off fishing with the boys." Ertta smiled as she handed Katrina the apron. Tentatively, she grabbed the garment and followed Ertta into the kitchen.

"Kat!" shouted Mary Lou, as she jumped into Katrina's arms. "Your boyfriend is not here."

"I know, maybe today I'm just here to visit you, girly." Kat gave

Mary a kiss, swung her around, and then returned the toddler to the floor.

"I'm glad. When my brother is around I never get to talk to you much."

"Well, you know what? I think we need to change that starting now!"

"Yeah!" shouted Mary. Satisfied by Kat's greeting, she resumed to her duties of mixing her mother's concoction of flour, sugar, spices, and eggs.

It was a very enjoyable time for both women and the little girl. Most importantly, they all benefited from the therapeutic, consoling conversation. Katrina asked Ertta how she was able to deal with Delbert's departure to Korea and, of course, her thoughts about Eugene going away to school. She was surprised to hear that Ertta was at peace with both.

"Honey, I pray constantly for Delbert. I pray for Eugene, too, but for different reasons. I hate that game of football. I'm not sure I can bring myself to watch him play. You know his father played, and I couldn't watch him either. I know Eugene loves it, so. . .It's just so violent! I pray that Delbert stays out of harm's way, and I pray that Eugene doesn't get hurt. I know this sounds strange but I'm just as worried that Eugene doesn't end up hurting someone else. I know, dear, you care deeply for Eugene. But if you spend all your life worrying about the men you love, you will not only make your life miserable, but theirs too." Kat embraced Ertta, for she received what she came looking for, some solid comforting advice.

CHAPTER 8

The summer of '53 shot by like a fiery meteor. Labor Day was only a week away and that meant the start of school. Eugene was already staying in Fairmont at Coach Shumaker's Monday through Thursday for two-a-day practices. He was not warmly received by the rest of the team; especially its two senior captains, quarterback Jack Rude and tight end Chris Creek. They had not yet realized his athletic ability nor how his skills would greatly improve the team. They just looked at Gene as the intruder from Point Marian that was staying at the coach's house.

The practices were long, ho, and brutal, and Jack and Chris did everything they could to instigate grief against the newcomer. So when Gene's helmet would come up missing or when the ladle was gone when it was his turn to drink from the water bucket, or an extracurricular kick was administered in the back or side during tackle drills, a fight would begin. For the first few days the coaches were constantly breaking up skirmishes. Fights, fights, and more fights. The two-a-days were mostly for conditioning—lots of running, weights, and agility drills. Coach Shumaker realized what was going on with his team and their unwillingness to accept the new kid. He knew that if he would step in and single out or punish the responsible players, it would only make it harder on his future superstar. So every time a fight would break out, he would make the entire team run. The more they fought, the more they ran. Eugene never backed down and usually delivered the most punishment, even if the fights involved multiple opponents. The fourth day it finally sank in and the fights stopped. For his courage and brute strength, Gene was slowly gaining respect, especially from the linemen. Shumaker's first week of conditioning practices were referred to as hell week, for the obvious reasons. By the second week the coaches introduced the pigskin and started doing football drills.

For the skilled players like Rude and Creek, this is when they started to put their jealousy behind them and began to notice Eugene. Especially for Quarterback Rude, it was as if a light bulb went off. Suddenly, he recognized he had a weapon.

It was the last weekend before school resumed and Eugene was about to make the best of it. As soon as he was dropped off at his house, he threw his bag down, kissed his mother, and then flew out the door. He couldn't get to his friends fast enough. Kat was standing on top of the rock waiting to leap into Gene's arms, while Jimmy killed time by tossing stones over the edge of the cliff. From out of the pines Eugene appeared, jogging toward his friends, sporting his normal contagious grin. As soon as he was near enough, Kat leaped in his arms like a cheetah pouncing on its prey. She had vaulted her petite frame hundreds of times into the arms of Gene, but this time Jimmy spontaneously joined her by jumping on Gene's back. The weight of the two, or the initial impact, didn't alter Eugene's footing. He spun the two around like a merry-go-round until dizziness overcame them, with everyone collapsing to the ground in hysterics.

"So you're a polar bear now," said Jimmy with a smirk.

"Yep, I guess so. A Fairmont Polar Bear."

"How's practices been?"

"Hell! Coach Shu is a deranged tyrant during the day at practice, but at night he's an okay guy. His wife is a great cook. I think anticipating her good cookin' is the only thing getting me through his brutal practices."

"I was hoping that it would be me on your mind getting you through the week," Katrina said teasingly. "We missed you, big guy!" were the words that preceded Kat's kiss to Gene's lips.

"Oh, I just about forgot. How's your mom and dad?"

"Ah, thanks for remembering. They are wonderful, sweetheart! They said they would look after you and keep you safe while you are away from me. They also said they would keep away any of those West Virginia girls who had a notion to make you their beau."

"Oh brother. See, Briggs, what I have to put up with while you're gone?" Jimmy asked.

"Well, the part about keeping the West Virginia girls away, I made that up."

The Cheat River Three spent the rest of the day and most of the night just hanging around, talking and laughing. And never left that clearing and overlook rock till the wee hours of the morning. They were pretty much inseparable the remainder of the holiday weekend. There were plans made and bonds consecrated between the three for every weekend up until Christmas. Jimmy had been scrimping and saving for years to buy his own car and because of his diligent efforts he was now living every young male's American dream. Jimmy was the proud owner of a 1948 Ford, in which, of course, he vivaciously agreed to drive Kat to every Fairmont Home game. In exchange, Eugene was to introduce him to all the available Fairmont girls. The most important pact, according to Kat, was the one she requested late Monday afternoon between Eugene and her. She dubbed this pact the "Dance and Sock Hop Agreement.". Katrina's request was that dances at either school were not to be attended unless accompanied by the other.

"Hey, Kat, since I can't go to our dances without you as my date, well. . ."

"Well, what!" Katrina's vocal tone changed and her arms folded.

"Well, does this mean that you are my steady gal?" The nervous and confused teen anxiously awaited her answer.

A smile returned to Katrina's face, and with a twinkle in her eye she said, "I was your gal the first time I laid eyes on you! The silly boy digging holes in the earth."

CHAPTER 9

Back to school for the three seniors! Kat and Jimmy felt a hollow void deep in their bellies that Tuesday morning as they headed off to school in Jimmy's car. This same emptiness was felt eighteen miles away by their pal Eugene. Eugene's eyes stared pensively through the passenger side window of Coach Shumaker's car at a fence row as it perpetually zipped by his face on the rural West Virginia road. The car was headed to Gene's new high school. No words were spoken by either the coach or his passenger, just the sounds of crackly, static-mixed music from the dashboard radio filled the car. The quality of the sound resonating from the radio was inconsequential because neither one was listening to it. It was just background noise. Finally, the coach broke his silence as he grabbed a pack of Lucky Strikes from the dashboard.

"You're not nervous about your new school are you, Eugene?"

"Maybe a little, sir."

The coach chucked as he flicked the flint on his lighter and took a deep draw on the cigarette to ignite the tobacco.

"You'll be fine. Most of the faculty and many of the students already know about you. You are Fairmont's new star polar bear.

The coach was exactly right. The anointment began from the moment they pulled into the gravel parking lot of the school. Stares and finger pointing from groups of congregating students greeted them as they rolled to a stop.

"Who are they lookin' at?"

"They are looking at you, son."

The awestruck reception continued as Eugene and the coach entered through the front doors of the large school.

The crowded and noisy hall suddenly became silent, as all heads quickly turned toward the direction of the new arrivals. The doors banged shut behind them, sending echoes reverberating through the corridors. With a supportive nudge on Gene's his shoulder, the coach directed Eugene to continue forward, then disappeared into the administration office. The still-hushed crowd parted and gave way to Gene as he cautiously walked down the center of the long marble-floored hall toward his senior locker. As the sea of teens filled in the void as he passed, muffled whispers began filling the air. The boy from Point Marion was visibly and understandably made uncomfortable by the examining mob. Finally, familiar faces! Leaning up against a locker with a smirk on their faces and shaking their heads were Jack and Chris.

"I think I'm going to puke!" snarled Jack as he gave Gene a playful shove. The three boys laughed, and that ignited the crowd. The silence was broken as cheers and applause erupted. Truly, there was a bigger than life hype that preceded Eugene, but fortunately, none of the off-the-field accolades went to his head.

When Friday night arrived, all the hype was solidified. The first game of the year was on the road with Grafton, and the Polar Bears, like the fierce carnivore whose name they sported, mercilessly devoured their prey. Eugene was the real deal. He was unstoppable, rushing for one hundred thirty five yards and five touchdowns. This was a school record that would be broken four other times that season by Eugene. In the locker room, the team's schedule was taped on the wall: Grafton, Clarksville, Kingwood, Bruceton Mills, and then Farmington. A big gold star was stuck beside October 9, marking their biggest game against rival Farmington.

"Each Friday, Another Victim," was the headline of the local paper on the 26th of September. But that wasn't the headline for Fairmont's paper; that was the headline for Farmington's. They were also running over their competition, and they also had their star player, Sam Huff. As a motivational tool, Coach Shumaker used the newspaper headlines to his advantage and taped it up in the Polar Bears' locker room.

Every Sunday afternoon, Fred Briggs would drive Eugene to Coach Shumaker's in Fairmont and most every Friday night Mr. Briggs would drive him home from wherever the football game was. Home games were a different story. Mr. Briggs and Mary Lou would, of course, always attend the games, but so did Jimmy and Katrina. And, of course, Eugene, like most teenagers, would always elect to ride home with his mates. Ertta, however was a different story. She was terrified of the game of football. More so, she was terrified of Eugene getting hurt. Even when the Cheat River Three played over at Jimmy's on Sunday afternoons, Ertta could not bring herself to stay and watch. She justified her absence by telling her family that Gene would be a lot safer if she were sitting at home praying instead of sitting in the bleachers worrying.

Eugene did not have to worry about being true to his promise with Katrina. She and Jimmy were fixtures at every home game, and the three attended the sock hops that followed. Gene always found a way to get his hands on a pint or two of Wild Turkey, one bottle for them and one for the punch bowl. Jimmy, the responsible one, would take a sip or two, but was always mindful of his responsibility of driving his wild friends safely back home to Point Marion. Eugene and Katrina were the complete antitheses to their tea totling, reserved, and deeply religious families. It wasn't how they were raised that made them free spirit adventurers; sometimes God just throws an extra crazy chromosome in just for societal contrast. Some might think that when it came to Eugene and Katrina, God may have dumped in the whole crazy chromosome jar. A funny side note: Ertta used to blame football for the reason Eugene was always ill on Saturday mornings. This was the start of Eugene's personal, "Three P Agenda" that he would carry forward in his football career. Practice, play, and then party.

"The Big Game! Two Undefeated Teams. Two Football Stars. Only One Team Can Triumph!" Finally, some mention by the *Morgantown News* Sunday , even though they had to share print with Farmington. The following Friday night was the big game, and the tension was mounting in practice. Coach Shumaker was using the "we don't get any respect" strategy to motivate his team. It was a home game so they had that advantage going for them, and they would need it.

The tension in the locker room was so thick you could taste it in the air. The uniformed warriors all stood lined up in a row, side by side, backs to their locker, heads poised forward, listening to the carefully chosen rants asserted by the coach as he patrolled the aisles of the home field locker room. Well-chosen words of motivational fire that would make George S. Patton proud sprayed like machinegun fire from Coach Shumaker's mouth. His short, controlled sentences were followed by a brief pause intended to give the players a window for response. And they obliged with a thunderous roar. The team was now in full frenzy, barely able to contain themselves through the brief pregame prayer. It was "Amen" and out the door.

Out from between the bleachers and on to the field the all-white uniformed Polar Bears stampeded onto the gridiron amidst a sea of enthusiastic fans. After the national anthem and coin toss, the stage was set. Two lines, two teams, eleven gladiators staring thirty yards apart, waiting for the referee's whistle to signal the start of the war. *Thud!* The rambunctious crowd went silent moments before the cleat of the Farmington player met the pigskin ball, sending it awkwardly rotating end-over-end through the West Virginia night sky. Waiting on the receiving end was a young freshman back who masterfully made the catch at the twenty-five yard line only to be greeted by a swarm of angry blue jerseys that piled on top of him like a pack of hungry hyenas pouncing on a rabbit. The moment had arrived, what Marion County had been waiting for, when onto the field trotted both stars: Briggs on offense and Huff on defense.

Huddled up in row twenty-two, seats nine and ten, on this chilly Friday evening in October were the other two components of the Cheat River trio. Katrina and Jimmy's roles had greatly diminished. Once they had played a significant role in Eugene's game of football, but were now relegated to merely fans. Yes, they were no different than anyone else in the sea of sardines in which they now sat. Jimmy had no real issue with this. He was very much content with being Eugene's groupie, as long as the perks continued to be post-game sock hops and introductions to cute girls. Katrina, however, still believed she played a vital role in Eugene's success. No, she did not want to be down on the field physically, but mentally, well, let's just say that, clairvoyantly, she was. To the dismay of the fans that sat behind Kat, she would always stand up, no matter what down, when the Polar Bears broke huddle. And she only sat briefly when the play concluded. Gene always knew exactly where she was and always looked up to her after each play. There was no doubt this game was the biggest so far of the season. The fierce, fiery look in Eugene's eyes as he charged the huddle for the first time in this game was no different than the look in Katrina's beautiful eyes, which were intensely watching from the wooden grandstand.

Everyone on the field and off, including the other team, knew that Gene would be receiving the handoff from Jack. The question was, which direction he was going to run. In the previous games, it really did not matter. The other team had no answer for him. Eugene would run right, he would run left, or he would run right up the middle and usually right over any would-be tackler. But tonight was different. Farmington had an answer. Or did they? A record six thousand people were in attendance to witness the clash of the two gladiators, to see which would prevail.

Finally the snap. Channeling all of her energy to Eugene, Katrina tensed her female frame as she screamed at the top of her lungs. As she screamed, she gripped Jimmy's arm, and she gripped hard, very hard, sinking her nails deep through his sweatshirt and embedding her fingerprints into his skin. Kat's adrenalin rush caused Jimmy to scream even louder than her.

Coach Shumaker wanted no part of the hype of Briggs versus Huff. Sam Huff played middle linebacker, but they floated him all over the field. It really did not matter with his speed where he started, in the end, he was always right there, abruptly and mercilessly ending the play for the opposing offense. Shumaker was not going to tempt fate. Even though he had confidence in his stud, the game plan for tonight was to try to avoid Sam Huff at all costs. Nothing up the middle, all plays were to be outside sweeps, with the hope of setting up a rare pass play from Rude to Creek.

For the first play, Rude handed off to Briggs as he hit the outside corner past the tight end, Creek, and quickly gained six yards before a crowd of unfriendly jerseys greeted him, led by, you guessed it, number seventy, Huff. For play number two, Rude handed off opposite field to Briggs, who ran for eight and a first down. The third play from scrimmage went from Rude to Briggs, and with a quick burst, Gene had seven, and this time he had open field, but not for long. Out of the corner of his eye, a blue speck appeared and was closing fast. Gene knew who it was; he lowered his head and shoulders and prepared to deliver a blow that would normally dispatch anyone who dared get in his way. Anyone that is, but Sam Huff. The horrific sound of shoulder pads and helmets crashing together summoned the silence of six thousand. There was not a breath drawn for what seemed like an eternity. Both Sam and Gene lay motionless, miraculously with the ball still firmly lodged in the cradle of Eugene's arm. Before their teammates arrived at the scene, both boys jumped up. They momentarily stared at each other in what could only be summed up as respectful disbelief; no one player had ever before laid a lick on them that neutralized their physical domination. Again, Gene looked up toward Kat and smiled as he ran back to the huddle.

As the rest of the people around her began to sit, Katrina remained standing. Eugene smiled as if he somehow heard or felt the one word muttered from Kat's mouth after the collision. "Ouch!"

As drawn up by the coach, after two more running plays, Fairmont indeed scored with a pass from Rude to Creek. The long run by Briggs that ended with a collision to Huff proved to be the climax of the game. Briggs and Huff battled on both sides of the ball for the rest of game. Both players had small victories, but no one, clear champion.

The game of football is a team sport and no one player usually determines the outcome. This was true in this game as well. At the end of this gridiron war, Farmington was too much for Fairmont. Farmington won by six points, but dominate they did not. Both teams knew their paths would cross again during state playoffs.

Eugene was disappointed, but he left nothing on the field. Sore and extremely exhausted, he limped alongside his teammates back between the stands and toward the locker room. The proud and faithful applauded the valiant efforts of their team as they disappeared from sight. There were more than just students, parents, alumni, and faculty of Fairmont and Farmington attending this highly profiled game. Sprinkled amongst the fans, sitting anonymously in both visitors and home bleachers, were coaches. These coaches were scouting players. They were not just coaches, they were collegiate coaches, and they weren't just evaluating any players; they were appraising Briggs and Huff. One might say it was more like salivating, than appraising.

Eugene had no idea what a scout was, and the thought of some college coach coming to watch him play was nonexistent. Heck, the thought of even going to college had never even entered his mind. So Eugene didn't notice the two men in dark grey overcoats standing stoic and out of place against the backdrop of empathetic fans. Eugene didn't notice, but Katrina did. While the boys were leaving the field and the fans were watching and applauding, Kat was studying these two men. They caught her eye because they seemed out of place. Not once did they applaud for either team.

They mostly talked exclusively between themselves and jotted down notes on paper after plays. "How bizarre," she thought. And this coming from a girl who cornered the market on bizarre. One of the men must have felt the burning gaze of Kat's eyes on the back of his head because he deliberately, but slowly, turned his head around when the rest of the audience was looking tentatively one hundred twenty degrees the other direction. His eyes were shadowed by the brim of his hound's-tooth hat. But Kat knew their eyes had met so she greeted him with a smile. The man took a second or two to study her before finally returning her greeting. His smile was warm but guarded, barely stretching his lips. He gave Kat an acknowledging nod and then turned back around.

Eugene was in no mood to attend the sock hop following the game. Sore, both mentally and physically, he elected to go back home immediately with dad instead of riding back with Jimmy. Katrina also chose to ride with Fred and Gene, leaving Jimmy to fend for himself. Jimmy understood and really did not mind; he now knew almost as many students at Fairmont as he did at his school in Point Marian. Going to the hop alone was no big deal.

Katrina sat in the front seat alongside Mr. Briggs, giving Gene the entire backseat to stretch out. Katrina serenaded to the men on the way home. She had a captive audience and she took advantage of it by singing every song that Nat King Cole had released to date.

"Mr. Briggs." Katrina stopped mid-song about a mile from her house.

"Yes, Katrina?"

"Sir, what do you know about WAF?"

"WAF?"

"Yes, sir. Women in the Air Force."

"Oh, brother, not that again," a voice muttered from the backseat.

"Shush, Gene!" Fred wheeled his head around and gave his son a stern look for his rude comment. Katrina ignored Gene and stared at the road.

"Well, darlin', I've heard about the WACs, but not the WAFs."

"Some really nice women came to our school and talked to the senior girls about volunteering in our armed forces. When I heard the air force lady speak, I was very fascinated with what she had to say. It sounded so exciting! Wouldn't it be great to fly, Mr. Briggs? Oh, well, whenever I talk to the Brownes about it they quickly change the subject. And Eugene thinks I'm crazy."

"Well, you don't listen to that bonehead in the backseat. If it's something you have interest in, then you should pursue it. Don't let anyone tell you that you can't do something just because you're a girl. Sorry, I mean a young woman!" He turned and smiled at Katrina as he pulled into the Brownes' driveway.

"Thank you, Mr. Briggs! That's the same thing my mother and father tell me." Kat leaned over and gave Mr. Briggs a peck on the cheek, then turned and stuck her tongue out at Eugene. She opened the door, and in front of the headlights she skipped, waving and smiling as she ran toward her front door. Eugene leaned forward, hanging his arms over the front seat adjacent to his father. "She kinda floats like an angel."

Fred shook his head and smiled, pausing for a moment as if

to reflect. “Did she just say, that’s the same thing her mother and father tell her?”

Eugene acting like a protective big brother responded quickly.

“Now do you see what I hafta put up with? If she weren’t so darn cute!”

As the porch light went black, Mr. Briggs backed out of the drive and they headed for home.

CHAPTER 10

"Breakfast!" Eugene's bedroom door flew open and in barged Mary Lou. She stood at the end her brother's bed staring at a motionless slab of humanity. "I said, breakfast is ready! Mother sent me to get you." Mary raised her voice a few octaves to enforce her message, only to have Gene retaliate by hurling his pillow blindly toward the direction of his sister's voice. The billowy projectile narrowly missed her head; nevertheless this reactionary response sent her retreating back through the door to the safety of the hallway. Mary understood that her big brothers next launch may not be so forgiving, and more on target. However, she didn't leave without one last verbal assault before descending the stairs. "Eugene Briggs, you are a barbarian, and I'm telling Dad that you tried to hit me."

"Ohhh, I ache everywhere!" Eugene muttered as he swung one leg over the side of the bed. Scratching his head with one hand and his rear end with the other, Eugene hobbled down the hall to the staircase. His teeth clenched in reflex to the pain as he began to negotiate the steps. This was the most post-game pain he had ever experienced. When he made it to the first floor he made a beeline straight to the bathroom to relieve himself before joining his family in the kitchen.

"Mom, Dad, Kat invited me to the Point Marion High School Winter Wonderland Dance."

"That's wonderful!" Ertta smiled.

"Well, not so wonderful is the fact that I need a suit. My Sunday church suit is getting too small and worn from wearing it every week. Mrs. Browne is making Kat a new dress, and all I have is this old, stupid suit."

"Well, maybe I can sew you a new suit too; we just don't have any extra money to buy you a new Sears and Roebuck suit now." Ertta looked at Fred waiting for his opinion.

"You are right Mother. Sears' suits are expensive, and our boy Eugene here used all his summer job money to fix Mendel's truck after they used it as a submarine." After Fred spoke, Eugene looked back to Ertta.

"Mom, please don't take offence, but I'd just as soon wear my old suit as one made by you."

"Well, the boy's right, Ertta, a seamstress ain't one of your strong points. Remember the pants you made the boys a few years back and forgot to put in the flies? And the shirt you made me for Christmas last year that had a different length for each sleeve?" Fred stood up and walked over to Ertta and gave her a hug. "By the way, that Christmas shirt, Ertta Briggs, is my favorite present from you of all time!" Ertta pushed her husband away momentarily and looked into his eyes and smiled.

"Okay, Eugene, you're safe, no Ertta Briggs specials!" They all three laughed. "I have another idea anyway. Delbert's new suit that he bought for his graduation last year."

"Mother, there ain't no way that Delbert will let me wear his new suit, and besides he's in Korea. Even if I could ask him, I know what he'll say. No!"

"Well, you could write him," said Fred.

"That's a grand idea! We'll both ask him, by letter," responded Ertta. "You have not written your brother yet anyway. I will add your letter to mine and we can send it off first thing Monday." Eugene was delighted; he gulped down the rest of his milk and jumped up from the breakfast table.

"Wait just a moment, mister.! Where do you think you're off to?" inquired the elder Briggs. "I see your aches and pains have suddenly left."

"I promised Kat and Jimmy that I would meet them at the rock at nine. I'm sorry, but I forgot. Mom and Dad, may I be excused?"

"Don't be gone all day. I have got chores for you to do around here."

"Got it!" With that, Gene was out the door.

As Eugene entered the clearing, he could see the backs of his compatriots already perched on top of the rock from across the way. Despite the brisk temperatures of the fall morning, his friends were huddled uncharacteristically close. Katrina had her arm around Jimmy, and they were saying nothing. As he drew closer, he could feel heaviness in the air.

"Good morning gang!" Kat turned her head slowly toward Eugene, exposing her sorrowful, heavy eyes and deliberate, but concerned smile. Jimmy's head remained forward and down. Gene's heart instantly began pounding harder.

"What's wrong?" He climbed up on the limestone and crawled, placing himself directly in front of Jimmy.

"Oh my God, what the hell happened to you?" Eugene immediately stood up, repulsed by what he saw. Jimmy's face was disfigured from swelling. Dark blue splotches pigmented his skin over his jaw and cheekbones. One eye was almost completely swollen shut and the other was black as a lump of coal. Jimmy was embarrassed, humiliated and struggled to respond to Eugene. Feeling Jimmy's awkwardness and anguish Katrina interjected. Her arm, still firmly embracing Jimmy, constricted slightly, showing her support.

"It's okay, hun" said Kat, unlocking her grip on Jimmy and standing up. She grabbed Gene's arm and escorted him off the rock and out of Jimmy's earshot. Softly and calmly she began explaining Jimmy's predicament to her excited and concerned mate.

"Jimmy got beat up last night."

"Who did it? Where?" Gene's voice rose as he looked at his dejected friend, then back to Kat.

"Please, Gene, shush! It took him forever to open up to me with that much. Let him tell us more details in his own time." Katrina sighed as she looked at Jimmy, and then continued. "Earlier, Jimmy was sitting and waiting on the curb in front of my house.

You know how he usually waits for me and then we walk to the woods together. This morning I sensed something was wrong even before I approached. Jimmy said nothing, not even his normal sarcastic greeting. He just stood up and started walking a step or two ahead, shielding his face from my view. Of course his odd behavior only brought attention to himself. I had to speed up my stride, practically run just to get alongside. My jaw dropped when I saw his poor face. I cried out for him to stop. I finally had to step in front of him. I tried to touch his face but that only caused him to flinch. "It's nothing!" he said. "Can we just go?"

"There were four of them, okay!" Jimmy interrupted with a broken voice and abruptly concluded Eugene and Katrina's conversation."My gosh, I can hear everything that you two are saying. Listen, I just got into a little altercation with some Italian thugs who thought they owned the jukebox at the Red Dog Tavern. The bottom line is that it was my fault, my problem, and I will deal with it." Jimmy was now standing up on the rock and staring down at his audience of two. "Trying to impress the two girls I was with by going into that Mafia bar last night sounds like some boneheaded stunt you would pull, Briggs. I'm supposed to be the smart one." Disgusted, Jimmy turned away and stared off to the distant river below.

"What did your mom and dad say, Wilson?" Gene yelled up at Jimmy.

Kat responded first. "They haven't seen him yet. They were asleep last night and he left this morning before they woke. This is why many adults including the Brownes, think the drinking age should be raised. Maybe this wouldn't have happened if you weren't allowed in that tavern."

"What are you saying, Kat? Are you nutty or something? You're constantly wanting me to get us hooch." Gene rolled his eyes and shook his head.

"I didn't say I wanted the law to be changed. I said many adults do. Pay attention, jerk!"

"Well, whatever," said Gene, "I'm going after those assholes tonight. We'll see how tough they are."

"Oh no, you're not, Eugene Briggs!" Kat cried.

"You are right, Kat, he's not. It's my fight, not his!" Jimmy jumped down off the rock to the eye level of his friends.

"You are not fighting my battles, Briggs! And I don't need your pity either, Kat!"

"Look at you, Wilson. You are in no shape to go out tonight, and besides, once you go home and your parents see what happened to you, they won't let you out."

"Who said anything about me going home? Mom and Dad are going to Morgantown this afternoon. I will slip back home while they're gone and leave them a note that I'm staying all night with you, Briggs."

"Then what, Wilson? Go back to Fairmont and get beat up again?" Gene asked. Jimmy looked away in anger.

"I can't take them all on at once, but I sure as hell can take them on one at a time, especially with me wielding a baseball bat," said Jimmy.

"Oh lord!" chirped Katrina. "Listen boys, we are a team. We're family, remember? Cheat River Three?"

"And nobody messes with my family!" Gene tagged on to Kat's oration, but didn't quite get it, as he began to walk away.

"Where do you think you're going Eugene? I meant that we would all *three* help Jimmy with his revenge!" Kat responded.

Jimmy had heard enough and yelled to Gene.

"All right, if you two really feel you must be involved, I think I just might have a plan." Eugene stopped to listen.

"That's the James Wilson I love!" Kat clapped, and jumped up and down with excitement. They all three sat down on the rock and listened to Jimmy as he formulated his plan.

The three teens had no idea what they were getting themselves into with the thugs. They had heard of the mob or Mafia, but had no idea what they were about or how dangerous these people were. Like many small towns in West Virginia in the late forties and early fifties, Fairmont's naive citizens opened their doors to organized crime. Crime families migrated away from the big cities like Pittsburgh to small mining towns, especially union towns, to set up shop. The Red Dog Tavern had been acquired by a family named Amato when the original owner suddenly left town in 1942, for what was rumored to be a debt settlement.

KERBOOM! The windows of the Red Dog rattled as Mendel's rusty beast of a truck pulled up and stopped parallel to the curb across the street of the establishment. It was ten o'clock; signs of human activity had subsided for the night. The empty street and sidewalks were slightly illuminated by the gas streetlamps pitching their lonely and cold shadows upon the dank, urban brick buildings. The exception to this deserted scene was a two-story, dingy grey building at the end of the block. This particular establishment was seemingly abuzz. A red dog painted on a wood plank supported by a stanchion hung over the entrance. Glowing red neon beer and tobacco signs decorated the otherwise blacked-out picture windows. A handful of cars were crammed perpendicularly in front of the tavern with a few more squeezed down an alley next to the building. Two men smoking cigarettes under the sign at the entrance laughed, reacting to the backfiring truck. Enthralled and amused, they watched as a male figure wearing a grey trench coat and sunglasses exited the vehicle and walked toward them from across the street.

"Hey, Hollywood, the sun went down hours ago!"

There was no hesitation or reaction from Jimmy, even to the jeers of the thug-like gatekeepers. He briskly walked up and grabbed the handle to the entrance. As he pulled open the door he could hear the engine in Mendel's truck revving up behind him. *BANG!* The loud clap that rolled through the open doorway sounded like a shotgun blast, causing some to dive for cover under their tables. The noise from multiple conversations inside the dimly lit den immediately ceased. Every startled eye in the room was now pointing directly at Jimmy. To his right, a long bar extended the length of the room. The red topped barstools were mostly empty, with the exception of three, which were occupied by thick-necked thugs in undersized sports coats. From behind the bar stood a weathered old man wearing a white apron over a blue shirt. Empty round tables with black and white checkered linen cloths burnished the center of the smoke filled room. Rows of booths lined the left wall; all filled with men and scantily clad women sitting on their laps. The thick, smoke-filled room combined with the stench of whiskey and sweet perfume caused Jimmy to swallow hard. This odorous cocktail triggered a recall of the terror of the night before. Suddenly, he felt the presence of the two centurions from the front door now standing behind him and realized there was no turning back. The surprise entrance was over; every male in the room began to make their advance, so he made a beeline directly over to the jukebox.

"Hey, it's that kid from last night!" a voice from the dark announced. The glow of the Wurlitzer jukebox illuminated Jimmy's face as he stood staring down at the music menu. Before his hand was able to dethatch the final button of his coat, a shove from behind pushed him into the music machine.

"I thought we told you not to come back here anymore!" a gruff voice from behind"I guess this time we won't be so nice!"

Just then the front door flew open, and once again a serenade of explosions from the street came bellowing inside the tavern. In the entry stood an imposing silhouette of a tall male, ruggedly chiseled in stature, with what appeared to be a larger than normal head.

Once again all eyes turned toward the entrance, including the thug's that just assaulted Jimmy. The silhouette stepped though the threshold and the lights revealed that he was wearing a football helmet.

"What the hell!" Uttered the enforcer in the dark blue sport coat, right before his knees buckled and he hit the floor. Standing over him was a smiling Jimmy, with a Louisville Slugger in his grip. The pine bat that was previously concealed under his trench coat just hit a home run. A war cry came from Eugene as he ripped off his shirt and the rumble was on as he began to deliver punishment to whomever and whatever approached him. Dispatching bodies, booze, glass, and chairs, Gene was a one-man wrecking crew. A full-fledged donnybrook had just erupted. Men who were not supposed to be there flooded the exit, leaving the chaotic battleground to employees and hired protection, all of whom were now engaged in the fight. Screaming topless women ran wildly from one side of the room to the other, finally taking refuge on top of the bar. With his initial deliberate swing of the bat, Jimmy had his moment of sweet revenge, taking down the main culprit from the night before. To celebrate his triumph and to cap off recapturing his bravado, he grabbed one of the fleeing, frenzied female floozies and planted a long and hard kiss on her lips.

A loud *BOOM* rang out, but this time it came from behind the bar. Pieces of the ceiling came floating down like snowflakes. All movement in the room came to a complete stop. *Chick, chick.* The bartender advanced another shell into his shotgun and lowered the barrel directly at Eugene. Jimmy's enforcer nemesis with the dark blue sports coat revived himself and stood up from the floor. He reached into his coat, pulled out a revolver, walked over to Jimmy, and placed the cold blue steel barrel to his temple.

"Say goodbye, Romeo!" Just as his thumb cocked back the hammer, the front door flew open again.

"Stop!" cried the female voice. The thug reacted and pointed his gun at the shadow in the door and pulled the trigger. *Click!*

Jimmy opened his eyes and broke away running as fast as he could toward the door, leaving the angered thug examining his firearm, bewildered as to why it didn't shoot. In the confusion the bartender looked away long enough for Eugene to bolt too. The boys arrived simultaneously at the doorway and before Kat could turn and exit, Gene picked her up and threw her over his shoulders like a sack of flour. A blast of pellets splintered the door as it shut behind the three. But they were already on the sidewalk.

"Run! Get to the truck!" yelled Gene. The bloodied crowd followed with guns drawn. When they hit the street, they were running at full speed. What a sight! Jimmy with his undone trench coat flowing in the wind like Superman's cape, and Gene with Kat over his shoulder, her butt in the air and her legs kicking. They passed right in front of a car that had to lock up its brakes, narrowly missing them. This was not a normal car; this was a Virginia State police cruiser. Jimmy reached the truck, opened the door, jumped in, and slid across the bench seat. Gene leaned forward and released his female package. The momentum sent Kat flying like a rag doll into the truck, landing in the seat next to Jimmy. Eugene followed, grabbing the door and pulling it shut behind him. The idling old farm truck quickly converted into a getaway vehicle. Gene crammed it into gear, stomped down on the accelerator, and before you could say Cosa Nostra, they were gone.

Days passed and nothing was ever publically acknowledged regarding the incident. The newspaper was absolutely quiet. Almost as quiet as the inside of Mendel's truck on the quick ride back home that night to Point Marion. The biggest newsworthy event to hit Fairmont since the fire at Clines Grocery ten years prior and it was as if it had never happened. Jimmy was a nervous wreck. He just knew that at any time a police vehicle would pull up outside of his house or at his school and cart him away.

Every morning for nearly two weeks, Jimmy retrieved the paper from the front porch expecting to read a front page exposé regarding the riot at the Red Dog, but nothing. Being arrested should have been the last of Jimmy's worries. Revenge from an embarrassed Mafia family should have been his main concern. For whatever strange reason—maybe it was indeed the shame of being upstaged by three teenagers—there was no retaliation. This was perhaps a night best left forgotten for the Amato family.

CHAPTER 11

Several weeks had passed since the rumble at the Red Dog. Football had concluded, with Eugene owning almost every single rushing record in school history. And once again the Polar Bears were defeated at the state tournament by their arch-nemesis, Farmington. This time was a much more decisive game than the prior match-up earlier in the season.

It was the Saturday after Thanksgiving, and a cold one at that.

Katrina was deliberately hurrying at a swift pace along the frost-covered sidewalk on her brisk morning journey over to the Briggs' house. For every step she put forward, she would exhale a short burst of warm breath that turned to white steam as it was introduced to the cold morning air. Kat was chugging along at high speed, looking like a steam locomotive, but her gait wasn't fast enough. A large black Plymouth passed her like she was standing still, then pulled to the curb a half a block away. The car had stopped in front of the Briggs'. Immediately a man jumped out from the driver's side and walked around to join another man who had exited from the passenger side and was now standing on the sidewalk. Katrina observed the taller gentleman who had exited the passenger side. He appeared to be studying the Briggs' home, and then looking up and down the street at all the surrounding houses. When satisfied with his quick study, he took one last draw on his cigarette, then flicked the butt into the street. With his other hand he placed a hound's-tooth hat firmly on his head, nodded to his subordinate, and began to walk up the steps toward the door. This hesitation by the men allowed Kat to catch up to them.

"You're going to see Eugene, aren't you?"

The men stopped and turned around to see the smiling face that had asked such a surprising question.

"Why yes, ma'am, we are." The tall man tipped his hat.

"Oh, I'm not a ma'am, sir, I'm a Kat, Katrina's my name, and we have already met. Well, at least from a distance, that is." She extended her arm as the bewildered man grabbed her mittened hand to shake.

"Paul Bryant, and this is Mr. Jerry Claiborne, but you have me at a disadvantage, Miss. I'm—"

"I sat a few rows behind you at the Farmington game," Kat said. "I was watching you watch Gene!" Bryant furrowed his brow, and then slightly tilted his head as if to recall the situation.

"How could I forget such a pretty face? You must be Eugene's sister?"

"Ha!" retorted Katrina. "He could only be so lucky. Come on

gentlemen, follow me." The two men looked at each other and smiled as Kat skipped around them and up the walk to the door.

"Well, you heard the lady, Claiborne." The men fell in line, escorted by the brassy young Miss Garretson.

"Good morning! Hello!" It was common for Katrina to let herself in; after all she was considered family. Ertta, however, was surprised to find her standing in the front room with two strangers.

"Who is it, dear?" yelled Fred, as his elevated voice preceded his appearance from the upstairs.

"We have visitors!" responded Mrs. Briggs as Fred entered the room just as she and Katrina gathered the coats and hats of the two men.

"Let me introduce myself, I'm…"

"No introductions needed, I know who you are. Ertta, this is Coach Paul Bryant and Coach Jerry Claiborne. It's an honor to meet you gentlemen." Fred smiled at the men. "Coach Shumaker said you would be a callin'."

"Let me first apologize for our rudeness. It's not my habit to just drop in uninvited, but Coach Shumaker thought that might be the best way to catch you all at home," said Coach Bryant.

"I don't like sending off letters, your son's too important to me and I'm too impatient to wait on the U.S. mail. And I understand that you have no telephone, so Jerry and I decided just to take a chance and drive over from Kentucky. But if you don't have time to visit today, we understand. We certainly would come back at a more convenient time of your choosing."

"We wouldn't hear of it, would we, Ertta?"

"Certainly not, I'll go make a fresh pot of coffee," confirmed Mrs. Briggs.

"I'll fetch Eugene!" Kat excitedly volunteered as she scampered up the steps to the second floor.

The three men shook hands, then ambled off to the kitchen. Shortly, Kat showed up with Eugene, and then excused herself to go play with Mary Lou. He shook hands with the coaches and took a seat.

"Well, I'm going to cut right to the chase, Mr. Briggs. I want your son to play football for me," said Coach Bryant.

"Well, Kentucky is close. Not as close as West Virginia, but—" replied Ertta.

"I'm not talking about Kentucky, ma'am," Coach Bryant continued. "I want Eugene to play for me at Texas A&M. Tomorrow, the Sunday papers across the nation will all have the story of me resigning at Kentucky and accepting the head coaching job at A&M."

Eugene's ears perked up. "

Where is Texas A&M?" he asked. "And what is A&M?" Coach Claiborne laughed, but Coach Bryant kept a straight face and responded to the younger Briggs.

"That's the same question Coach Claiborne asked me two weeks ago when I told him of my decision to leave Kentucky. Texas A&M is located in a town called College Station, a little northwest of Houston. A&M stands for Agricultural and Mechanical. It's a proud and good university focused on preparing students for a career in either the military or farming, but Eugene, you need not worry about either of those fine vocations.

"Yes, you will receive a formative education," Coach Bryant continued, "and the college will pick up the tab, but, son, with your athletic talents, football will be the vocation that will open unlimited doors for you. Up until now A&M has never had a football history. I will change that and make the Aggies a winning football program. Eugene Briggs, I want you to be a part of my team, the team that changes A&M history. I want you to play fullback for me. I want to tandem you up with another boy I have recruited from Springhill, Louisiana. His name is John David Crow. The running ability of both you young men will give our team a rushing threat that will be unstoppable."

Coach Bryant had a totally captivated audience. He was charismatic with his southern charm, but plain spoken and absolutely no nonsense. They talked for two hours and over two pots of coffee. Jerry set up a projector and they looked at film of the campus, and before the two men left, Coach Bryant invited the four Briggs to fly to Texas to personally see and tour the campus. As a parting thought, Coach Bryant told Eugene that his rival Sam Huff had signed a commitment letter to play for the University of West Virginia. He said, "Son, would you honestly want to be on the same team, of someone that beat you twice in one season? I know I wouldn't. I'd want to be on another team that may give me opportunity to play against and beat him someday. I know that you all need to discuss a lot of what we have talked about, so we'll get out of your hair. It certainly has been a pleasure, and with your permission, I will be back in touch. We'll talk about a good time for you all to fly out there." The men walked through the door and down the walk where Katrina was waiting for them at their car.

"I know you are going to take Eugene away from me. I knew it the other night at the game. But my heart is not too heavy. My mama and daddy assured me that even though we would be some distance apart, our souls will never separate. They also told me that a bear would take good care of him. I wasn't sure why they said that then, but I think I know now. Are you that bear?" The coaches were momentarily dumbfounded at Kat's prophetic articulation.

"Some folks call me Bear," said Coach Bryant. "And yes, I've always looked after my boys. Eugene will come to me as a boy, but he will leave as a man." The men got into the car, and before they pulled away, Coach Bryant rolled down the window.

"You know, Missy, you are always welcome to come to Texas anytime to visit Eugene."

"Oh, you can count on it, Mr. Bear Bryant, sir!" Bryant gave a slight nod to Kat as the car sped away. Then he turned to his assistant coach behind the wheel, smiled and said,

"I get the feeling that while we were recruiting Briggs, that gal was recruiting us!"

The Briggs did accept Coach Bryant's invitation and were flown out to visit the university. This in itself was a tremendous undertaking, which took days of coaxing by the Briggs men to convince Ertta to get on an airplane. This was Ertta and Eugene's first time out of the Appalachian Mountains, let alone their first time flying. Ertta was understandably terrified. She finally yielded her fears to her faith and agreed to go. And it proved to be the right decision. She had a wonderful time, as did the men. The Briggs were so impressed with the campus and their hosts, that Eugene signed a letter of intent before they returned home. Even Ertta who had much trepidation before with the trip, was put at ease. As a mother, she had concerns with the distance of the college, but mostly the fact that her son was going to continue playing the violent game of football. Coach Bryant's calm, fatherly demeanor comforted her worries, though, and she felt confident her son would be in good hands.

The Brownes, Kat, and Mary Lou were all at the airport in Morgantown to collect the Briggs to return them home. Eugene was excited to announce to Katrina the news of his commitment to attend school and play football at Texas A&M, but had some reservations too. He was feeling some concern and angst about being away from his family and friends. His greatest concern was how he would break the news to Kat. What would he say, and how would she react?

He would soon need to tell her the news that would potentially break her heart. His happy news was not so happy if it meant breaking up the trio of Jimmy, Kat, and himself. To his surprise, or lack of her surprise, Kat had already accepted the fact that he would be leaving home next fall. She confirmed this to him as he struggled to break the news on the ride home from the airport. Lisa Browne, Kat, Mary Lou, and Eugene all were all crammed like sardines in the backseat of the Brownes' car when Eugene told of his decision.

"You silly boy, I already knew that you would be going off to play football with that man named Bear. There was a whisper in my head at your football game when I saw him in the grandstand. That whisper got louder when I met him at your house."

"Who whispered in your head?" the consortium in the car answered in unison.

"Oh, brother," Gene responded in disbelief to what Kat just said out loud.

"Now, Katrina, dear, we know that no one really whispered in your head, don't we?" said Mrs. Browne. Kat said nothing until Gene nudged her in the side with his elbow.

"Yes, Mrs. Browne, we know no one really whispers in my head." Kat turned and softly spoke in Eugene's ear. "She's right, no one does whisper in my head. Someone does!"

CHAPTER 12

The Point Marion High School Christmas dance was a week away and Eugene still had not heard back from his older brother regarding borrowing his suit. In July, President Truman had announced that the Korean conflict was over, but many troops still remained deployed. Their new mission was to serve as deterrents against further skirmishes and assist the South Koreans with cleaning up and rebuilding their war torn country. Nevertheless, war or no war, there was no letter and Eugene needed a suit. So Ertta and Fred took it upon themselves to render permission on Delbert's behalf. This turned out to be a huge mistake.

Delbert had been very proud of his new suit. He had scrimped and saved for months to come up with enough money to purchase it from the Sears and Roebuck catalogue. He had it packed in mothballs and boxed away in his closet, only to be brought out and worn on the most special of occasions. But his brother Eugene didn't share the same respect and reverence for the garment, even though Eugene promised his mother and father that he would treat the suit as if it were his own. It wasn't the promise, but the interpretation of the promise, that would be compromised. It was inconsequential to Eugene who owned the suit. The promise to his parents should have been to respect the suit as much as Delbert would respect the suit.

Saturday night, at six o'clock on the nose, Jimmy's car rolled up to the curb in front of Eugene's house. Out jumped a dapper young man, dressed in a black suit. Jimmy looked like his hero Clark Gable in *To Please a Lady*. He had even grown a mustache, which had taken weeks, but was nevertheless now a part of his ensemble. Up to the Briggs' door he strutted to retrieve his buddy.

"Good evening to my partner in debonair!" was Eugene's vainglorious greeting to his chum as he crossed over the threshold and into the living room of the house. Gene was equally as well-dressed, but was in contrast to Jimmy. Delbert's suit was a little tight fit for the rugged, rawboned younger sibling. Gene's larger physique pushed the elastic limits of the wool garment, which would prove difficult later when dancing. One thing both boys had in common this evening was their generous use of Brylcreem. This didn't go without notice and teasing from Mary Lou, and even Fred Briggs. After the accolades from Mom and the posing for pictures, the boys were off to pick up their dates.

Jimmy dropped Eugene off at Katrina's, then headed off to pick up his date. His plan was to pick up Tiffany Trump, a fellow classmate and honor student, then return back to collect Kat and Gene.

Gene patiently bided his time in the Browne's living room waiting for his date. Behind the wall and down the hall, Katrina sat on a chair in front of the bathroom mirror. She was meticulously applying makeup and lipstick, while Mrs. Browne stood behind Kat, preparing her hair. Streams of tears rolled down Lisa's cheeks as she methodically worked to sculpt Kat's locks. As a mother she was well aware of the implications of this event. This was the defining moment, the rite of passage of a girl turning into a woman. Only a parent who had experienced this transformation of their children could relate to this emotion. Lisa Browne might not have been Kat's real mother, but maternal or not the emotions behind the tears were just as genuine. She experienced the private moment between a mother and daughter, and the parental emotional paradox somewhere between joy and sorrow.

Eugene had no way to anticipate or prepare for what his senses were about to experience. The little girl in a ragged dress with the soil-smudged face and big brown eyes that came into his life years earlier was now gone. That little girl was now a breathtakingly beautiful woman!

Katrina was wearing a full length red dress that Lisa had made.

Her brown hair was pulled up in a bundle and laced with baby's breath and fake pearls and, of course, one red ribbon to secure it all in place. She stood before Gene and smiled, and he nearly fell out of his chair.

"Are you ready to go, handsome?"

Eugene swallowed hard and opened his mouth to speak but nothing came out. He shook his head and tried again. On his second attempt, he managed to sputter, "Is that you, Kat? I, I mean, you are so pretty. You look like a movie star."

"Ah, you are so sweet! You look very handsome, too, Mr. Eugene Briggs."

Not taking his eyes off of Kat, Eugene clumsily stood up, knocking over the manger scene on the coffee table. She had him in an enchanted trance, an unintentional spell that rendered his motor skills totally paralyzed. Gene was so numb that he didn't even notice that Jimmy and Tiffany had joined them in the room. What a mess he was. Katrina had to physically maneuver him around the room in order for Mr. Browne to take pictures. When Gene failed to respond to two separate questions, it became very apparent even to Jimmy that something was up with his buddy.

"Hey, Kat, what's with your zombie date?

"I think he just needs some fresh air," replied Kat.

"I think he needs a lot of fresh air," said Jimmy. "So what do you say we head to the dance?" With that, Kat grabbed Eugene's arm and led him out the door behind Jimmy and Tiffany.

Eugene gawked at his newly discovered beauty all the way to the school. About halfway through the dance, Eugene snapped out of his trance when the band started to pep up. They began playing music called "rock and roll" that was the new rage sweeping the nation. This musical phenomenon was like rocket fuel that ignited the kids. They went crazy, especially Gene and Kat, who were all over the gym shuffling, jumping, bumping, and sliding.

The teenagers were emulating dances they saw at intermission at the movies from their counterparts from the West coast. Eugene and Katrina's antics drew a crowd, and their classmates loved every minute of it. The louder and faster the band played, the faster they danced, and the faster Gene and Kat danced, the more the crowd clapped and egged them on. Soon Gene's jacket came off, and then his tie. And with Kat, the first to go were the high-heeled shoes, followed by her hair. What took Lisa nearly an hour to sculpt up high fell down in less than two seconds. It was all about the fun despite the frowns of the teachers and chaperones.

"A dance doesn't start becoming fun until the punch gets spiked." At least that was what one senior was heard to say as he dumped a pint of Wild Turkey in the bowl. Eugene also subscribed to this theory, but he was a little less willing to share. Apricot brandy was the prescribed poison and several trips were made to Jimmy's car by the four marauders to partake in this libation. Very soon the booze began to take effect and, of course, bad decisions followed.

"Hey, Wilson, what do you say about blowing this joint and driving to Morgantown?" inquired the half inebriated Briggs, with Katrina nestled beside him.

"What's in Morgantown?" asked Jimmy, raising the volume of his voice to compete with the band in the background.

"It's not 'what's' in Morgantown, it's 'who's' in Morgantown," slurred Eugene.

"Okay, Einstein, who's in Morgantown?" Jimmy asked.

"The Farmington football team, that's who. They have been invited by the governor of West Virginia to a fancy dinner at some highfalutin hotel to honor them for winning the state. I think we should go crash their party. Come on, it will be fun!" It must have been the effects of brandy, because no one in the group objected to Gene's scheme, not even Jimmy. So the gang jumped in Jimmy's car and they were off to the big city. In thirty-five minutes they arrived at the city limits. Eugene wasn't sure exactly where the hotel was, or even the name, but he thought it was downtown.

So that's where they headed. Actually, he wasn't exactly sure that this was the right night either, but he elected to keep that little detail to himself.

Eugene lunged forward in his seat as the car turned on High Street. "There it is! The Hotel Morgan! That's it!" He pointed at the name on the awning of the front door of a multistory, majestic building as they drove by. "I'm sure that's what the paper said!" Jimmy pulled over to the curb about a half block away.

"Okay, Briggs, what's the plan now?" Before Jimmy could finish his sentence, Katrina jumped out of the car.

"Come on, slow pokes. Let's go!" Kat turned around and motioned to the car. Eugene jumped out behind her and lifted her in the air, twirling her around, then returning her to the ground. Their contagious laughter spread to Tiffany and then to Jimmy, who were all now huddled together.

"There ain't no plan, Cat Daddy Wilson." Eugene extended his arm to Katrina and she grabbed ahold. And like Dorothy and the Scarecrow, they skipped down the walk toward the hotel. Through the door they strutted, acting as if they were the Rockefellers on a visit to the White House. Katrina and Tiffany's eyes lit up as they entered the massive entry hall of the grand palace. Pretty strands of Christmas lights draped the mahogany banisters and walls, while red poinsettias were potted strategically throughout the room. From the crystal chandelier to the white marble floor, the lobby was as magnificent as Oz to the four friends. As if on cue, Katrina broke from the other three and did a pirouette in the center of the room. Her brown hair and red dress fluttered outward in the self-made breeze. She completed her twirl, raised her arms, and then gave a full bow to the crowd of bewildered onlookers at the front desk.

"Excuse me, may I help you four?" asked a staunch maître d' as he approached.

"I say, will you be joining the honorable Marland for his inaugural awards dinner?"

"Why, yes, we will, sir!" Jimmy replied without hesitation. Jimmy, of course, had no idea what he was committing them to, but knew he had to say something quick or risk being expelled from the premises. His assumption was that the Marland Inaugural Awards Dinner was what Eugene had been alluding to regarding Farmington's state football championship. The maître d' assumed by their formal attire that they were just stragglers arriving late to the occasion.

"If you would be so kind as to follow me." The arrogance of the master of the house incited Gene and Kat to mock the little man as he marched off toward the grand ballroom.

"Miss Katrina, would you be so kind as to follow me?"

"I would be more than delighted to, Mr. Briggs." They all four marched in single file, mimicking their stuffy leader down the corridor and through the large door of the ballroom. As the snooty host opened the massive door to let them in, they were immediately inundated by the beautiful sounds of the season spilling out from the room like champagne spilling over a crystal chalice. The sounds of a string quartet playing traditional Christmas music mixed with the chatter coming from rows of round tables filled with people. At the front of the room was a podium, and behind the podium a large, draped banner with the words, "Governor Marland's West Virginia Democrat Fundraiser Awards". The four stood at the back of the room gazing over the tops of the heads of the many seated individuals, none of which looked a day under thirty.

Eugene turned to Jimmy and said,

"These cats from Farmington sure look old!"

Jimmy couldn't believe what he was hearing and looked at Eugene to see if he were serious.

"Well, I guess I got the wrong night!" said Gene with a grin.

"Why am I not surprised by this, Briggs?" scoffed Jimmy. "Well, we're here, so let's make the best of it."

Jimmy nodded toward Kat and Tiffany who had already found a vacant table in back. The bussers had already begun to clear the tables in preparation for the speakers. Back in the car, Eugene had been playing out in his mind various embarrassing pranks he could play on the Farmington football team while they were being honored. But this droll dinner of staunchly old politicians totally decimated his plans. The four friends now sat fidgeting in their seats, listening to the monotone voice of the master of ceremonies as he read from his written speech. It was only a matter of time before the lack of excitement would kick in and cause Eugene to take action.

"What we need is a little more apricot brandy to liven things up."

"I thought we drank it all on our drive over to this very boring place," said Kat.

"Nope, and like a boy scout I am always prepared." Gene opened up his jacket and, sure enough, pulled out another pint. He twisted the cap off and raised the bottle to his lips, gulping down at least two healthy shots before passing it. Only two times around the table and the bottle was dry.

"Come on big boy, let's dance." Even though the band had long since stopped, Kat was motivated. She jumped up, shimmying and swaying around the table, returning to Gene and extending her hand, which he accepted. And just like at the gym in Point Marian, the two were at it again. This time, however, there was absolutely no music. But like at the high school gym, they did draw attention. First, from the closest surrounding tables, and then the whispers spread like wildfire all the way to the podium. No one in the room was listening anymore to Governor Marland. As soon as he sensed this, he stopped reading and looked up. The governor squinted to try to see the commotion at the other end of the hall, but the string quartet had already dialed in their vision. As if the quartet had rehearsed it all day, they led into a fast tempo rendition of "That Christmas Feelin."

Jimmy looked over at an uneasy Tiffany and said,

"See, what did I tell you about these two? Believe it or not, even in this room, we now look like a couple of bumps on a log."

"You don't mean. . . " Tiffany suddenly became terrified at Jimmy's next request.

"That is exactly what I mean, baby!" Jimmy sprang from his chair, knocking it over, clutched Tiffany's arm, and suddenly, the floor no longer just belonged to Eugene and Kat.

The tables awoke. Smiles replaced blank-slate faces. Hands and toes tapped, keeping time, and even a few heads bobbed to the music. The guests were momentarily set free from their political captor, but not for long. The governor was not one of the amused. After realizing he had lost his audience, he gave a stern glare to his musicians, then summoned the hotel heavies. But like the Von Trapp family, Gene, Kat, Jimmy, and Tiffany made their escape moments before security arrived. They waved to the room as they hastily exited back out into the hall. A few timid well-wishers hesitantly applauded during their departure.

"Follow me!" Instead of heading for the front door, Katrina skipped off toward the grand staircase. "I must see the beautiful hall from the balcony." Running up the steps they went, following the lead of Katrina. When they reached the top, they were all winded, but headed over to the banister anyway.

"Isn't it lovely?" asked Kat. While Kat and Tiffany were awed over the spectacle from that height, the boys seized the opportunity to clown.

"Look, I'm Errol Flynn!" proclaimed Eugene as he mimicked a swashbuckling sword fight against Jimmy. Flinging around

Delbert's suit coat as if were a sword, Gene jumped from chair to chair chasing after his make believe foe. At one point he even jumped up on the banister to emulate the whole effect. This charade was not received well by Tiffany, who shrieked at him to get down. She pleaded with Jimmy to get involved and so he did.

"Alright, knucklehead, get down. You are acting more like Johnny Weissmuller than Errol Flynn. Ape boy."

"Who's the ape boy?" Gene stopped and put his hands on his hips as if to taunt Tiffany and then threw up his hands. When he did, the suit coat came flying out of his hand and over the balcony. It shot straight out and became lodged in a chandelier. Eugene climbed down to the hysterical laughter of his friends. Jimmy was rolling on the floor in tears.

"Okay, Tarzan, now what are you going to do?" Jimmy nearly hyperventilated laughing, but managed to get out his question.

"I can jump out there and get it," offered Kat.

"No. Me, Tarzan, you, Jane." Gene pounded his chest and started to climb back up on the banister.

"You are *not* going to jump over onto the chandelier!" Tiffany said. "Katrina and Jimmy, tell him not to do it!"

Tiffany could not believe what she was hearing, but this time Jimmy was not much help.

"Briggs, if you're going to act like Tarzan, then you should dress like Tarzan," said Jimmy.

"What do you mean, Wilson?"

"You know, dress like Tarzan. All the ape man ever wore was a loin cloth."

"What the hell is a loin cloth?"

"The thing that looked like a diaper."

"No way, this ape man doesn't wear diapers."

"Oh, so you're saying that you are a chicken ape man."

"Well, the next best thing if you don't have a loin cloth is your birthday suit." The boys bantered back and forth for minutes regarding the appropriate attire worn by a jungle man, with the occasional comment opined by Kat. Tiffany, meanwhile, lectured the three about the safety concerns of jumping off a second-story balcony onto a crystal chandelier then somehow climbing down to the floor. No one was really listening.

Eugene convinced them to go downstairs and stand below the chandelier while he prepared for his leap. He would then toss several articles of clothing until it was just him and his loin cloth.

Then he would jump to his makeshift chandelier perch. While swinging over poinsettias and assorted winter greenery, the gang would drag one of the many leather sofas under him. At that point, he and Delbert's coat would fall, landing safely, and then they would be on their way.

As with most unrehearsed plans, there is always something that doesn't exactly go the way it should, and this plan was no different. The three looked like they were at the baseball field ready to shag flies. All were staring up at the balcony, including Katrina, who was already holding Gene's shoes and socks. Over the side and down came Eugene's shirt, followed ten seconds later by his pants. Then, to the shock of the Tiffany and the uncontrollable laughter of Jimmy and Kat, down came his underpants. Finally, their Tarzan of Point Marion appeared wearing a white towel that Gene had apparently swiped off of a maid's cart. He climbed up on the rail of the banister and gave the patented Tarzan of the jungle cry just as the doors of the banquet room opened up. The crowd poured out into the hall. They joined Jimmy, Tiffany, and Katrina and looked up at Eugene, standing vulnerable before them. With the merciless grace of a cheetah pouncing on his prey, Gene leaped toward his target, but with one problem. The towel in which he was adorned decided to part ways and fell limp, straight down to the floor. Tiffany screamed and covered her eyes, leaving Kat and Jimmy to drag the heavy couch under the human pendulum. Ladies shrieked and men groaned as they witnessed a sight that most of them were not prepared to see. A naked man on a crystal trapeze. However, there was no embarrassment for Gene. He was grinning from ear to ear, realizing how terribly funny his predicament must look. Swinging back and forth, he released one hand to try and free the snagged garment. When he did finally grasp a fistful of cloth, he timed his dismount. As he let go with one hand, he tugged with the other, and down he went, him and the suit coat. Well, at least some of the suit coat. Gene did miraculously land on the couch, but the chandelier refused to let go of the coat. Half of Delbert's beloved suit coat remained up on the chandelier.

"Oh, mother of God, it's those damn dancing kids!" the governor said as he witnessed Eugene's awkward descent.

Gene bounced up off the sofa and grabbed his trousers from

Kat. There was no time to dress, so he wrapped his waist as best he could and sprinted toward the door. The stunned crowd watched in disbelief as if they were witnessing a jail break. Even the arriving hotel security stood paralyzed and confused. Gene was a white blur, running faster than he ever had in his life. He breezed through the front door as if it were the turnstile on the first day of the state fair. His cohorts followed suit, but could not keep up.

The maître d', at his post like an expressionless guard at Buckingham Palace, stood fast as the four marauders went by one at a time. The suddenly sober youth all had varying dispositions and expressions as they passed though the exit. Eugene was still grinning, but now a shade of red embarrassment tinted his face. Second through was Jimmy with a look of terror in his eyes, followed closely by Tiffany, who was openly sobbing and mumbling to herself. Bringing up the rear was Kat. Her exit was not nearly as urgent as her friends. She'd had the time of her life; and the glow on her face exemplified that. In fact she really didn't want to leave without first trying her hand at balcony jumping. When she passed by the maître d', she stopped momentary to thank him for his hospitality. By the time she made it to the sidewalk, Jimmy, Gene, and Tiffany were already in the car and ready to go.

Tiffany was convinced she was either going to prison or hell or both. Her sobbing turned into hysterical bawling as Jimmy's car squealed away from the curb. She did stop caterwauling long enough to tell Jimmy that she hated him and his two heathen friends in the back seat. Those were the last words that Tiffany ever spoke to Jimmy. Ever.

When Eugene got home, he opened his front door, but before walking through, he stopped momentarily to slip off his shoes, as to be quieter. Then he walked directly across his living room to the stairs, anticipating that his parents would have long since retired.

"How was the dance?" his father's deep voice fired across the room. Eugene looked over to see his father sitting with the paper in his lap in his favorite chair. The only illumination in the room came from the lamp next to his chair. "I reckon I must've fallen asleep."

"Oh, hey, pop. Ah, I guess the dance was okay." Gene remained sheepishly in the shadows. "Well, goodnight." Gene turned to start up the stairs.

"Wait, I'll walk up with ya." Fred moaned as he crawled out of his chair. "I bet our little kitty Kat looked beautiful all dressed up. Your mother was hoping Pastor or Mrs. Browne got some good pictures." By the time he had finished his sentence, Mr. Briggs was next to his son. "Hey, where's Delbert's suit coat?" Fred stepped back to closer examine his boy. "Are your pants ripped? And why is your shirt all dirty? Did you get in a fight?" At that point the questions were being fired at Gene faster than he could respond. Which was a good thing because he had no answers, and the truth was the last thing he was prepared to give. But the questions kept coming and they were getting harder and Mr. Briggs was getting angrier with each word. "You smell like a drunken sailor. What's in your hand?"

"My shoes."

"Your other hand."

"Ah, it's Delbert's coat, or some of it."

And then it hit Mr. Briggs. "You destroyed your brother's suit!" Eugene could feel the heat radiate off his dad's head. He was hot, and Gene knew he was about to blow. So fearing for his life, he bolted up the stairs, fleeing for the safety of his room. At the top of the stairs he dropped one of his shoes, but no way was he stopping to pick it up. *Slam*. The door shook the pictures on the walls in the upstairs hall and woke up Ertta. She raced out of her room, nearly running into her husband as he arrived at the second floor.

"What's wrong?" she asked, startled.

"I'll tell you what's wrong." Fred reached down and picked up Gene's shoe. "That son of yours got himself drunk and in a fight or something, and ruined Delbert's suit. Now, I'm gonna kill him."

"Not if I kill him first!" Ertta's fear turned instantly into aggravation and she stepped in front of Fred and opened the door to Gene's dark room. She reached along the wall and turned on the lights.

"Get your rear end out of bed this minute!" Gene slowly reacted to his mother's order.

"Where's your brother's suit?"

Gene pointed to a pile on the floor. "It's not my fault." That was the best response he could muster up in his condition. Ertta walked over to the pile, reached down, and pulled up a shred of fabric that used to be Delbert's coat.

"It's not so bad. I think it can be sewed." Gene's absurd comment did nothing but toss gas on the fire. At that moment, Mount Fred erupted. He was so angry he stammered and spit trying to talk. But when nothing but incomprehensible babble came out of his mouth, Fred was left with no other option. So he reared back and launched the shoe. It sailed past Eugene's ear, barely missing him, and then hit the plaster wall behind. The force of the impact created a six-inch hole, enabling the momentum of the leather projectile to be swallowed instantly upon impact. The shoe disappeared and it was as astonishing as any trick ever performed by Houdini. Eugene looked at the wall, then looked back in shock at his father. He was not going to make the same mistake twice. Not ever remembering seeing his father so upset, Eugene knew that it was best to keep his mouth shut.

"Get in bed! Your mother and I will deal with you in the morning," Fred said.

"And you better pray hard for God to forgive you for whatever you did tonight, young man," said Ertta. Both parents stormed out of the room, leaving Eugene to collapse on the bed.

The shoe was never recovered and it remains entombed still today somewhere between the first and second floor wall.

Eugene spent most of his childhood paying for his sins. Literally! The boys had just finished paying off the debt owed to Uncle Mendel for the truck repairs from the baptism in Cheat River during their wild canoe adventure. Now Gene would need to begin work immediately to buy Delbert a new suit. Conveniently for him, Mother Nature would lend a hand. The next month the East would be hit with a blizzard, and viola', instant work. There would be lots of drives and parking lots that would require shoveling. He and Jimmy wasted little time before going to work. They even got themselves hired by the town of Point Marion to shovel sidewalks for fifty cents an hour. That was big money at that time, and a lot more than the boys were used to from working on the farm during the summer. Every penny that Gene made, however, went directly to his father, who kept custody over the new suit account. Snow shoveling didn't satisfy his debt but it did go a long way toward it. It was really irrelevant for Eugene, because it was all about the fun. No matter the cost of the debt or the severity of the punishment, he would do it all over again in a heartbeat.

CHAPTER 13

The first day of March was unseasonably warm and the boys were taking advantage of it. They were sprawled out, soaking up the sun on top of the rock, viewing from a distance the awesome roaring rush of Cheat below them. The gates to the dam were broached to the maximum, releasing the pressure of millions of gallons of water from the record snowfall received after the blizzard a few months earlier.

"It came! It came!" The boys wheeled their heads around to see the commotion. Kat was running toward them waving a paper over her head and smiling from ear to ear. "It came, guys. Colonel Mary Jo Shelly, Director of WAF—that's an agronym, Jimmy, for Women in the Air Force.

"Acronym," responded Jimmy.

"What?" Kat asked.

"Acronym. The word you are trying to say is acronym. It's formed from letters of a compound term to make the term shorter," Jimmy said.

"Who cares? Other than you and the Webster dictionary."

Jimmy shrugged at Kat's cold stare. "WAF wrote me back. They want me to consider joining the air force. She also included a copy of a newspaper article of this female pilot named Jacqueline Cochran who broke the sound barrier, and set speed and altitude records last year. She's amazing. She could fly circles around Amelia Earhart, maybe even Colonel Chuck Yeager. And boys, this says she is an orphan like me." Kat sighed, momentarily looked at the ground, and then looked through the trees to the sky. "Guys, I want to fly. I want to be like Jackie Cochran!"

"But you're a. . ." Eugene stopped before finishing his sentence. He could feel the fiery passion radiating from her.

"Mama and Papa said I can do anything I want when I grow up. Even your Daddy said the same.

He said, 'never let anyone tell you what you can or cannot do.' You heard him, Eugene." Gene looked at Jimmy, then looked back at Kat.

"Damn right, you can do anything you want. Anyone who says any different is going to hafta answer to Wilson and me." Kat was touched by their support, and with a tear in the corner of her eye, she gave her very best friends a long embrace. "The best part, Gene, is once I enlist, they will be sending me to Lackland Air Force Base in, *ta-dah*, San Antonio, Texas! I looked on a map and it's about one hundred miles from College Station, but at least it's in the same state." Kat sat down on the warm rock between the boys. "I wish Jimmy here would go to college somewhere in Texas too. Are you still wantin' to go to Duck in North Carolina?"

"How many times do I need to tell you? It's Duke, Duke

University. I am still waiting to see if I've been accepted or, more importantly, if they will offer me the academic scholarship I applied for. You guys know it's my dream. I want to be a surgeon, and Duke would be a great start towards that goal. But I don't know. It's going to cost my parents a lot of money." Katrina reached over and grabbed his chin and lifted it up, then looked him in the eye.

"Weren't you listening? You can do anything you want. Heck, if I can go fly jets you, surely, can be the greatest surgeon of all time." They all laughed, and then Kat concluded, "I know this creeps you out when I do this, but, hun, trust me, they did accept you."

"Don't mind me if I don't celebrate just yet." Jimmy smiled. "Although you are usually right with your unexplainable clairvoyant talents." That was the first time Jimmy even acknowledged Kat's gift. However, by Jimmy using the word 'clairvoyant,' neither Gene nor Kat had any idea that he acknowledged anything. "Until I get my letter from Duke, I won't check off the college deferment box on my draft registration card."

"You know there are a lot of our schoolmates that are perfectly content with never leaving Point Marion.

They are just as happy working the rest of their boring lives working in the mines or Houze Glass," Gene contended.

"What's boring to us may not be boring to others. The big world out there may not have the same allure to everyone as it does to us. And that's okay." Jimmy had just attempted to rationalize the behavior of most of their relatives, as well as the entire community.

CHAPTER 14

High school graduation is always a big event in most small towns and Point Marion was no different. Every family in town knew every family in town. Whether actually blood-related or not, if you lived in Point Marian, you were family. In fact, following commencement, many homes had open houses, regardless of whether they had graduating seniors or not. Even though the dropout rate was very high, the community celebrated just the same. One might say that they even celebrated with a bit more sense of accomplishment, perhaps realizing that the cards of fate were not stacked in favor of their kids. Because of the poverty among the families, many males were persuaded to quit school and begin work just as soon as they could. There was such a need for additional income to the households that staying longer in school was a luxury, not a necessity. But what usually happens is the young males end up marrying and marrying younger females. The immature girls unwisely look to their future mates as providers of their security. But their false knight in shining armor, of course, caused them to drop out of school too. Then they start their own family, and the mouths to feed increase and the poverty cycle continues.

Eugene's statement of classmates being content with never leaving Point Marion, and Jimmy's profound response, were not entirely true. Some, yes, but to others, their desires and dreams were squelched by the harsh realities of a world that held no other options for them.

Today was the big day, and Point Marion was abuzz. Pomp and circumstance abounded in the small Appalachian town. Fairmont held their graduation ceremonies the night before, so the Brownes and the Wilsons loaded up their cars and followed the Briggs over to watch Eugene receive his diploma. Coach Shumaker and his wife had a simple reception following the commencement. Eugene, excited as he was, was not impressed with the gown and mortarboard cap provided by the school. And he couldn't wait to discard of them after the ceremony. Even though not part of the Saturday commencement at Point Marian, Ertta, to the chagrin of Eugene, made him wear his different-colored cap and gown as a spectator to the graduation, as well as all afternoon for his open house at the Briggs'. She told Eugene that it was to prove to any doubters that he really did graduate, even if it wasn't from the same school.

Katrina and Jimmy were just the opposite; they didn't see the cloak as silly. They saw it as a symbol of twelve years of hard work, an emblem of many accomplishments. Especially Jimmy, who narrowly beat out his old flame Tiffany Trump for valedictorian.

Subsequently, they took no issues with leaving their gowns on all day, even while visiting their classmates' homes.

Later in the afternoon when the crowd began to thin, Katrina excused herself to make some quick visits to her friends' homes. But before she did, she ventured out to the woods and to the rock. Earlier, she'd felt the whispers in her ears of her proud mother and father as she walked down the aisle to receive her diploma. Now she yearned to have them near. Katrina knew she was blessed to have two sets of parents who loved and supported her. She graciously gave her time to the Brownes on this special day, but now it was time to be alone with her biological parents.

CHAPTER 15

The summer of '54 was not a summer of leisure for the graduates. It turned out to be a year of whirlwind, life-changing events for all three families. The kids took jobs immediately after graduation in preparation for leaving home. Jimmy took a job as a bag boy at the town grocery, while Kat babysat and housecleaned to earn her money. Gene spent at least the first part of spring continuing to work on Mendel's farm. He was able to satisfy his debt with his dad and buy his brother a new suit, and still had a little cash left for school. However, Gene would quickly realize that cash would not be an issue for him. And of course as foreseen by Kat, Jimmy got his acceptance letter along with a full academic scholarship to Duke.

Technology finally made its way into Point Marian. The Wilsons got their first television set, and the Briggs got a telephone. The Brownes got both.

The Briggs' new telephone would provide an information conduit that would have an immediate impact on their household. Two phone calls would pull their family in two different directions.

First, a call from Coach Claiborne informing Eugene that he and a select few boys from the football team had been offered summer jobs in the oil fields of Corpus Christi, Texas. Claiborne wanted to initiate the call on behalf of the Texas Oil Company and to highly recommend Gene take the job that would last until football conditioning camp in August. When Claiborne mentioned that they would be paying him nearly ten times the amount his uncle paid—plus sending a Greyhound bus ticket and spending money for the trip—it was really an offer Gene couldn't refuse. But that was the good news; the bad news was that he would need to leave as soon as the ticket arrived. This was much sooner than Eugene, and especially Fred and Ertta, had expected.

Ironically, the next day a second call came, but this one was for Fred and from Washington D.C., the Bureau of Mines. They, too, were offering a job that couldn't be refused.

The Korean War was over, but some say the conflict was just beginning.

Wars destroyed architecture. Wars took the living, ravaged the innocent, but rarely changed political views. They were always a battle of attrition, even back to the destruction of Jericho and the burning of the Rome. It's as simple as, who ever blows up or destroys the most, wins. It was as true in ancient history as it was in both World Wars. Korea was no different than Europe. The Armistice was signed in July of '53, and the 38th parallel was redeemed. Like Europe, much of South Korea's architecture, modest as it was, was destroyed. It was the same, but to a much greater degree in North Korea, where most of their architecture was leveled. The invasion of the Communist occupiers was driven back north, but communism was not defeated. Thus the conflict still remained. The occupation of Europe was also driven back, but rest assured; the evil was not entirely destroyed. The battles of good and evil are cyclical, and it will remain until Armageddon. But as in Europe, post-World Wars, the United States' role as liberators morphed into rebuilders. Rebuilders of the destroyed architecture, as it were. So now it was Korea's turn, specifically South Korea, as it directly involves the United States and NATO.

As a result of the armistice agreement, millions of U.S. tax dollars flowed into South Korea. And it wasn't just the military that received our money for their involvement. Most of the other governmental agencies such as the Department of Mines also put in their time.

Fred Briggs had been getting noticed for some time for his hard work and savvy managerial capabilities. He had been steadily advancing up the management chain and capturing the attention of his superiors. In government, no matter what branch, being noticed was no easy task.

So when the Washington bureaucrats began to pick over their flock of managers to look for the right person to ramrod a group of thirty civilian miners in Seoul, Fred Briggs name came to the forefront. The bureau's mission was to train the Koreans on mine safety as well as production and twentieth-century mining techniques. Restoring South Korea's coal mining industry was crucial to restoring their economy, and preserving and sustaining their newfound democracy.

So just when Ertta was about to receive her son Delbert back from Korea, she found out her husband Fred had accepted a six month temporary position that would send him to the very same country that had haunted her every waking hour for the last eighteen months. The only solace she could take was the fact that the war was over and the Communists were driven back north of the 38th parallel. Well, actually there was one more selling point that Fred emphatically maintained. Their income would double and a high level promotion was certain upon his return to the States. Fred failed to tell her that at the end of that six month period in Korea, coinciding with the promotion, was a relocation. If he were to head up the Division of Mine Safety for the Bureau of Mines, it would be from a permanent office in Washington D.C. It would be awfully hard to live in Point Marion, Pennsylvania. But he felt that with all that was going on, this little bomb could wait until later before it was dropped.

Eugene would be leaving Point Marion before his father, so that's where Ertta was concentrating her worries. She was driving Gene crazy, hovering over him as if he were a newborn. She was more nervous about him going away to college than about Delbert going off to war. She was livid at the fact that the university coaches had lured her son to leave earlier than planned with the insidious high paying job and the beautiful beaches of the Gulf of Mexico. The truth was that Coach Bryant was not the slightest bit concerned that his prized recruit had a summer job or not. He was concerned that some other college would steal him out from under his nose.

Bryant needed to keep his boys close; his "million dollar boys," that is—a term he dubbed his recruits. So like most coaches worth their salt, he turned to the university boosters to help him. And help they did.

A Corpus Christi, Texas, oil executive named Gregory Leppert, a faithful and loyal Aggie alumni who was always eager to help the cause, whatever the cause maybe, would provide the assistance the coach would need. Bryant's needs or "the cause" was for someone to watch over his investments until football training camp began in August. Some would call him a den mother, others a sugar daddy, but for the next couple of months, to Gene and a couple of other boys, he would be known as Uncle Gregg.

As forecasted by Coach Claiborne, Eugene received Mr. Leppert's introductory letter in the mail, along with a Greyhound bus ticket and two hundred fifty dollars in crisp, new bills. More cash than Eugene had ever seen in his life was stuffed in the envelope and the letter was signed, "Yours truly, Uncle Gregg." To say Eugene was excited was an understatement, but he wasn't the only one. Mom and Dad Briggs were also initially thrilled, but that feeling wore off and was replaced by reservation and skepticism. In Ertta's own words, "Why would anyone pay for a service before the service was rendered?" They were not sure if it was a loan or a gift.

Jimmy and Katrina were also very enthused about their bright horizons. Both their households were energized, too, even Pastor Mike and Lisa. Despite weeks of endless advice and encouragement from the Brownes to pursue an alternative career choice, Mike and

Lisa finally relinquished to Kat's desires. Reluctantly, Lisa Browne drove Kat to Morgantown to enlist in the air force. She not only enlisted, but scheduled an officer's test, a test that Jimmy had been working with her on for weeks. Katrina joined the United States Air Force to fly, and she knew that in order to become a pilot she needed to become an officer. Arithmetic was not her strong suit, but Kat wasn't flying blind, so to speak. She had been researching and studying hard, and she was ready.

"I've been accepted to officer's school!" Kat was grinning from ear to ear as she whispered into Eugene's ear as he slid next to her before church services began.

"Yahoo!" Gene's exuberating cheer drew the attention of the parishioners around them, including Ertta and Mary Lou.

"Does Wilson know?"

"Does Wilson know what?" Jimmy stuck his head in between theirs from behind.

"Kat got into officer's school!"

"Whoopee!" cried out Jimmy as the pipe organ began to play, this time drawing shushes along with the stares.

"We'll all meet at the rock after church. Okay?" whispered Kat, winking at Jimmy.

CHAPTER 16

Pastor Browne's sermon was about letting go of the ones you love. Like birds pushing their offspring from their nest, or lions nudging their young from their den. Tears were welling up in the eyes of the adult congregation at his moving sermon, but the passionate words were wasted on Kat, Jimmy, and Eugene. They were all three a thousand miles away, daydreaming and fantasizing about their future.

Kat broke from her thoughts about what lay ahead in life and remembered something she wanted to give to Gene. She reached in her purse and pulled out a white, tissue-wrapped cylindrical package, about one inch in diameter and eight inches long. It was tied up in a bow with a red ribbon, one of the favorites she used to pull back her hair. Kat had carefully planned this final detail—the fragranced strand of ribbon, naturally scented with jasmine, was from Katrina's hair and was intended as a personal, heartfelt touch. A special, intimate reminder of her that he could take to Texas. She laid it on the pew and slid it over until it touched Eugene's leg. He immediately awoke from his trance, looked down, then over at Kat. He smiled and looked back at his gift. Gene picked up the modestly wrapped gift and held it in his lap until the end of service.

This Sunday, Eugene did something totally out of character. When the final prayer ended and Pastor Browne dismissed the congregation, Eugene remained seated. Normally Gene fired out of his seat faster than an Olympian sprinter reacting to the starter's pistol at the beginning of a race. But as the pews emptied, just he and Kat remained. Even Jimmy filed out with the crowd. Moments later, though, Jimmy stuck his head back in the door, but seeing his friends having a private moment he immediately retracted and went on his way.

Katrina pressed closer to Eugene, threading her arm inside of his to nestle close. Eugene gently untied the ribbon and tore away the tissue exposing the silver serving spoon.

"Mom's serving spoon," he muttered in a soft voice.

"I think you called it your digger," Kat sweetly replied. "For years I slept with it under my pillow. My hero, Eugene Briggs, even as a small boy, stood up for me."

Gene lifted the ribbon to his nose.

"It smells like you. Mom will never get this spoon back" He turned to Kat, whose eyes were already waiting; so too were her lips. They met and the passion took over. They were reaching a fever-pitched frenzy when suddenly Kat pushed Eugene back.

"What's wrong?" His desperate voice quivered.

She nodded toward the statue of Mother Mary.

"Not here!" Kat grabbed Gene's hand and led him out the door and down the sidewalk. A few parishioners lingered out front in the yard conversing as she quickly pulled Eugene along, avoiding any eye contact that would cause delays. Before their shoes met the street, the familiar voice of Mrs. Browne rang out. "Kat, where are you two headed?"

"We'll be back after a while!" Kat quickly waved to Lisa as she picked up the pace to elude the crowd and to make their escape.

"Where are we going? To the rock?" inquired Eugene.

"No, we might run into Jimmy there."

"So where are we headed?"

"I don't know somewhere down by the river or by the ovens." Furiously sorting through their minds for secluded places where they could be alone, Kat and Gene hastily walked hand-in-hand toward the river. Down the dilapidated service road they walked with purpose, even though they had no real destination. When they arrived at the T, they stopped to study their options.

Straight ahead a hundred yards was the river; to the right was a long, unused road leading to nowhere. Down the road to the left, paralleling the base of the mountain and rail spur, was the abandoned beehive row.

"We are not going in those filthy ovens!" Kat declared. "Maybe we should wait till—" "Come on!" yelled Gene

Before she could finish her sentence Gene spotted an old, abandoned car nested in tall weeds.

Kat was losing some of her lascivious enthusiasm but followed behind Gene anyway, marching through the tall grass. He could sense that she was cooling off and knew that his window of opportunity was fleeting. If Kat were to take him to Shangri-la he must hurry.

The rusted sedan sat on four flat and rotting tires. The front window was cracked and looked like a spider web. The front bumper was concaved as evidence of a lost bout with a tree. But regardless, its battered condition was inviting to Eugene. With Kat peering over his shoulder, he leaned forward and wiped the grime off of the rear door window, then looked inside the sedan. Surprisingly, the condition of the interior was not nearly as bad as its exterior, so Gene gripped the handle and gave a yank. He slightly budged the metal body as he pulled, but the door remained closed. He tried again, and this time it broke free. *Creak*! The metal-on-metal grinding sound made Kat cringe. "Yikes!" she said.

A burst of stale, hot air was immediately introduced to their faces as he pulled open the door. Gene grabbed the knob and started cranking down the window. He crawled in and over to the other side and started cranking that window too. After a quick visual inspection, Kat followed him. The earlier rush of romantic adrenalin she felt at the end of church was gone. Clear thinking was now taking the place of overactive, amorous hormones. Even though it was a step up from a dark and dirty beehive oven, no girl would ever dream of losing her virginity, even to the man she loved, in the backseat of a wrecked and abandoned car.

"What the hell was I thinking?" wondered Kat. "Was there real wine used for communion? What am I supposed to do about this horny monster sitting next to me? Can I talk him down from his libido-induced state?" The questions continued to race through Kat's mind, but the elusive answers still evaded her.

"So Gene, who do ya think owned this car?" When Gene didn't answer, Kat knew that casual banter wasn't on his immediate agenda. She quickly realized it was time to move to Plan B.

Kat leaned forward, looking over the front seat, pretending she was suddenly interested in the makeup of the interior, but Eugene intercepted, grabbing her waist and pulling her back onto his lap.

"Come here, silly."

As soon as she sank into his lap, she began to melt all over again. Clear thinking flew right out the window and was replaced once again by those amorous hormones. "Oh well," she thought, "it's not the Grand Hotel, and it's not our honeymoon, but damn, I do love this man." From her mind, to the words she spoke, as she looked into Eugene's eyes. "I'll love you forever, Eugene Briggs!"

They were all over each other in seconds. Passion-heated kisses, hands rubbing and touching areas that had been taboo before. Years of pent-up feelings for each other were suddenly released in crazed, carnal erotic play. Kat and Eugene relentlessly explored every inch of each other's bodies. Kat's hair, wild from impassioned wrestling, was now covering her lover's face. Within moments, Gene's shirt was completely soaked with sweat, so off it came. This was the start of a chain reaction. Within moments both were completely nude in the middle of the day in the very, very hot back seat of the junked sedan down by the river. Eugene, relentless and eager to concur, maneuvered himself on top of

Katrina, his ivory white rear end beaming upward and ready for rapture. But the hand of fate was soon to be played out naturally or more correctly by nature.

Out of the blue, an unwanted guest came a' calling, disrupting the romantic afternoon of the two oversexed teens. For when the yellow jacket flew in through the window, it took an immediate liking, or perhaps offence, to Eugene's lily white ass.

BONZI! The stinger was delivered just in the nick of time, before the dirty deed was committed.

"OUCH!" A blood curdling scream echoed down beehive row, followed immediately by a thud caused by Gene's head hitting the inside of the roof.

"Something bit my ass!" Gene wailed at the top of his lungs as the excruciating pain radiated down the left cheek of his gluteus. Kat screamed as he trampled over her, exiting the rear door. Eugene looked like a dog chasing his tail, spinning around and looking over his shoulder as to what had just stung him. When Kat realized what had happened, she burst into laughter, which did not set well with the young Romeo. Whimpers turned into curses as Gene slipped back into his trousers and Kat into her dress.

"This is not funny! I'm allergic to bees. I swell up bad."

"Let me look at it." Still laughing, Kat began chasing Gene, trying to examine his backside before he buttoned his pants. "Hold still; let me pull out the stinger!" Kat giggled.

"Stop it, Kat. I am embarrassed enough as it is. I don't know how I'm going to explain this one. I probably won't even be able to get my pants on or off later." Gene hesitated, searching for his next words. "For some reason, I can't help think that your parents had something do with this." Kat smiled at him and gave an endearing look.

"Maybe so. You know, I was ignoring them when they told me that we weren't ready yet." Kat placed her hands on Gene's shoulders, beseeching his full attention. "Don't you feel weird now? Can you imagine how much more awkward it would be had we succeeded? I know this sounds funny, but I'm not sure if I could have seen you for a while if we had done it. When it finally happens for us, it will be a beautiful thing, and it sure as hell won't be in back of a car either." Kat gave Gene a kiss and grabbed his hand, leading him back to the road. "Come on, let's get you home before you have to cut yourself out of those pants."

It was unclear if anyone really bought Eugene's story on how he got stung on the butt, especially Jimmy, who was waiting for them at the rock. Gene contended that he was on his way to catch up with him when nature called. Seeking privacy in a clump of tall weeds he inadvertently disturbed a hive of bees. The trouble was that his story kept changing slightly daily, when re-interrogated by the skeptical Jimmy. The swelling did subside in a couple of days with the help of vinegar and baking soda compresses, and not a moment too soon.

CHAPTER 17

It was time for Eugene to head to Corpus Christi. Saturday morning, Mr. Briggs loaded up the car with two suitcases full of everything imaginable that Eugene would need for the summer. Soon the packed car carrying the Briggs and Katrina was headed for Morgantown. Kat and Eugene were tired after staying up all night with Jimmy talking. All three eventually fell asleep in the Briggs living room. That's where they left Jimmy after repeated attempts failed to raise him from his slumber on the couch.

This journey to Morgantown was eerily similar to the trip made a few years earlier with Delbert, sending him off to the military. Mom and Dad Briggs were almost as nervous about sending their unbridled, fun-loving Gene off with limited supervision and an ample supply of cash, as they were about sending his older brother off to war.

Waiting at the bus station seemed like an eternity for Gene. He was anxious to get his journey underway. Finally over the speakers came the announcement to board, which in turn triggered the emotions of the women. Ertta had been carrying around a paper bag of snacks and sandwiches she'd packed; she placed it in her son's hands, wiped her tears, and gave him a hug and kiss. Katrina handed Gene three letters that she had intended originally to mail, having decided that he needed something to read on the long trip. Ertta and Fred's eyes popped wide as Katrina delivered a long, open-mouthed kiss to their son. After what seemed to be an uncomfortable eternity for those waiting, Eugene broke from his kiss, composed himself, and turned his focus to his younger sister, patiently waiting. He crouched down to receive Mary Lou's hug, and she then gave him some pictures she had drawn with specific instructions to hang them in his room for decoration.

Gene, still in the embrace of Mary, picked her up and twirled around, giving her kisses on the top of her head for the complete 360-degree trip. Then he returned his giggling sibling to the floor. Awaiting him was the outreached hand of his father. Gene welcomed his hardy handshake and parting words—*Make us proud son*—and then picked up his bags, walked out the door, and boarded the bus.

After handing over his luggage to the attendant, Eugene took a seat towards the back of bus and settled in for the marathon of a trip. The route would have stops in Lexington, Louisville, Memphis, Little Rock, and Shreveport, all before the final destination of Houston. That's where Uncle Gregg would pick him up and drive him the rest of the way to Corpus Christi.

Eugene waved from his window seat to his loved ones huddled on the sidewalk as the loaded bus pulled away. Gene stared out the window at the constantly changing scenery until his mind started wandering, into deep random thoughts and somewhere around fifty miles out of Morgantown, he succumbed to sleep. Sleep would be Gene's solution to this long, monotonous trip. He would nap, wake up, chat a while with the person next to him, snack from his mother's goody bag, then fall back to sleep. This routine seemed to suffice until the sleep just wouldn't come anymore, and then the struggle began. Gene was not one of those individuals who could be perfectly content with just sitting, reading, or writing—he had to be doing. Especially when fully energized by all the sleep he had just received. There was a new fellow sitting next to him that had boarded in Little Rock, but the problem was, the man was now asleep, so that meant no conversation there. As Gene glanced around the bus looking for someone to talk to, he remembered the letters that Kat had given him. He pulled them from his rear pocket and began examining them further. Gene opened each of the three addressed, sealed envelopes, pulled out the inserted paper, and began reading. Kat's letters were more like journals or a diary.

There wasn't much structure, just random reflections of her life. Amongst the minutia, Kat scribed some personal secrets she'd apparently needed to share. Eugene started reading and instantly became enthralled. She felt the need to explain many of her quirky habits and many of her silly anecdotes, bringing an instant smile to Eugene's face. But not all she wrote was light. She wrote that she would often walk over to her old house and stand across the street, sometimes for several minutes, staring numbly at the boarded-up windows. Other times she would just sit on the curb and cry. She went on to confess that as a small girl she would sit and cry until her Grammy would rush from the house to attend to her skinned knee. Then after Grammy would make things all better, they would be off to bake cookies or go fishing. Her grandmother was quite adept at either activity. Kat concluded by saying that the saddest, and most confusing thing was that, unlike her Momma and Daddy, she'd had absolutely no communication with her Grammy since her passing. Kat thanked Eugene, as she had verbally on several occasions, for always believing her and understanding her God-given gift.

It was a sad time after losing her grandmother, but Kat never felt like an orphan. God had immediately blessed her by bringing her to the Brownes, and of course, Gene's mother, Ertta, Kat explained, "always treated me like a daughter." But most of all, she contended, if it were not for her two very, very close friends that she loved dearly, she would have never made it past her childhood. And for that, she wrote, she would be eternally grateful.

Gene read through the first two letters progressing from past to present, leaving for last the letter that delved into more recent events, as well as the deep, personal feelings she was having for him. She felt that despite her heartstrings being tied to him, destiny might be pulling them in different directions. Flying was all she could think of (she had very high expectations), but she knew her journey would not be easy. She was well aware that by becoming a pilot she would be entering into a male's-only club, and fair or not, she would need to deal with.

She was indebted to Jimmy for all his tutoring, especially in math. "Despite his extreme lack of patience, he was determined to teach me geometry and he never gave up. More importantly he never let me give up. He was tough on me. I actually wanted to kill him at one point!" Kat's proclamation made Gene laugh out loud. She boasted that she got revenge by pulling Jimmy's chain by pretending she didn't know the answer to a question that they had been working on for hours. "He went berserk! That is until he noticed I was smiling. Then he realized he'd been had."

Kat finished the third letter by explaining how she struggled with writing the word "deceased" after her parents' names on the enlistment papers and again on the officer's test.Kat's letters helped entertain Eugene on the trip, but they also provided a window for him to see into her soul.

Gene was able get off and stretch his legs at the various rest stops and designated bus stops along the way, but the trip was still grueling. When the bus driver announced that Houston was ten miles ahead, Gene let out a jubilant, "Yahoo!" The Houston skyline, with its magnificent skyscrapers glowing from the mid-morning sun, was a sight right out of a picture magazine. Eugene's nose was pressed against the window and his eyes were as big as silver dollars.

A man sitting in the seat beside Gene took notice of his enthralled attention to the scenery and spoke in a low, smooth, Southern drawl.

"Son, those are what you call manmade mountains." Gene turned to him and smiled.

The air brakes announced the end of the trip for Gene. When

the bus stopped, he anxiously jumped up and filed in line down the aisle with the other exiting passengers.

Gene stepped off the bus, and there he was, holding a cardboard sign with "Briggs" written on it. "What in the world?" were the four words that popped into Gene's head when he saw who was meeting him. Did Ringling Bros. and Barnum & Bailey send one of their clowns to pick him up?

After God created Gregg Leppert, he quickly broke the mold. Eugene was not quite prepared for the flamboyant and gaudily-dressed Texan. Uncle Gregg stood about five foot eight inches tall and three foot six inches wide, wearing plaid, short pants and an oversized, orange Hawaiian flowered shirt. He was sporting slicked back hair and sunglasses, and was smoking a huge cigar. Eugene sheepishly approached the man.

"Are you Mr. Leppert?"

"Does a Leprechaun shit green?" the man responded. Gregg then tossed the cardboard sign in the air and grabbed Gene's hand to shake. "And you must be the stud Briggs kid from PA. I'm your Uncle Gregg. If you call me anything else, I'll kick your ass!" The man had a grip like a bear, and with his piercing eyes, he gave Gene a cold, hard, intimidating stare. Not to be dominated, Gene tightened his grip and sternly stared right back. Their little machismo competition seemed to last for an eternity. Both competitors intensified their vice-like grips, saying nothing and giving death stares. Finally Uncle Gregg took a big draw on the Havana dangling from his mouth, turned his head, and blew out the white smoke. He then turned back around and smiled.

"Son, you can call me anything you damn well please. I'm just funnin' with ya. Welcome to Texas! I think you and me are gonna get along just fine. Nice grip, by the way. Come on, let's get your bags, we gotta little drive to go. I think you'll like your housemate; he's a tall Lanky boy from Kentucky. He's got a good grip too! Tells a lot about a man, you know. I wouldn't trust a man with a bottle of piss, let alone something of value, if he had a wimpy limp handshake. You grab your bag, Briggs. I'll get your car."

"My car?" Gene watched the Texan walk away without responding to his question After picking out his bags from a row of luggage lined up along the curb, Eugene walked through the open building to the other side, past the ticket counters and out to the street. Standing on the sidewalk he looked down both directions of the street, but no Uncle Gregg. Just as he was about to set the suitcases down, he heard the squalling of tires and looked up to see a bright red convertible sliding around the corner about a half a block down.

The car sped down the street toward him, and then at the last moment, darted over next to the curb, sliding to an abrupt stop. Low and behold, driving this long, sleek, Cadillac Eldorado was good old Uncle Gregg.

"Well, stop gawking and get in!" Gregg reached under the dash and pushed a button, popping the trunk. Gene tossed the two suitcases in the truck, closed the lid, walked around, and climbed in beside Gregg in the passenger seat.

"Are all the folks in Point Marion, Pennsylvania, as slow as you? Damn it, son, we got places to go, things to do, and ladies to screw! You got to put it in a higher gear." Gregg stuck the cigar back in his mouth, turned his head forward, and floored it. The tires squealed once again and they shot away. The sudden exertion threw Gene back into the seat, but he loved it. Eugene was grinning ear to ear as the Eldorado rocketed away from the Houston bus station and toward Corpus Christi.

"So how do you like your car? It will be you boys' transportation in Texas. Pulled it right out of the lot myself. I'm just working the bugs out, and then I'll hand over the keys. Oh, by the way, your roomy, Stanley—Stanley James—he's afraid to drive it. The only thing he's ever drove in Kentucky was Daddy's old truck. What about you, you afraid to drive this?"

"No, sir," Gene confidently replied.

It was a long drive down 59 toward Corpus Christi, but it wasn't boring. Once they were a few miles out of Houston's shadow, the highway became a lot less crowded, and the Cadi's speed increased. At one point they drove for over an hour on that long, flat, two-lane road, without even seeing another vehicle. Uncle Gregg was flying at speeds near one hundred m.p.h. Eugene was loving the moment, the adrenaline rush, the open air, the excitement of what lay ahead.

"See those, son?" Gregg extended his arm, nearly hitting Gene's nose. He was pointing to some objects speckling the landscape of the pastures a half mile or so from the highway.

"Yes, sir," Gene responded. "What are they, some sort of farm machinery?"

"Oil derricks! Those bastards suck the oil out of the ground and make me a rich man. You and Stanley are going to be watching some of those for me this summer." Gene looked at Gregg, then stared back at the black iron towers.

"There's hundreds of them, they look like dinosaurs grazing on the pasture grass."

Finally, on the horizon was evidence of civilization. The derrick and cattle-dotted pastures disappeared and were replaced with the occasional ranch home. Coming into focus from the distance and rising up from the ground were the shapes and forms of buildings. As they drove, the number of homes and buildings increased and began to compose the landscape. As they passed the "Welcome to Corpus Christi" sign, a flash of blue appeared between the openings of artificial, manmade dwellings.

"Is that the ocean?" inquired Eugene, who momentarily broke away from the postulated mold of an adult man to a young, excited boy.

"That, son, is the Gulf of Mexico waving to you!"

Soon the highway turned into a street and the street turned into a series of streets, then a beautiful parkway that paralleled the scenic Gulf. Gregg pointed out various landmarks and points of interests as they passed them.

He explained they were heading to one of his cottage homes. It was normally used as a rental, but for the next month, it would be Gene and Stanley James' home.

"I'll get ya'll unpacked and moved in, introduce you to Stanley, and we'll go get some grub. Then you boys can drive me home.

After that, you're on your own. Well, at least until Monday. I'll send someone for you and we'll go to work."

The Eldorado pulled into the driveway of a modest, ranch style house in a middle income neighborhood.

"Your casa, hombre."

"My what?"

"Your damn house, dumbass!" Gregg looked at Eugene and laughed, then departed the vehicle.

Gene grabbed his suitcases and followed Gregg to the door, then on inside. Waiting in the middle of the front room stood a tall, muscular, rangy boy with a crew cut.

"Stanley James, this is your roomy, Eugene Briggs. James, here arrived yesterday." Gene set down his bags and extended his hand. Stanley moved forward, reached out, and shook Gene's hand, then returned back to the middle of the room. Both boys said nothing, just stood and stared at each other like prize fighters sizing up their opponents.

"Lord, have mercy!" Gregg shook his head." Is that the best greeting you two hill jacks can muster up?" Both boys broke their stares and looked down at the floor. "I reckon social skills are not the priority for you all in Kentucky and West Virginia, or southern Pennsylvania, or the Appalachians. Damn, wherever the hell you're from." Gregg motioned for Gene to follow him, so Gene picked up his luggage and trailed him down the hall. After Gregg showed Gene his room and gave him a quick tour of the house, he was ready to go.

"I don't know about you boys," Gregg said, "but my throat's

parched. I say we head for a watering hole, drink us a few beers. Then you can try to eat half of one of our famous Texas steers." Gregg paused and looked at Gene, then at Stanley.

"Unless of course you'd rather just sit around here, pick your nose, and stare at each other all night."

"I can't answer for Stanley, but I'm coming with you, Uncle Gregg."

"I've never drank any beer before," Stanley said, "but a big, juicy steak sounds mighty good. I ain't sticking around here. I'm going with you fellas."

And with that, the boys were out the door. Two slams of the Cadillac doors and the car was backing down the drive and out into the street. Gregg once again squealed the tires as he made his getaway.

"Oh, Uncle Gregg, I forgot to call home and tell my folks that I arrived okay."

"It's too late for that now. Once the Eldorado hits the street, it ain't turnin' around and going back until all the beers are drank and all the steaks are ate. Don't worry, we'll give Mom and Dad a call from the restaurant."

Before the boys could even settle into their seats, the red Cadillac pulled up in front of a two story brick building and parked along the curb. A flashing neon sign hung above them on the side of the building, sporting the name "Katz." Eugene looked up and slowly enunciated the word, "Katzzz. Katz? Katz! You have got to be kidding me!" Gregg and Stanley looked at him inquisitively as they climbed out of the car.

"What the hell, boy, you just learn how to spell?" asked Uncle Gregg.

Eugene was now standing on the sidewalk with his mouth wide open, pointing up to the sign. "My girlfriends name is Kat. Well, her real name is Katrina, but..." Gene's sentence was interrupted by the sound of the restaurant door closing. Apparently, the other two were not interested in Gene's discovery. With a smile on his face, Gene quickly caught up with the other two right inside the door.

"Mr. Leppert!" The warm greeting came from the hostess as she entered the foyer and walked up to Uncle Gregg. "Your table is ready, sir. Please, gentlemen, follow me." Gregg reached in his pocket and pulled out a long Cohiba and stuck it in his mouth while motioning the boys to follow the tall, slinky brunette. The boys were instantly mesmerized by the elegant lady in a tight, backless red gown. Their eyes grew big as silver dollars as they followed every movement she made—gathering up their menus, jotting something down on a tablet behind her podium, and then strutting right past them. She could have chosen any route to take in that spacious room, but the course she decided took her directly under their noses, as if to give them full advantage of her exposed cleavage. Fully aware of her bewitching abilities, as she passed by Gene, she looked up and gave him a wink. Eugene immediately turned and looked at Stanley to make sure he caught her flirt that was specifically for him.

"Pay attention, James where I come from, that's the way men handle themselves around the ladies." At this proclamation, Gene started walking forward while still smugly looking back at Stanley and ran smack dab right into the wall, knocking off a picture and sending it crashing to the floor.

"I do see how you handle yourself around the ladies. Real impressive!" Stanley responded.

Uncle Gregg grabbed Gene's shirt collar and lifted him up from a crouched position on the floor, where Gene was attending to the picture.

"Come on, knucklehead, they will take care of this."

The three men followed their escort past the bar, where the bartender polishing a glass greeted Gregg by name. Continuing through the elegantly decorated room, they arrived at a specific corner table. The hostess pulled out one of the large mahogany and leather chairs and invited Gregg to sit, then repeated the process two more times for the boys. When they were seated, she unfurled the linen napkins from the table and placed them in their laps.

Before she departed, she plucked a wooden match from a cardboard box she had concealed in her palm. With one efficient motion, she ignited it and positioned the flame directly under Mr. Leppert's cigar. With her ample breasts strategically presented, she leaned over from behind and held the flame steady until the brown tobacco end turned red from the heat. The appearance of white smoke was her clue that the service was complete.

"Thank you, Connie," obliged Uncle Gregg. "One more thing, darlin', this boy here needs to make a phone call." She smiled and motioned for Eugene to follow, he couldn't move fast enough to comply.

Gene returned to the table to find a green-faced Stanley choking on his own cigar and swigging on a bottle of beer. Waiting in Gene's place was his stogie and bottle.

"Coach Bryant instructed me to turn you boys into men, and that's exactly what I'm going to do. Step number one is to introduce you to the finer things in life. Did you get a hold of your Momma and Daddy?"

"Yes, sir, and now I'm ready to get started on those finer things in life!" Gene could tell that Stanley was struggling with his introduction to the vices of manhood. So as to one-up his new peer, he grabbed the bottle of beer and nearly downed the entire brew in one gulp. He then returned the bottle to the table, picked up the cigar, and stuck it in his mouth. With an ornery smirk on his face, he turned to Stanley and said, "How's that stogie, boy?"

Uncle Gregg could see his experiment was not going well, at least with Stanley, so he intervened. "Stanley, what do you say we save that cigar for another day?"

Stanley quickly stood up and walked around to Gregg, laid the smoldering cigar on the table, then darted off toward the men's room.

"Lightweight!" Eugene chuckled in delight, as if this were some sort of competition for who would be dominant male.

Gregg could see what was happening between the boys and realized it was time to even the playing field. "I guess that old James there just isn't cut out to be a man yet, is he, Briggs? Let's fire up that Cuban." Gregg motioned over the waiter and pointed to Eugene sitting back in his chair, gloating.

"Hey, how come I don't get the beautiful hostess to light me up, like you?" Gene inquired.

"You're right, son. I like how you think, first class all the way." When the waiter arrived, Gregg gave instructions for him to fetch Connie along with another whiskey.

"Say, Briggs, now that it's just us two men and I see that you're about ready for another cold one, how about having what I'm drinking?" Gregg looked up at the waiter.

"Make that two whiskeys."The waiter smiled and nodded. A couple of minutes later, Connie returned. She was carrying both drinks. Gregg winked and she replied with a smile. She sat his drink in front of him, then walked over to Gene.

The seductive hostess leaned over and placed one arm around Gene's shoulder and her other hand on his chest. She then softly whispered in his ear as she pressed against him, "May I?"

"I may. . .I mean, you may, please!" The dangling cigar from the corner of Eugene's mouth bobbed up and down as he nervously replied. She slowly moved her hand up from his chest, running it up his buttoned shirt till her fingers met his mouth. She then without mercy took the Cuban from his quivering lips. As his mouth gaped open and his heart pounded hard, she reached down her cleavage, and with two fingers, retrieved a cutting tool and clipped off the end of the tobacco cylinder. Sweat beads were forming on Eugene's forehead as she placed the cigar deep in her mouth, then rolled it between her closed lips before pulling it out. Before the wet leaves had dried, she had a match going and was billowing white puffs of smoke.

As a grand finale, she took in a long draw and, blew the smoke up to the ceiling, and stuck the cigar back in Gene's mouth. With a huge grin on his face, Eugene sat frozen in his chair, paralyzed by his male hormones. The hostess looked over at her instigator.

"That, Mr. Leppert, was one for the Aggies!" Gregg acknowledged her with a smile and a nod showing that he understood her intentions. He also realized by her tone of voice that she was expecting a tip worthy of her performance.

"Well, son, are you going to smoke that cigar or not?" Gregg's loud voice snapped Gene out of his trance.

"Yes, sir!"

Gene didn't need much taunting from Gregg. He responded to his request by taking a long draw on the cigar.

"Now we're talkin'!" One could see the devil in Gregg's eyes, as he took pleasure in playing the role of the tempter. "Now that it's just us men, let's raise our glasses and drink like men."

Gene reached down and clutched his glass of whiskey, then raised it, mimicking Uncle Gregg.

"Here's to us men!"

Gene brought the glass down to his mouth and took a large gulp as if it were beer, not whiskey. As he swallowed, he realized his mistake, but it was too late to avoid the consequences. The shock to his system of the alcohol burning his throat was tremendous. It was excruciated and took his breath. His gag reflex responded, and Gene began choking and gasping for air.

"Take another big draw on the cigar, that'll help!"

Gene did, and it obviously didn't. Gagging even harder, Gene's red face was beginning to turn the same shade of green as Stanley face earlier. Eugene withstood the initial trauma to his throat and chest, but when the fire water reached his stomach, he too set down his cigar and glass and quickly exited to join his cohort in the loo.

"Will your guests be returning, sir?" inquired the waiter.

"They will be eventually, but I doubt they will be very hungry. Seems a couple of little brown Cubans may have spoiled their appetite."

"Would you like to order then?" the waiter asked.

"What do they got good to eat here, Uncle Gregg?" Gregg looked up from behind his menu and the waiter spun around in response.

"Well, I'll be damned, here come the walking dead," said Uncle Gregg with a chuckle.

Eugene and Stanley came shuffling back to the table, looking like they'd just gone twelve rounds with Rocky Marciano.

"How about a nice juicy steak, boys?" asked Uncle Gregg.

"Sure," mumbled Gene.

"Sure," muttered Stanley.

"Three of your thickest porterhouses, my good man!" Gregg barked out his demand to the waiter. "And another round of cold ones! Ah, maybe this time just beer for my two warriors here."

It was obvious that Eugene and Stanley were struggling, but they weren't going to let their newly adopted Uncle Gregg get the better of them. What had come out of their little porcelain rendezvous was a realization that they had just been played.

Instinctively at that point they went from adversaries to allies, opponents to teammates. As crude as Uncle Gregg's spur of the moment scheme was, or the recklessness of his motives, the end result actually worked: the mutual bonding between Eugene and Stanley had begun. Like brothers, even though they were still very competitive, they had each other's backs when it became necessary for their own social survival.

The night carried on with a plethora of booze and food. Gregg got louder and more obnoxious, and the boys got drunk, sloppy, and tired. They were the last to leave the fine establishment, and even though this was apparently quite routine with Katz's best customer, this night Gregg had a new excuse. Several patrons, including the owner, came by the table to meet the new Aggie studs and offer their best wishes.

Some bought drinks, some took pictures, and some even sat down uninvited and wouldn't leave. Football was paramount in Texas, and the excitement of A&M's new football program, the hiring of a premier coach, and the recruitment of blue chip players had everyone, Aggie fan or not, in a buzz.

Finally it was time to leave, but only after they'd devoured their steaks and had practically drunk their weight in beer.

CHAPTER 18

The boys' experiences were a little blurry the next morning. Eugene woke from his alcohol-induced sleep around eleven to the sound of Stanley vomiting in the bathroom down the hall. Several seconds elapsed before Gene realized he wasn't in his bed of nineteen years. In fact, he wasn't sure where he was at all. Startled, he rose up, shoeless but still in his clothes. As soon as his feet hit the floor, the blood left his head and the room began to spin. Gene clutched the bed sheets to steady himself but to no avail. Then his stomach started doing summersaults and began feeling queasy. There were multiple things occurring at once, but on this morning his brain was slow to sort and register them. As soon as he recalled that he was in Corpus Christi, he cautiously stood and walked over to the window and peered through the shades.

The sunlight immediately being introduced to his sensitive bloodshot eyes was not a pleasant feeling, so he quickly recoiled back. Even though Eugene's gaze out the window was anything but long, his squinted eyes did see a red Cadillac sitting in the drive. "Well, I guess I wasn't dreaming," he thought. Suddenly, Gene recognized a familiar scent, the aromatic smell of breakfast. Most mornings he would welcome the tantalizing smell of bacon, but not this morning. He walked out of his room and stood in the hall, turning his head in the direction of the gagging and moaning sounds bellowing from a room a couple of doors down. Gene reluctantly shuffled toward the source of the disgusting noises. As he drew close, he could see the little white squares of tiles, so he quickly deduced it was the bathroom.

"Is that you, James?"

Silence.

Gene took another step forward to look past the open door and into the room. His hands went quickly to cover his nose and mouth. And in a muffled voice he inquired.

"Are you alright, man?"

On his knees, sitting on the floor with his arms around the commode and his face almost touching the water, was Stanley.

"Does it look like I'm alright? Go away!" Stanley lifted himself up just enough to stretch out his leg and kick the door shut, practically in Eugene's face.

"No problem, Daddy O!" Gene wheeled around and focused in the other direction, toward the kitchen and the unwanted scent of breakfast. The sounds of clanging pots and pans were now introduced to the mix of unpleasants.

"Uncle Gregg, are you trying to torture us?" Gene snarled. He'd assumed that Gregg was the culprit responsible for breakfast, but when he turned the corner from the end of the hall to the kitchen he was surprised to find it wasn't Mr. Leppert wielding the spatula, but a complete stranger.

"It's about time you got your lazy rump out of bed! Is your buddy still praying to the porcelain gods? I told Mr. Leppert I'd cook and clean from you boys, but ain't no way I'm playin' momma! Well, what are you staring at boy? Sit down and eat!"

"Yes, ma'am." Despite being sick with a hangover, and without question or debate, Eugene quickly took a chair in front of a place setting at the kitchen table. The heavyset, middle-aged women approached Gene armed with a frying pan heaped with scrambled eggs. She ladled out two large spoonfuls that covered nearly two thirds of his plate. Then she returned to the stove and traded in the egg skillet for one filled with fried potatoes. With her other hand, she grabbed a plate of bacon, returned to the table, and set both in front of Eugene.

"You can call me Minnie. I'll bring the food to you now, but I ain't waitin' on you after today. Starting tomorrow, we eat at six, twelve, and six, unless Mr. Leppert takes you boys to a restaurant.

You'll pick up your food in the kitchen and eat either at this table or the dining room table. When yer done, you'll bring back your dishes to the kitchen and put them in the sink."

Gene's head drooped and his jaw sagged. It was all he could do to muster up a, "yes ma'am" to this three hundred pound ogre. She did not care one way or the other for his unenthusiastic response, so she grunted, then left the room. Eugene was sitting motionless staring down at the mountain of steaming food, when he heard the wooden legs of the chair across from him drag back from the table. Like fingernails on a chalkboard, this hideous sound caused a reactionary cry of pain. Gene raised his tormented eyes to find that the cause of this ghastly noise was none other than his new housemate. Stanley was also grimacing in pain from his self-inflicted trauma. He then flopped down in the chair like a wet towel and both boys remained motionless, almost comatose, for a few minutes until Eugene spoke.

"Have you met Tiny?"

"You mean Minnie? Why do you think I'm here? She kicked me out of the bathroom. Man, I feel awful, Briggs. I think I'm having my first hangover."

"You think so, Einstein? I think Uncle Gregg's trying to kill us. He gets us drunk last night, then throws us in with a grizzly bear this morning. Where is that son-of-a-bitch anyway?" Gene looked over his shoulder to make sure the coast was clear, then picked up his plate, leaned over, and scraped half of his food unto Stanley's plate.

"What are you doing, creep?" growled Stanley.

"Shut up, moron. Do you want to eat a whole plate or half a plate? When Attila the Hun returns, she'll load you up too." Stanley reluctantly picked up his fork and stirred once through his eggs before stabbing a morsel and taking a bite.

"So, Briggs, do you remember how we got home last night?"

"Not really, but the Cadillac is sitting in the driveway. I'm pretty sure that neither one of us drove it home."

"Well, well, I see you finally found your way to the table."

Minnie returned and stood looming behind the boys. "Hurry up and eat! You two are going to learn the meaning of, *time to pay the piper.*

We're going to do a lot of work around this house, starting first with washing the dishes. Ha ha ha!" The agony in the boys' eyes quickly turned to terror at her evil laugh. Stanley turned and looked at Gene as Minnie's heavy footsteps creaked on the floor as she left the room.

There was a panicked look on Stanley's face at the thought of spending his day slaving under this sadistic beast of a woman. Even the cobwebs in Gene's head immediately dissolved after hearing her threat. Eugene's instinctive reaction was very similar to that of a wild animal that has become cornered. He quickly panned the room in search of his escape.

"Hey, Stanley, are those the keys to Uncle Gregg's car lying in the middle of the table?" Stanley shrugged, but joined Gene in focusing on a set of silver keys with a Cadillac insignia within an arm's length

"Didn't Uncle Gregg say that the Eldorado was ours to use while we were here?" Stanley sat straight up in his chair at Eugene's query.

"You're not thinking about…" Stanley sheepishly asked.

"ARE YOU LAZY JOCKS DONE EATING YET?" Minnie's horrifically loud request reverberated off the walls and down the hallway. "COZ IF YOU ARE, THAT TABLE BETTER BE CLEANED OFF, AND THOSE DISHES IN THE SINK AND READY TO BE WASHED!"

The boys said nothing, but stared at each other, perhaps waiting for the other to make the first move.

"If we're going to make our break, we gotta go now before she returns." Gene glared at Stanley.

"Are you with me?"

Stanley stood up and grabbed the keys and tossed them to Gene.

From the other end of the house, Minnie reared up from her task at hand, reacting to the sound of the front screen door slamming. But before she could manage her way to the front, the boys were backed out of the drive and spinning their wheels to freedom.

Both boys' grins were as big as Texas tacos. Stanley let out a Kentucky war cry—*yahoo*!—and Eugene gave a giant goodbye wave to the warden of Uncle Gregg's cottage as Minnie stood in the doorway.

"Where are we headed, Briggs?"

"When we drove into town yesterday I saw blue ocean from a distance. I want to see it up close. Hells bells, Stanley, I don't want to just see it; I want to get in it. I never been to the ocean. You?"

"It's the Gulf of Mexico."

"What!" responded Gene.

"The name of it is the Gulf of Mexico."

"Stanley, everyone knows if you can't see the other shore, then it's an ocean."

"Well, there was this one time we went to visit cousins in northern Indiana and I saw the Great Lake, Michigan. I couldn't see the other shore there. Is Lake Michigan an ocean?" Gene had no response, so he just shook his head, and his counterpart smiled.

The boys were having so much fun driving and sightseeing that they completely forgot about their hangovers. They also forgot they were underdressed and had no money. Because they left with such urgency, Stanley was shoeless and both boys had left their wallets in their rooms.

"Hey, Stanley, you got any money?" Gene inquired, but Stanley didn't immediately reply. He finally found forty cents in his front pockets.

"This is all I got. What about you?"

"I think I got fifteen cents, so at least we can buy a couple of sodas and have enough left over to share a hamburger. But that doesn't matter because look ahead." The car went over a crest in the road and it was as if they'd driven right into a postcard. There it was, at the end of the street, at the bottom of the hill, acres of white sand. This lovely white sand served only one purpose—it was the doormat to the deepest, bluest body of water that the boys have ever seen.

"Park the car, Briggs. It's time for this Kentucky boy to sink my bare toes in that white sand."

The pavement ended, but there were tire tracks that continued onto the beach, so Eugene drove right out on the blanket of sand. Within seconds the boys were within a few yards of the water, so Gene threw the car in park and shut off the engine. They were immediately captivated, overcome by the seductive beauty and omnipotent power of the vast, boundless sea. A reaction that most have, no matter how many times they view the magnificence of any great body of water.

The doors flew open and a warm Gulf breeze blew in, carrying carefree inhibitions that immediately commandeered their souls. Before their bare feet touched the warm, white sand, the boys reverted back to their childhood. They ran to the water's edge, yelling as loudly as their vocal cords would allow. Shirts were off and the boys were in, skipping and jumping and splashing. Nearly an hour of frolicking horseplay in the newly discovered salt water went by before the boys became aware that there were other interesting things going on around them than just swimming in the aquatic brine.

Girls! Girls in swimsuits! The beach was alive, but Gene and Stan had just become aware of it. As fast as they turned into adolescents by the lure of the sea, they transformed right back into young men, with the prospect of meeting females. The two red-blooded American boys were now walking out of the surf in soaked pants and ready to shift their focus. Miles of shoreline and beautiful white sand sprinkled with beach towels and sun-bronzed Texas cuties—this was now the attraction. Without hesitation and absolutely no debate, they began their quest to meet all the prettiest girls in Texas. So off they walked, leaving their new Eldorado sitting in the sand.

CHAPTER 19

Back in Point Marion, Mr. Briggs was loading up the car, preparing for his early morning drive to Pittsburg to catch a long flight to Los Angeles. From there, another long flight to Anchorage, Alaska, would be followed by an even longer flight to Seoul, Korea. The total trip would take an exhausting forty-eight hours.

A few blocks away the Brownes were also packing and loading their car for their early morning drive to Morgantown to put Katrina on a bus to Montgomery, Alabama, for a few weeks of basic training before heading on to Universal City, Texas, for flight school.

Jimmy spent the day with Kat, just hanging around, almost getting in the way at times. She tolerated his clingy behavior, sensing he was feeling a little deserted now that both of his friends would be gone. Jimmy wouldn't be leaving for college for almost a month.

Finally, the Brownes scooted Jimmy out the door. Kat followed him outside onto the porch to say goodbye and give him a care package she'd prepared for him for school. Jimmy turned around, but before he could speak, Kat put her hand on his shoulders and said,

"I love you, James Wilson. You have been my brother for all these years. I know we've had our differences and many times bickered like cats and dogs. But I know that you have always cared deeply for me. You're like that big rock in the woods. Our big rock in the woods! That rock has always been our home base. No matter what, no matter when, it's always there for us. You're my rock; you have always been there for me. And I know you've always been there for Eugene too." She threw her arms around Jimmy and embraced him for several seconds before giving him a kiss, then pushing him away.

"Wow, that was a little theatric, even for you, Kat!" Jimmy did not know how to express his feelings as fluently as Kat, so he made do with sarcastic humor. In past experience, this tactic would always squelch any uncomfortable situation, but tonight it had no effect. Kat stared into his eyes as if she were staring into his soul, then warmly smiled. Jimmy smiled back, then turned and walked down the driveway.

She stood on the porch until he drove away, her smile faded. With a tear running down her cheek, she whispered three words.

"Farewell, Jimmy Wilson."

CHAPTER 20

Two cars left Point Marion early the next morning heading in opposite directions. However, the emotions felt in both vehicles were very similar. Fred Briggs and Katrina's feelings ranged from sadness at leaving their loved ones behind to the exhilaration and excitement of the challenges that lay ahead.

Ertta and Mary Lou were obviously saddened by Fred's departure to Korea for the Bureau of Mines, but he assured them that the six months of his absence would fly by. He also teased them with an announcement of a big surprise when he returned. But the biggest comfort for them was the anticipation of Delbert's homecoming at the end of the week.

Katrina knew her departure was very hard for Mrs. Browne to accept. She also knew that Lisa's strong faith would help her cope. So on the car ride to Morgantown, Kat decided to ease the tension of the trip by leading them in singing some of Lisa's favorite hymns. And it worked; all three sang their hearts out, and joyful bliss replaced the anxiety.

The Brownes were running a little late, so there was not much time to linger at the bus station. As a result, as soon as they'd purchased Kat's ticket, she needed to board. Tight embraces and parental instructions were given for the hundredth time while ushering their only daughter to the bus.

Kat's bus pulled away from the station, leaving a proud Mike and Lisa Browne fighting back the tears. As soon as the bus left the lot, Kat reached inside her purse and pulled out her newspaper clipping of her heroine Jackie Cochran, smiled, then returned it. She laid her head back on the seat and began to drift off to sleep, but her slumber was interrupted. She thrust her head forward and opened her eyes wide. Then she spoke her warning.

"Eugene Briggs, you better behave!"

"Katrina!" wailed Eugene.

"Who's Katrina? My name is Jill." The tall blond pulled back from Gene's arms and gave him a dirty look.

"I don't know what made me say that," he replied.

Gene's response was apparently adequate for the inebriated, swimsuit-clad damsel. She took another swig of beer and went back to dancing with Gene. There was a huge bonfire and nearly a hundred of Eugene and Stanley's closest and newest friends were fraternizing in the sand. The furthest thing from Eugene's mind was Kat, until now. He truly had no idea what made him blurt out her name, but nevertheless he did and now Kat consumed all his thoughts. So much so that he couldn't continue holding a complete stranger in his arms.

"Where's Stanley?" he wondered, grabbing a cold bottle of beer from the ice-filled trough. Gene began trying to remember the last time he saw his friend. "Was it an hour or two ago? And in which direction?" Gene stood and looked both ways up and down the beach, but there were too many people and it was too dark. The last time he saw Stan he was doing the limbo, wearing nothing but his underpants and a cowboy hat that he'd acquired from who knows where. To make it more challenging, someone had lit the limbo stick on fire. This was certainly very entertaining to watch, but so was the tall and very female blond who insisted on dancing by the fire.

Gene and Stan had abandoned their car several hours earlier nearly a mile from where they were now. The fifty cents they'd started with earlier in the day was still in their pockets. Once the local beach dwellers had found out that they were the new coach Bryant's recruits, they'd been treated like royalty. The boys had no idea that they would be treated like movie stars. They hopped from blanket to blanket; it was like a buffet. They were fed, they were given beers and Coco Cola's, and they achieved their objective.

They literally met hundreds of girls! There was no shortage of Texas maidens on that beach who were all willing to let Gene and Stanley rub suntan lotion on their backs.

But the long day of fun in the sun had turned into late night and Eugene was beginning to feel fatigued. Thoughts of responsibility began seeping into his brain. He quickly forgot about the blond, the bonfire, and the beer and began to search for his counterpart.

"Hey, have you seen Stanley?" Gene repeatedly asked as he

passed new acquaintances while retracing his journey back toward the car.

"Briggs!" The shout got Gene's attention. With the backdrop of the moonlit Gulf, a tall silhouette stood next to a smaller silhouette. The smaller one seemed to be pointing his way. The larger form then took a beeline in Gene's direction.

"I see you found your pants!" Gene's observant statement got no reply from Stanley as he arrived at the small group Gene was standing with near the fire.

"I thought you ditched me, you jerk. What did you do with the car?" Stanley asked.

"I didn't do anything with the car!" Eugene responded.

"I couldn't find you so I headed back to where we parked the car, to see if you were there and there was no car. I thought you took off without me." Stanley paused. "Jeepers, Briggs, if you didn't take the car, someone must have stolen it." Without another word, they immediately broke from the group and took off running back to the scene of the crime. The curious group, overhearing their conversation, followed close behind.

"Briggs, doesn't this beach look smaller to you?" panted Stanley.

"It does, must be the moonlight."

When they arrived at the spot where they thought they had parked, there was no car. The area was just an empty space of sand, now secluded and void of any people, except for those just arriving.

"Maybe it's down farther," Stanley said, looking down the beach.

"No man, look, there's the entrance where we came in. But it did seem like it was a lot farther away from the water."

"What time and how far away from the water did you park?" one of the onlookers asked.

"Around one o'clock and about six feet away, I guess. Why?" Simultaneous to Gene's reply, the four locals all looked out at the water.

"The tide, Big Daddy! The tide took your car."

"What's a tide?" Gene looked at Stanley and both boys shrugged.

"Thar she blows!" It wasn't Moby Dick the local was referring to; rather, it was an elongated, dark, rectangular shape bobbing in the surf about fifty feet out.

"Are you saying that's our car?" Stanley reluctantly asked.

"About ten times a year, one of you Yankees drives down here and parks their car too close to the water; the tide comes in and washes it out."

"Uncle Gregg is going to kill us, Briggs."

"Worse than that, Coach Bryant is going to kick us off the team. We got to get it out of there." Eugene started for the water.

"You ain't never going to get it out of there without a winch truck. And it's too late; you won't get any truck tonight. You all will hafta come back tomorrow morning with a truck and hope the Gulf hasn't swallowed it up more."

"Swallowed it up more?" Stan's panic-stricken voice cracked.

The boys' day had started out badly and ended even worse.

"Briggs, we can't come back tomorrow morning! Tomorrow is our first day of work at the oil fields. Remember, Uncle Gregg is sending someone for us in the morning. We should call Gregg."

"We might as well call the undertaker while we're at it, Stanley."

One of the locals offered to drive them home, so they accepted. When they arrived back at the house, they found their dishes just as they'd left them, piled with eggs and sitting at an empty table.

"Do you think she's still here?" whispered Stanley. They both gingerly stepped through the rooms as if not to wake the angry giant. Gene went over to the table and picked up his plate, then headed for the kitchen. Stanley followed his lead and did the same. When they stepped into the kitchen they were greeted with a sink of waiting iron skillets and various dirty utensils.

"So what are we going to do?" asked Stanley.

"I guess wash them." Stanley looked bewildered by Gene's response.

"I meant, what are we going to do about the car"

"Worry!" Gene wasn't trying to be curt, he just had no idea. He turned on the faucet and began filling the sink.

"I'll wash and you dry." Gene tossed Stan a dishtowel. "You are not going to believe this, Stanley, but this is not the first time this kinda thing has happened to me. I don't know what it is about me and vehicles left unattended, but somehow they always end up in the water. Long story, but I know I won't have my Uncle

Mendel this time to bail me out." Gene found the dish soap and the boys dug into the mess. After they'd finished the kitchen chores they were done for the day. Totally exhausted, they headed off to their rooms and for the second night in a row, collapsed on their beds.

The obnoxious sound of a horn blowing was Gene and Stanley's alarm clock. *Honk! Honk! Honk!* Eugene crawled out of bed and over to the window to view a truck in the drive. Accompanying the truck was a man standing alongside, reaching though the window, honking the horn. Before the boys pulled on their jeans and laced their shoes, he was pounding on the door.

"Hold on, we're coming!" The boys entered the hall approximately at the same time, their hair a mess and their eyes still glazed over with sleep. Nevertheless, half asleep or not, they were now jogging toward the front door. When they opened the door, they were confronted by a short Mexican man with a big grin.

"Good morning, amigos." He was seemingly very amused by the fact that he'd ousted the boys from their sleep.

The boys stood at attention in the driveway waiting for their next command.

"Relax, amigos, my name is Hector. I'm not your foreman. My job for the next few weeks is to pick you up in the mornings, take you out to the oil fields, then bring you back home in the afternoon." The boys relaxed a bit listening to Hector's introduction.

"Why are you so damn happy this early in the morning?" Eugene asked.

"This is like a holiday for me," Hector replied. "I am on the maintenance crew. Is very hot and is very dirty. Hector is very happy boss picked me for this job." He motioned for the boys to get in the truck, and they were on their way.

"Hey, Briggs, did you notice something different about this morning from yesterday? I mean aside from the horn blasting from Hector here."

"Yeah, I feel a whole lot better!"

"Besides that."

Gene thought a moment than blurted out,

"No Minnie!"

"I know we left in a hurry, but I didn't smell breakfast or hear her banging around." chimed in Stanley.

"Oh, Ms. Minnie?" Hector asked. "Ms. Minnie, she quit. She is a very angry senorita. Don't worry, Hector made you breakfast." He reached below the seat and pulled out a paper bag. Inside the bag were individually wrapped tortillas in wax paper. They were filled with scrambled eggs, steak, and tomatoes, all diced up and ready to eat. The familiar aroma was so inviting, the boys didn't even question the unfamiliar thin dough wrap. Instead, they wasted no time in devouring the Mexican sandwiches.

Eugene nudged Stan with his elbow to draw his attention away from his meal to hear what he was about to ask Hector.

"These sandwiches are great, Hector! Thank you very much. Say, would you have time to run us by the beach before heading out to the fields? Stanley here lost his watch and we think he may have dropped it in the sand."

"I guess that would be okay. The boss told me you should get what you want. Mr. Leppert's orders."

Gene gave the directions to Hector and he drove accordingly, leading them ultimately to the same spot where they'd entered the beach yesterday with the Eldorado. He pulled down the street and then out onto the sand just as Eugene did.

"Right here is fine, Hector. Wait, we'll be right back." The boys jumped out of the truck and ran to the water's edge. They stoically stood looking out to sea, but to their chagrin, there was absolutely no sign of the car.

"I guess the Gulf has swallowed the car completely," Stanley muttered. "Now what, Briggs?"

"Maybe we tell Uncle Gregg that someone stole the car," Gene replied.

"What are you amigos looking at?" The boys nearly jumped out of their skin, unaware that Hector had followed them and was now standing at their heels. They were nervous, so it didn't take much to frighten them. Immediately, they began searching the ground as if they were looking for a watch. They made the silly charade last for a few minutes before calling it off. Then they piled back in the truck and off they went.

They left the confines of Corpus Christi and headed towards what one would describe as a no-man's land: from the beauty of the Gulf to flat, rocky pastures, almost barren except for the occasional cactus. After driving several miles on a narrow gravel road, they turned off at an unmarked entrance. Nothing significant, just an old iron gate chained to a concrete post. Hector jumped out, unlocked the chain, and swung the gate open. He then pulled the truck through, jumped out, and repeated the process only in reverse.

Kicking up a cloud of dust, they drove down the narrow dirt lane for nearly two miles. The road had a gradual rise in grade, but the higher elevation wasn't really noticeable until they reached the summit. When the truck crossed over the peak, there it was: a valley of black iron oil derricks. There were literally hundreds of acres of oscillating black monsters.

"Wow! That looks like a scene from a science fiction movie," commented an exuberant Stanley.

The truck continued down the road and pulled up alongside the first towering beast.

"Here we are amigos." Hector got out and was followed by the boys. The derricks, or wells, were in no particular pattern or row. Some were close together, some were far apart. There were various sizes and shapes; most looked like dinosaurs bobbing up and down, but some were stationary towers extending sixty to eighty feet high. Not only did it look like something out of a science fiction movie, it sounded like it too. Creepy creaking and shushing noises, or the sounds of wind whistling through the iron lattice of the towers created a ghostly serenade. Hector walked around to the back of the vehicle and lifted out a couple of lawn chairs, two umbrellas, and two, five gallon water cans. Then he walked back to the cab and grabbed two clipboards from behind the seat and pulled two stopwatches from his pocket.

"This is everything you hombres need." Hector began giving

his orientation. "Every one of these wells has a number on it. You will write down the number of each well, then you will count how many times the big arm makes a cycle in one hour." To make sure the boys understood, Hector stood back and demonstrated by sweeping his arm around, emulating the boom on the derrick.

"Comprende, amigos? Okay, boys?" Hector nodded and they nodded back.

"So is it supposed to rain?" inquired Eugene, grabbing for one of the umbrellas.

"Shade, amigo." Hector laughed, then jumped back into the truck.

"I'll be back to check on you." He started the engine, put it in gear, and then drove off. The boys stood and stared at the gear lying on the ground.

"Well, I guess I'll take this one, number fourteen." Gene looked up at the towering iron machine. "You know James, we gotta tell Uncle Gregg something tonight. It's too late for the "car got stolen" story. He'll know right away that we're lying; any normal idiot would have called the cops last night."

"We could call now!"

"It's too late. He's going to think it was a little strange that we didn't even mention it to Hector this morning. Besides, how are we going to call him now anyway? You got a telephone in your pocket or something?"

"You're right, Briggs, I guess it's time to be a man and do the right thing. I just hope that Uncle Gregg will loan me money so that I can buy me a bus ticket to get back home." Stanley kicked a rock lying on the ground. "Boy, I'm going to get a beatin' when I get home. All this is because of you, Briggs, you dumbass. Why did you hafta park right next to the water anyway?"

"Hell, I didn't know!" Gene paused. "You're right, though. There's no sense in both of us getting kicked off the team. Takin' the car really was my idea, anyway. I'll tell Uncle Gregg that you pleaded with me not to park the car on the beach, but I wouldn't listen."

Stanley stammered around for a few seconds, then picked up his water cooler, folded the chair and clipboard, and walked about a hundred yards to another derrick. The boys spent the day apart, but were always within eyeshot of each other. Hector would come by occasionally, honking his horn to notify his arrival. They would convene, eat a quick snack—or lunch around noon—then move on to two different derricks. This process would be repeated throughout the day. They were pretty much left in seclusion. The only other sign of human inhabitants of this valley, other than Hector, were the maintenance or work crew vehicles driving by the derricks.

By the end of the day, Eugene and Stanley were mentally exhausted from the combination of the heat and the mundane, repetitive task of their new job—and worrying. Sitting around all day staring and counting the strokes of the arm of a derrick proved very hypnotic. No matter how hard they tried to concentrate, their minds drifted away and they began dwelling on the car. Thoughts of guilt and projected scenarios of their fate consumed them. Would they be arrested and sent to prison? Would they have to pay for a new car? Would they be kicked off the team? What would they tell their friends and family back home?

The boys loaded their stuff in the back of Hector's truck and handed him their clipboards. Their first day of working the oil fields had come to a close. Hector put the truck in gear and they were headed back to town.

"Well, amigos, I have some good news," reported a smiling Hector.

"They found the car!" Stanley blurted out, followed by an elbow to the ribs by Gene.

"What car, amigo? I heard a rumor that Mr. Leppert has hired a new housekeeper for you. You are dos lucky hombres!"

The boys were not sure what Hector was saying, but let it go. The rest of the ride home was quiet. Both Gene and Stan were mentally preparing what they would tell their families and how they would get home. The truck passed a strange car sitting in front of the house and pulled in the drive.

"You fellas have fun tonight!" The boys gave Hector a strange look and told him they'd see him in the morning.

"What's up with him?" Eugene commented. He and Stanley quickly found out what Hector meant when they walked into the living room. Perched in a large leather chair, looking like Venus, was Connie, from Katz's. With a cigarette in one hand and a cocktail in the other, her goddess-like appearance had an abstractly risqué, erotic flavor.

She took a draw on her cigarette and set down her drink, then stood up to receive her two male subjects.

"Hello, boys. I guess I'll be taking care of you now, that is, if that's okay with you." Eugene and Stanley stood frozen and speechless.

"That is okay with you two, isn't it?" She smiled, knowing full good and well it was.

"You're going to be our housekeeper?" Stanley's voice cracked with excitement.

"Normally, I would have said no, but Mr. Leppert made me an offer that I couldn't turn down. So you are stuck with me. By the way, I'm taking the master bedroom, so whoever has their stuff in there needs to get another room."

"You're staying here?" both boys asked in unison.

"It's my house now, so, yes, I'll be staying." It was all the boys could do to withhold their jubilation.

"Your house?" inquired Eugene.

"Oh, I guess that slipped out." She smiled confidently. "Wasn't supposed to let you in on my little arrangement with Mr. Leppert. That's our little secret, right, guys?"

There was no mistaking it: she was proud of her accomplishment, and was more than willing to boast. Far from a dumb beauty, she was very street smart and certainly knew how to handle men. Connie was indeed a master at the art of feminine manipulation.

Contrary to her provocative and flamboyant demeanor at Katz's, she led a quiet and private life. However, because of her anonymity and the fact that she was a single woman, she was quite often the center of speculative tales and scandalous gossip. Some said she was a retired madam; others say a former blackjack dealer from Los Vegas; some even whispered that she was a widowed wife of a mobster. Her one allied confidant, was Uncle Gregg. She and Gregg had shared several affairs, business and otherwise, over the years. Connie was Gregg's first choice for housesitting the boys, but she'd turned him down.

After the disastrous one day with Minnie, he'd returned to her and upped the ante.

"By the way, where's my car?" asked Connie.

"Your car!" The boys' high-pitched collective response brought Connie over to within an arm's length.

"So do you two always answer in unison?"

"Yes, ma'am, I mean no, ma'am." The boy's responded together again and Gene shook his head realizing how silly they sounded.

"We. . ." Gene paused and then started over. "*I* parked the car on the beach too close to the water and the tide came in and. . ." Before Eugene could finish his confession, the telephone rang. Connie held up one finger to shush him, gave them both a hard stare, turned around, and walked over to answer the phone.

"Hello. Hi, Gregg. What's wrong? The boys? Yes, they are here. They seem okay." There was a long pause as Connie listened to the voice on the other end. "Hold on, I'll let you talk to them." Gene and Stan dropped their heads in submission as they listened to Connie's reply. She held the phone out for Eugene who was beginning to tremble with fear. Slowly, he walked over and took the receiver from her hand, cleared his throat, and put the phone to his ear.He sat down on the couch and began to speak.

"Hello, who is this?" Gene asked as if he didn't know who was on the other end of Alexander Graham Bell's invention. Stanley waited intensely to hear what he was anticipating to be his orders of execution.

Gene was still and said nothing for a few seconds before giving a couple of quick verbal responses of, "I'm okay, sir," and "He's okay, sir." sounding a lot like the responses given by Connie only moments before.

Connie leaned over to Stanley while Gene and Gregg continued their conversation over the phone. She whispered, "Apparently the Corpus Christi police found the car washed up on the beach this morning and traced the license plate back to Mr. Leppert." Gene then went into his explanation of the events which led to losing the car to the Gulf.

At the end of his admission, Eugene apologized repeatedly and offered to pay for all the damages. Stanley perked up when he heard Gene take full responsibility for this "bone-headed event." He also asked Uncle Gregg not to mention Stanley's involvement to Coach Bryant.

The telephone conversation lasted a while longer with Eugene doing more listening than talking. When the discussion concluded, Eugene thanked Gregg and said goodbye. As soon as the receiver rested back in its cradle, Gene exhaled the breath that he'd been holding since he first grabbed the receiver. He then leaned forward and rested his head in his hands.

Stanley immediately walked over and sat beside him.

"I don't know what to say, Briggs. I can never thank you enough for what you just did. You would have been one hell of a teammate." Connie sat back down in her chair, lit up another Lucky Strike, and acted as if she were entertained by Stanley's syrupy speech.

"I'm going to miss you, too, James." Gene rose up and without expression fired back. "And I agree, I would have been one hell of a teammate. But you'll never have the chance to find out when you're back at your family farm in Kentucky." Gene jumped up, looked over at Connie, and winked just as she blew out a thin stream of smoke.

It took a couple of seconds before what Gene said sunk in with Stanley. Then he exploded, and then imploded.

"What! What are talking about, Briggs?" Stanley jumped up and followed Gene to the kitchen.

"Briggs, stop! You got to tell me what he said." Stanley was right on Eugene's heel, pathetically pleading with him to reveal his conversation with Uncle Gregg. Gene kept repeating, "I'm sorry, man. I'm sorry, man." Gene filled a glass with water from the tap and walked out of the kitchen and back to the couch. Stanley was beginning to become angry and the tone in his voice started to change. Gene sat the glass on the table and plopped back down beside Connie.

"Okay, James, here's the story." Eugene sat on the couch and stared at Stanley anxiously standing before him.

"Apparently Uncle Gregg was so moved by my courage and honesty, as well as my valor, for accepting the entire blame, that he is willing to forget about the whole incident. He was quite impressed that I was willing to sacrifice my career so that a fellow teammate could continue on with theirs." Eugene smugly shook his head and paused in silence.

"Well, what did he say about me? Why did you say I would be going back to Kentucky?"

"Well, I didn't want to tell you this, but. . ."

"But what, Briggs?" Stanley shouted.

"He said he knew you were just involved as I was, but acted like a coward. And the fact that you were willing to sacrifice your teammate, for your own benefit. . . that didn't sit well with him either. Right before he hung up, he said he was going to call Coach Bryant and recommend you be cut from the team."

Stanley stood for a moment in shock from what he just heard. Totally dejected, he turned and started walking away, then stopped and turned back around.

"Hey, Briggs, thanks anyway for taking a bullet for me. You're right, you would have been a hell of a teammate. The thing is, Uncle Gregg is right. I don't deserve to be your teammate or be on this football team." Stanley walked down the hall to his room, and the sound of his door shutting, even though softly, thundered through the deafening silence.

"So when are you going to tell him?" Connie asked.

"How did you know?" Eugene laughed. "That was a pretty good story, though, wasn't it? To tell you the truth, I was scared to death. I couldn't believe how well he took it. He didn't even act mad."

"Honey, Gregg was more worried about two of Bear Bryant's

prized studs drowning in the Gulf of Mexico under his watch than losing one of his many Eldorados."

"Well, I think it's probably been long enough. I'm startin' to feel a little guilty, so I'll go pay a visit to Stan. Maybe I'll tell him that Uncle Gregg called back and changed his mind. I'll tell him that he left the decision of whether he should be on the team or not totally up to me. I'm going to milk this as long as I can."

CHAPTER 21

Katrina was wide-eyed with excitement as the Greyhound bus pulled into the station in Montgomery. From her window she spotted a brown station wagon parallel to the curb, with "USAF" and an American flag on the door. Leaning against the vehicle was a man wearing an olive uniform and holding a clipboard. The backseat of the government vehicle appeared to have silhouettes of passengers, but she couldn't make out their faces. She patiently waited her turn to file off the bus, keeping an eye on the car. Kat stopped briefly to thank the bus driver as she exited past him, but didn't hesitate further, not even to stretch her legs or collect her suitcase. Wearing a smile that she could not contain even if she'd tried, Kat ran immediately toward the car. There was absolutely no trepidation in this young lady. The air force was her calling, her destiny, and she wasn't going to delay her waiting chariot that was poised to take her to her future.

"Sir, are you going to Maxwell Air Force Base?" inquired Kat upon her urgent arrival. The uniformed man stepped away from the car to converge with Kat. He looked at his clipboard, then looked down at Katrina, who, in turn, was staring up at him.

"Are you Garretson? K. Garretson?" He looked again at his clipboard, then back again at her. He eyed her from top to bottom, even walking around her for the full inspection.

"My name is Katrina Garretson, sir!" she responded sharply "Is there something wrong?"

"I guess I was expecting a man, not a petite little girl." Amused by his sarcastic comment, he gave out a snide chuckle.

Kat was now completely irritated by his disrespectful behavior. As he started his second inspection trip around her, she reacted.

"With all due respect, airman, I would appreciate you looking at my eyes instead of my rear end when you talk to me, unless, of course, that's how you greet all new arrivals, including those boys sitting in the backseat of your car." Kat paused briefly to compose herself before completely finishing him off. "In a few months, this *petite little girl* will be your superior, so I would suggest you tread lightly whenever you're in my presence from this point forward, in the hopes that I might forget this little incident."

That stopped the airman in his tracks. He looked over at the four boys sitting in his car. They were all starring back with grins on their faces. It was obvious they had seen and heard everything.

"Get your bags, Garretson, and get in the car!" ordered the airman.

Unfortunately, this encounter with a chauvinistic pig would not be the last for Kat.

The short ride to the base was uncomfortable; no one spoke,

not even a whisper. The car stopped at the main entrance gate of the base and after a flash of credentials and a brief look over by the guards, the car continued. One more security gate and they were inside the base. Five new residents to Maxwell—well, at least in their vehicle. The station wagon pulled into a large parking lot full of air force buses, making its way up to a designated drop off area in front of a complex of buildings. There were a couple of buses and another wagon ahead of them unloading their human cargo. Their car pulled in behind and Kat and her companions in the backseat exited. As if orchestrated by a Hollywood movie director to greet their arrival, the United States Air Force had their own spectacular reception. Just as soon as Katrina stepped onto the sidewalk, she (along with every other new arrival) threw back her head to view the sky. The low-pitched buzz of a B-52 bomber announced its arrival as it glided—seemingly barely—over the top of the tall flagpole and then disappeared over the tops of the buildings. Katrina screamed with excitement, but her sound was drowned out by the rumble of the turbine engines.

Amongst the masses of newbie's carrying luggage were uniformed airmen directing traffic—people traffic, that is. They were herding the arrivals through a pedestrian gate and toward a large building that turned out to be a gymnasium. Kat grabbed her suitcases, gave a parting, dirty look to the chauvinistic chauffer, and funneled in with the crowd.

Kat quickly learned that basic training was a series of lines—get in this line and get in that line. And then there were the forms. Filling this out and filling that out; most of the questions were duplicates from a previous form or had been answered in her original registration. The question that appeared on nearly every form—and caused her the most angst—was the question about notification of a recruit's family or guardian. For whatever reason, providing the names of the Brownes whom she'd lived with for the last eight years never crossed her mind. She decided to be consistent with what she wrote on the original registration, which was simply writing down the word "deceased."

After the admissions process, she checked her personal belongings, then skirted off to the auditorium for a thirty-minute orientation from the base commander. Then it was back to the gymnasium to stand in line again for a physical screening; this time her line was a little shorter. *Women to the left and men to the right* were the repetitive orders being shouted. This was where her fellow male airmen parted. Kat was quickly accumulating male admirers who followed her around like a puppy. Despite the ongoing instructions, three mesmerized males followed her to the wrong line. Aware of their blunder, she turned around and warmly directed them to the right line.

"Ah, boys, I think you have wandered into the girl's line by mistake." Embarrassed by their error, the three scurried away.

There were about ten females per every fifty males, or around 20 percent. Even though the percentages were low, they were significantly higher than during World War II or the Korean War. There were no surprises for Kat during orientation; she had been researching this day for months.

Some of the women were surprised and a little apprehensive

when it came time for them to receive their U.S. military grade haircut of above the shoulder length, but not Katrina. If it was good enough for Jackie Cochran, Mary Jo Shelly, and Lillian Keil, it was certainly good enough for her.

Katrina used to humorously prod Jimmy about which sex was the more dominant. She really didn't care, but she knew it infuriated him so she kept at it. She used lots of examples to make her point, but her favorite was pointing out that Katharine Wright had as much to do with the first flight at Kitty Hawk as her brothers, Orville and Wilbur. To really send him over the top, she would say that, in her opinion, the analogy, *Behind every good man is a good woman,* was totally flawed. "The more accurate statement should be, *Beside or ahead of every great man is a great woman.*" The final line of orientation day was to accept her new clothes, the only material that would touch her skin for the next several years. She received two sets of fatigues and one pair of shoes, and then it was off to the women's dormitory.

The other female enlistees were not as willing to be as social with Katrina as their male counterparts, with the exception of Gail. Gail Harden was from a small town in southern Mississippi. She was a tall, skinny girl with distinct, somber facial features, and wore no makeup to disguise her life of hardship. Gail was not accustomed to being approached and greeted by strangers, especially in a kind and friendly manner. So when Kat turned around in line with an inviting smile and a warm hello, Gail was a taken aback for a second. But as soon as she realized Kat's friendly greeting was genuine, it was as if a veil had been lifted from her face and she lit up with a beautiful smile. Gail's reasons for joining the air force were totally different from Katrina's. She wanted out of Mississippi and wanted to pursue nursing as a career, but had no monetary means to do either, so this was her ticket.

Finally, day one of orientation was complete and it was off to the women's dorms to unpack and enjoy an hour of free time, then to the mess hall for supper.

There was nothing feminine about the dorms; they were long, gray metal Quonset huts. No pictures on the walls, no flowers in vases, just beds. Bunk beds, one after the other, on both sides for the entire length of the building. Purposely, one could not tell the difference between a male and a female dorm by physical appearance. The women's showers and restrooms were in another building completely. Kat and Gail grabbed a random bunk, and Kat immediately offered to take the top, because of her smaller size. But as not to embarrass her new friend, she told Gail that because she was going to be a pilot, she wanted to sleep closest to the stars.

Kat put all her stuff away in minutes except for her stationery. It was time for her to write letters. The first one, of course, was to Eugene. She'd made sure to get his address before she'd left.

My dear Eugene,

It's only been a couple of days since we've been apart, but it seems an eternity. My first day at Maxwell was unbelievable; almost as exciting as the first time I laid eyes on you! Tee hee! Every time I hear or see an aircraft fly over the base, I get a charge. Believe it or not, I can see myself piloting it.

Don't worry about me, Mother and Father are close. Just a few weeks until I'll be there in Texas with you.

I know it's been hard for you to be good, but I'll keep sending you reminders to keep you in line.

Love you forever,

Your gal, Kat.

She kissed the letter, imprinting it with lipstick, and inserted it along with one of her scented red ribbons into an envelope.

The other letters were to Mike and Lisa, Jimmy and Ertta. She wanted the Brownes and Ertta to know she'd arrived okay, that orientation had gone well, and that there were no surprises. She reiterated over and over just to ease their worries that she was excited and very happy to be there.

She also told of meeting this really nice girl from Mississippi, and that she was certain that they would become very good friends. Jimmy's letter was a little more detailed as to the first day's events. She told him about the jerk driver that had picked her up at the bus station and how she'd put him in his place. She also mentioned the low flying bomber that'd sent shivers up her spine.

Gail was observing Kat's writing and glanced over her shoulder as Kat finished her last letter.

"You have pretty handwriting, Katrina. I guess that's as it should be. Everything you do and say is pretty. You're even very pretty. I saw how all the boys look at you." Kat looked up and sheepishly smiled.

"Thank you, Gail. I guess all roses have their share of thorns;

you just haven't seen mine yet. You're welcome to help yourself to some stationery, hun, if you'd like to write your loved ones."

"Thanks, but my momma can't read and my daddy don't care." Gail turned away quickly and started attending to her locker. It was rare that Katrina couldn't think of an appropriate reply, but Gail's glib response caught her by surprise. Kat stood up and touched her arm.

"Well, girl, what do you say we walk over to the mess hall and get some, what do they call it, grub?" Katrina's humorous request snapped Gail back to life and her face lit up again.

"I'm starving, Kat, even for grub. Let's go!" The girls walked down the center aisle and just as they were about to walk through the door, they were met by a senior airman, or more specifically, airwoman, entering the building. Kat froze and immediately brought herself to attention and saluted. She could tell with her peripheral vision that Gail was still relaxed; this prompted her to deliver an elbow to Gail's side with her free arm. Unsure and startled, Gail then awkwardly jumped to attention, too. The short, stocky woman said nothing, but gave them a sharp stare. She then walked up to within inches of their faces.

"Where do you two trainees think you're going?" Before Gail had a chance to say anything, Kat responded.

"Ma'am, Trainee Garretson and Trainee Harden reporting, that we were on our way to the mess hall."

"You were, were you? What ranking airman gave you permission to leave your unit, to do so?" barked the superior.

"No one gave us permission ma'am," Kat responded, still holding her salute and looking forward.

"Are you two bimbos always going to abandon your unit?" asked the superior.

"No, ma'am!" said Katrina.

"We didn't know, ma'am." Gail's first verbal response moved the sergeant from directly in front of Kat to directly in front of Gail.

"Trainee Garretson, I was unaware that your acquaintance Harden here could talk. Now that I've heard her talk she sounds pretty ignorant. Do you agree with my assessment, Trainee Garretson?" Kat hesitated, then spoke.

"I must respectfully disagree, ma'am. Trainee Harden is very smart. We both were selfish and put ourselves in front of our unit, ma'am." Katrina's reply seemed to satisfy the sergeant.

"I see. Well, I hope you're right. I can fix selfish, but there is not a damn thing I can do about ignorance." She pulled back and walked around them to an awaiting barracks of saluting young women that now had her complete attention.

"Let's see how many other selfish bitches there are in here." It was eerily quiet as she walked from bed to bed, individually examining each of her trainees as if she were a lioness inspecting her pride. When she completed her tour of the bunks, she walked to the center of the aisle in the middle of the building.

"Listen up, trainees! My name is Sergeant Whitehead, but you will never address me by my name. You will address me in the same manor manner as this selfish bitch Garretson did:

'Yes, ma'am' or 'no ma'am.'" The sounds of snickering made the Sergeant pause. "There is nothing funny about being selfish! Take a look at the trainee beside you. If that individual is selfish on or above the battlefield, then you will surely die. You are all a team. No one trainee is any more significant than the other. Just as important, you are no less significant than any of your male counterparts on this base.

"I will be your main military training instructor while you are here at Maxwell. You will do what I say. You will not question what I say. You will never go anywhere without your unit of twelve. Not to the mess hall, not to the latrine, unless you have specific orders from me. You will never address your fellow trainee as either bitch or bimbo; those names are reserved for my use only. Got it?"

Twelve "Yes, ma'ams," responded in unison.

"One more thing. Because we are a team, one unit, you are no longer individuals. And because you are all the same as Garretson and Harden, you're all selfish bitches. So your punishment for being selfish bitches is that we will be the last unit to march to the mess hall tonight. I will be back to get you, and you will line up and we will march over to the mess hall as a unit, eat, then march back." With that, she stormed out of the barrack. As soon as the screen door slammed, twelve girls relaxed, but things did not remain quiet. Muddled choruses of "selfish Bitches" echoed off the metal walls. Ten angry women were now all staring at Gail and Kat.

"Thanks for sayin' I was smart," Gail whispered, "but why did you say we were selfish? We didn't know we were supposed to all go together. Now we got everybody in trouble. Lordy, girl, all I wanted was just to fit it in and now look at them. They all hate me."

"I told Sergeant Whitehead that because that's what she wanted to hear. Trust me, she was going to scold us for something, regardless. I just helped her out. See, I read all about this. It's called *role playing,* a teaching process used by the military. Sergeant needed to establish who was boss and find out which one of us girls was going to be her problem." Kat noticed some of the trainees walking toward them and decided to address the group. So she jumped up on her footlocker.

"You girls did great! The sergeant knows you're not selfish bitches; she just wanted to poke our cage just to see who'll growl back. Since no one questioned her authority or caused a scene, she was very pleased. We just made her job easier."

A big girl named Betty from Detroit was not so happy with Kat's explanation. She walked over to Kat and shoved her off the footlocker and down on the concrete floor.

"I ain't no selfish bitch, but I can be a mean bitch. I don't like little goody two shoes princesses waltzing around making my life hard. Sergeant, she wants to punish us all, but I'm gonna punish you. Maybe putting some dents in that pretty little face will teach you to keep your mouth shut." Big Betty clenched her fists and stepped toward Kat, still on her backside on the floor where she had just been deposited by Betty.

"You're not punishin' anybody!" Gail stepped in front of Betty, but she didn't need to. Betty stopped in her tracks, her hands unclenched, and she gasped as if she were suddenly startled. She stopped her advance toward Kat and made her way over to a bunk and sat down. Everyone, including Gail, stared and was speechless by her sudden change in behavior. Kat jumped up and went over to where she sat.

"Are you okay, Betty?" Kat asked.

Gail came up behind Kat and grabbed her arm. "Have you lost your mind? Why are you asking her if she's okay? She was about ready to mop the floor with your head." Kat didn't respond to Gail; she just stared down at Betty, who was desperately trying to gather her thoughts.

"I'm fine." The rage in Betty's eyes was replaced with bewilderment as she looked up at Kat. "You'll think I'm crazy, but I just heard voices in my head."

Katrina leaned over and whispered, "It's okay. You're not crazy you just met my parents. We'll talk later." It was obvious that Betty was shaken and what Kat said to her didn't help. Betty felt an emotion that she wasn't accustomed to and certainly didn't know how to express.

Betty stood up abruptly and the female trainees, including Gail, braced, but were surprised to see what occurred next. Looking like a mother grizzly bear receiving her cub, Betty opened her arms wide and embraced Kat in a loving hug. Their teammates let out sighs of relief, but were totally blown away. However they didn't have time to dwell on Betty's transformation because in through the door came the sergeant, announcing it was their turn to march to the mess hall.

Air force life began that day for Katrina, but a human bond was formed that evening with her fellow trainee teammates. Betty left Kat alone from that point on; most importantly, she never threatened her or anyone else on their team again.

When the team returned to the barracks, each trainee was given an hour to do what they needed to before lights out. They would quickly find out how precious and valuable their rest would be.

Routine wasn't just a way of life, it was the only way of life in the military, and the United States Air Force was no different. Every morning at five a.m. a recorded version of reveille played over the loud speakers, and the trainees had five minutes to rise, dress, make their bunk, and report out in front of the barracks in a designated row. They were then inspected and barked at by their TI (Training Instructor).

Every day, someone else didn't live up to the expectations of the US Air Force and, of course, they all paid the penalty. They did a quick ten minutes of calisthenics and then they ran. The first day it was two miles and increased a mile every day after. Of course, they were always being penalized and that tacked on additional miles. And every day Kat would remind them about *role playing* and encouraged them to stay positive and focus as a team so they would get through it. When the running concluded they marched to the showers, then to the mess hall, and from there it was on to the classroom. After lunch, it was back to the classroom before finishing the day with military training such as hand-to-hand combat, obstacle courses, and the use of weapons and firearms.

There was absolutely no fraternizing with trainees or any

airman of the opposite sex. However, the female teams and the male teams were mixed during classroom time.

Military training usually concluded around four o'clock—or 1600 hours—every day. A couple hours of free time would afford Kat plenty of occasions to write letters and read or study.

Gail's aspirations were quite different than Katrina's, however, their paths of accomplishing their goals were parallel. In a few weeks both girls would be heading to Lackland Air Force Base in Universal City, Texas. Katrina would be in Phase One Flight Training School and Gail in Education and Training Command for the Fifty-Ninth Medical Wing.

Kat insisted it was fate. She knew they would make a great team. She would pilot the plane, Gail would be the ranking medical officer on the aircraft, and they would save the world together.

The days, as hellish as they were, sailed by quickly. The grueling runs and difficult obstacle courses were becoming easier as their team became more cohesive. They were faring well in their competitions against other teams, including the male teams.

Kat was a good coach for Gail as well as the other girls. She was a source of strength; no matter how tough it got she always remained upbeat and positive. She was constantly telling her team that basic training was merely a hurdle and they should focus on the prize—their careers, which would begin in a little over a month.

CHAPTER 22

After Stanley stewed in his room for a few minutes, he ascertained that Eugene was pulling his leg about being kicked off the team. He came storming back out of his room and met Eugene halfway down the hall to demand the truth. As soon as Gene saw the pathetic despair on Stanley's face, he couldn't help but smirk, which in turn gave away the farce. Stanley was so relieved he could kiss Gene, but after realizing he'd been had, the horseplay began. In their rough celebration ceremony, the two strapping males looked like a couple of burly moose colliding. They knocked into the walls and tumbled on the floor, sending hung pictures crashing. This activity lasted for a couple of minutes before running its course, then the boys broke, took their showers, and were ready to eat.

Connie was not much of a cook but the boys didn't mind. The first meal she served was pancakes. In fact, pancakes were just about all she had in her culinary repertoire, so they got pancakes about every other night. Breakfast would become the boys' favorite meal, not because of what she prepared, but because of the flair of her service. She brought them peanut butter and jelly sandwiches in bed, sometimes wearing only a flimsy negligee. Connie loved to sadistically tease the boys. She found amusement in torturing them, prancing around the house half naked, sending their overactive hormones into overdrive.

Connie also loved her vodka, and the boys quickly learned that the more she drank the more provocative she became. Vodka was the great equalizer and it would quickly turn the tables. She went from teasing the boys to performing for them, but no matter how drunk she got, she never lost complete control.

She never allowed prolonged physical contact, and when the show was over, it was over, and she'd wander off to her room, leaving the boys panting and begging at her locked door.

The day after Eugene's confession to Gregg, the boys returned from the oilfields to find a surprise sitting in the drive: another new Cadillac, this one a bright yellow.

Because of their God-given athletic talents, these two country boys of modest backgrounds were now living the life of movie stars. But soon the life of luxury would be put on a shelf—when it came time for them to report to Junction, Texas, for training camp.

Unlike Kat's daily agenda, a much more liberal routine was established for Eugene and Stanley—but nevertheless, it was a routine. Monday through Friday, bright and early, Hector would arrive to take them to the oilfields. On the return trip, as soon as they pulled into the drive, Eugene would jump out of the truck and run to the mailbox to retrieve Kat's letters. He treasured her letters and saved every one. Although he cherished every word she penned, he was not as proficient at returning the favor. Writing down his thoughts and feelings was hard for Gene; he had trouble translating what he felt in his heart to paper. So most of his returned letters consisted of one short paragraph, but Katrina thought no less of them than if they were several pages long.

On the weekends Connie would drive them to the beach. She'd sun herself while Gene and Stan socialized up and down the sand. Once a week Gregg would come by and take them to Katz's or another one of Corpus Christi's finer restaurants. Payday for Gene and Stanley came twice a month when Gregg would send someone for the car to wash and service it. When the car was returned, in the glove compartment were two envelopes, each containing two hundred dollars in cash.

Despite the royal treatment, by the third week both boys were becoming a little homesick and weary of all the superficial attention. Connie sensed this, so she persuaded Gregg to fly both boys home to their families for a week.

This was Stanley's first time on an airplane and Eugene's second, but both were scared to death. Gregg's advice was to drink heavily before boarding and the fear would subside or they would pass out. Neither boy took his advice but did sleep most of the time in the air. Gene couldn't wait to tell Kat that he had actually flown before her. The timing of this trip home was great for Gene. Besides seeing his mother and sister Mary, he was able to see his brother Delbert, who was home, and this time for good, from the army. Besides Eugene's reunion with his family, he was able to do a little fishing on Cheat with Jimmy before Jimmy headed off to college.

When Gene and Stanley returned back to Corpus Christi, they were both refreshed and recharged. Eugene, though, had a little extra kick in his step because he knew that in a week his girl would be coming to Texas to see him. Kat would be graduating basic training and then put on a US Air Force bus to Lackland in San Antonio.

CHAPTER 23

It took Gene three days of lobbying Connie—not Gregg—to get permission to drive the Eldorado to San Antonio to pick up Kat. But Connie finally conceded in the name of love. That's what she told Gene, anyway. So Saturday morning at six a.m., Eugene was off, heading north on US 37 just as fast as he could. The trip from Corpus Christi would normally take approximately two hours, but Gene got a little lost trying to find Lackland, so it ended up closer to three. Regardless, he was an hour early. After his arrival on base, he received instructions from the guards at the gate directing him as to where to wait for military arrivals. He parked his car where instructed and impatiently waited. Finally, there it was—her bus. He jumped out of the Cadillac and jogged over to where the bus had stopped. He walked along the windows, peering in to catch an early look at her, but was unable to find her. Everyone looked the same, just like a uniformed football team; all dressed identically in their blues. The only contrast was their height and weight.

Gene didn't see her step off the bus and was still up on his toes looking in the window when he felt a tap on his shoulder.

"Who ya lookin for, stranger?" Gene spun around, totally unprepared for what he was about to see. There, waiting for his embrace, and staring up at him with big brown eyes, was a beautiful woman in a formal military uniform. Gene didn't know how to react or what to say. He reached up and touched her hair that dangled down only inches from the side of her garrison cap.

"It's short," she said softly.

"You are so beautiful." Eugene's voice broke. She reached up and touched his cheek and they locked together, entwined as one.

They hugged for what seemed to be an eternity until they were interrupted by the sound of someone clearing their throat. That someone was Gail. She had been patiently waiting for their reunion to end, but gave them a little sign acknowledging her presence.

"Oh, Gail, I'm so sorry!" Kat said. Gail smiled "Gail, this is Eugene. You've heard me talking about him so much. Sweetheart, this is Gail."

"Hi, Gail. I feel like I've known you forever, from Kat's letters. She says you are going to be the Florence Nightingale of the air force." The girls laughed and then quickly collected their bags and the three walked to the reception center.

Katrina and Gail had to check in and fill out more forms before they were granted a customary three-day furlough. Kat and Gene invited Gail to go with them back to Corpus Christi and she accepted. So three hours later, after the paperwork, quick orientation and moving their stuff into their separate barracks on opposite sides of the base, they were on their way south.

Connie felt the house would be a bit crowded with her there, so she was gone when Gene and the girls returned from San Antonio. Stanley, however, was not, and that worked out great. He and Gail hit it off from the start and this allowed Kat and Gene plenty of quality time for just the two of them. Just like Eugene and Stanley, Gail and Katrina had never seen the Gulf of Mexico, so that's where they spent most of their time in the two and a half days of their leave. At night they would party up and down the beach at the local watering holes.

On the last night of the girls' leave, the boys wanted to treat them to a nice meal and also introduce them to Connie, so they went to Katz's. It was actually the girls—more specifically, Katrina—that wanted to meet Connie. Eugene had actually been a little relieved that Connie was not home when they got back from Lackland. He wasn't sure how Kat would react to her casual displays of nudity, or worse yet, her vodka-induced exhibitionistic theatrics. As free-spirited as Kat was, he didn't think she'd appreciate Connie's behaviors, especially if Connie chose to be promiscuous and not act reserved.

He was hoping that tonight she would be a little more covered up and a little less sexy. After all, she was supposed to be the house mom not the house madam. At least that's the perception that Gene had to sell. Connie was, in fact, a little more conservatively dressed that evening, but far from frumpy. The introductions were quite cordial, and even hugs were exchanged between Katrina and Connie. That's when things got a little interesting.

There was a reason Kat was so persistent about meeting Connie. She had something to tell her. Katrina whispered something in Connie's ear as they formally embraced that surprised and noticeably shook her. Connie recoiled instantly; she looked at Kat in disbelief, and then turned away, hiding the look of humiliation on her face. Connie couldn't get them to their table fast enough and disappeared quickly after the group was seated. Whatever Kat had said to her remained a secret despite the urgings of her friends. Whatever it was that Kat whispered in her ear it had a tremendous impact. For the remaining time that Gene and Stanley spent in Corpus Christi, Connie acted more like June Cleaver than Gypsy Rose Lee.

There was no more subtle drama for the rest of this particular evening. Katrina handled her issue with Connie like a lady and then quickly moved on to other things. It wasn't long before the table for four became crowded and romance took over the night. Succumbing to the candlelight and soft music, Katrina and Eugene decided to drive to the beach for a moonlight walk. Gail and Stanley had ideas of their own, so Gene dropped them off at the house on the way.

Holding hands, Gene and Kat walked barefoot along the water's edge. The three-quarter moon illuminated everything, accentuating objects to virtually another dimension. Katrina's eyes glimmered like diamonds from the reflecting moon as she looked up at Eugene. Inebriated by passion, they plunged their bodies together and entwined as one, falling into the surf. Articles of saltwater-soaked clothing were tossed carelessly along the shore waiting to be retrieved; but that was inconsequential now for the two lovers.

Unlike in the backseat of the junked car, this time the timing was right; there were no interruptions from uninvited bees. Years of love were consecrated on the South Texas beach that night.

Before sunrise, the car was headed north and all but the driver, Gene, was asleep. The girls had to be on base by 7a.m. to keep from being AWOL and they barely made it. The time on the dashboard clock read 6:52 when the car passed through the security gate. The girls jumped out, grabbed their bags, kissed the boys, and checked in with two minutes to spare. Because Katrina and Gail were not in the same schools, they did not share the same dorms. In fact, they were almost on opposite ends of the base. The women assigned to Gail's dorm were in the Air Education and Training Command and every bunk in her building was occupied. Katrina, on the other hand, was only one of four other girls accepted into flight school as a navigational student, so Kat's dorm was nearly empty.

After basic training Katrina was given a rank of airman. Not just a rank, but a new first name. Now that she was in the United States Air Force, she would only be addressed as Airman Garretson, by her supervisors. After a few days, her fellow airmen all called her Kat.

No females were accepted into flight school—this was the Golden Rule of the US Air Force. The air force would not train female pilots, however, they would accept female enlistees who already had a pilot's license and allow them limited duties as pilots. Up until now, most female enlistees did not even bother to apply. This was notably due to the real underlying reason, which was discrimination. Since the inception of the WACs in 1947 and the WAFs in 1948, the armed forces put a limit on the number of female enlistees and officers. This in itself sent a discouraging message. The rule was, women shall not be used in combat situations or intentionally put in harm's way. Most of the females enlisting in the Air Force were no different than any of the other armed forces; they enrolled in the more acceptable, female friendly programs like clerical or medical. But Kat was confident that she'd somehow buck the system and go through flight school, even if it meant only flying non-tactical aircraft.

She didn't let the archaic regulations of the past and present stymie her enthusiasm. She was optimistic, but she was also realistic too. She had a constant reminder taped in her locker of how hard it would be. It was the picture of her hero, Jacqueline Cochran, a very skilled pilot who was never given the chance to fly in combat. Kat wanted to break through the discriminating barriers that held back her pioneering heroes, but she also had selfish motives. Kat's response on numerous occasions to individuals who questioned her motives was, "Forget about the male female equality thing. I just want to have a chance to protect our country while soaring amongst the angels." She was optimistic that fate was on her side, and perhaps she was right.

CHAPTER 24

"Oh, I wish Jimmy were here!" Kat thought as she sat in her first class. She was feeling a little unconfident about learning all of the required geometrical and mathematical formulas. Simultaneously, thirteen hundred and seventy five miles away in Durham, North Carolina, Jimmy stared out at the hundreds of faces at the university student union and said, "I wish Kat were here!" Jimmy was terrified at the mass of humanity and the ensuing frenzy that went along with freshman orientation. Katrina had always been his social liaison; she was a magnet and strangers seem to migrate to her. Not just the males but also with the females. Girls are always interested in what or who the guys are interested in.

However, both Kat and Jimmy were on their own now, but soon after turbulent starts they settled down and acclimated to their environments. Coincidently, a major part of both of their times, at least initially, was spent in the classroom.

Even though Kat and Jimmy couldn't help each other in person, they did communicate quite often via letters. Jimmy's letters were a lot more substantive than Eugene's. He wrote several pages detailing his studies or inquiring about hers. His letters both offered and welcomed suggestive advice; usually, her advice to him was social in nature, while his suggestions were more academically-based.

One of the main topics penned in their letters that kept growing over the weeks was the Cold War. Even though the country was not quite up to speed yet with this contentious competition between the USSR and the U.S., Katrina and Jimmy were immersed in it. This subject of the Cold War was spreading like wildfire on the collegiate campuses, as well as the military bases. At Lackland, it was more than just a subject of discussion, it was urgent.

World War II and Korean War pilots were retiring and the air force needed to replace them, and replace them quickly. The Communist Soviet Union was aggressively accelerating the growth of their military, causing much angst for the United States and their free world allies.

This meant an expeditious pilot training program with the goal of getting trainees into the air and logging cockpit hours as quickly as possible. There were changes to the curriculum too; along with the normal aeronautical-related classes, the air force added two classes—one on Russian geography and the other on Soviet aircraft. Katrina was hoping that this whirlwind training philosophy would act as a vacuum and pull her in with the males to the advanced phases of flight school. And that once she'd trained—and because of the post-war pilot shortage and the Cold War concern—the air force would have no choice but to allow her to fly tactical aircraft like bombers or fighters.

CHAPTER 25

In the eyes of Coach Bryant, Uncle Gregg's summer watch over Eugene and Stanley in Corpus Christi had been a success. Gregg was able to keep the highly sought-after recruits hidden away from the pilfering hands of other coaches and football programs, as well as treating them to the spoils of the privileged. But the high life was over for the boys, because training camp was about to begin.

The boys said their farewells to a tearful Connie. She hugged them as if they were the sons she never had. Indeed, she had changed since her moment with Katrina at the restaurant. Gregg noticed the transformation of Connie, too, and he was not totally pleased.

They loaded up the car, and Uncle Gregg headed north to training camp. Not to College Station as the boys were anticipating, but to a new location out in the middle of nowhere. The destination was called Junction, Texas. The boys were clueless as to what was waiting for them in Junction. The next ten days would be as close to a visit to hell as they would experience. A complete antithesis of what their summer had been.

Coach Bryant took over a habitually losing football program at Texas A&M. Bear knew that if he had any chance of turning that program around, he would need to weed out the chaff. He needed to know which of the players he'd inherited was wheat and which was chaff. A grueling preseason camp would do the trick, but he needed a secluded location without any meddling from boosters or the faculty. On campus in College Station would not work. It took a few days, but with the help of his coaches, he found the perfect location. A cactus-infested outpost in a drought-stricken western part of Texas. The boys' palatial living quarters were two beat-up, World War II metal barracks with busted-out windows. It was just as well, having no windows, because there was certainly no air conditioning.

And at night when the temperature dropped to a chilly ninety degrees Fahrenheit, anything that potentially restricting ventilation was not good.

An adversarial climate was formed almost immediately as Eugene and Stanley arrived in their new Cadillac. Arriving at approximately the same time were a few of the other privileged Bryant recruits. They were also chauffeured by their own sugar daddies. These privileged boys were dubbed by one of the team managers as Coach Bryant's "million dollar boys." The manager was responding to the "who the hell are they" inquiries from the crowd witnessing the Hollywood-style grand entrance. The reference stuck. An hour earlier, before the million dollar boys arrived, two university buses delivered the majority of the team. The buses were filled with the wheat and chaff; and those boys were eventually dubbed the "Junction Boys."

The genius of Coach Bryant was not to drive a wedge between his team, just the opposite. He wanted his acquired team to develop pride. He wanted them to come together and compete as a unit. He wanted them to be jealous. He wanted them to prove to him that they were every bit as valuable as the freshman studs he'd brought. In fact, he wanted the rest of the team to be hard on the freshman. Their days of being coddled were over—now it was time for hard work to earn the rest of the team's respect. Coach Bryant needed to find leaders, and he looked to his upper classmen to emerge by the end of the hellish ten days and bridge the gap between the Junction Boys and the million dollar recruits. Coach Bryant's strategy did work, but it was a rough way to go.

Coach Bryant and Coach Claiborne walked over to the Cadillac to greet the new arrivals. Coach Bryant went directly to Gregg, shook his hand, and thanked him, while Claiborne went directly to Gene and Stan. After the gregarious exchanges and the unloading of luggage they all posed for Polaroids.

Eugene and Stanley thanked Uncle Gregg for all his hospitality, and even though Gregg extended his hand, the boys circumvented that exchange and gave him a hug. Gregg was not prepared for that, but he did appreciate them acknowledging his efforts and even limply returned the hugs. To keep his macho persona intact, he growled one final departing instruction to the boys.

"Enough of the touchy feely bullshit! I invested a lot of time and money on you two knuckleheads. Besides that, you drowned one of my new cars in the Gulf and turned my mistress into June Cleaver. So I expect you two to bust your balls and contribute to the Aggies winning the Southwest Conference."

Overhearing this, Coach Bryant opined.

"With all due respect, Mr. Leppert, I expect this team to win a national championship." Gregg nodded his head, as he climbed back in his car.

"Well, what are you ladies waiting on? Grab your bags and let's go." Claiborne signaled to the boys and they followed. He took them into the brutally hot Quonset hut and found them an open bunk bed. Obviously, because of the heat, the barracks were empty and as soon as the arrivals got a bunk they were out of there. Some of the boys had found shade under the few trees around, including one large one at the entrance where they'd been dropped off earlier. But most, including Eugene and Stanley, made their way to the stream that meandered its way through the property. The coaches had made it clear that after the first day there would be no more swimming. Their philosophy was that if any boy had enough energy after practice to go for a swim, then the coaches had been too soft on them. That would result in more running, not just for that player, but for the entire team, and not the next day, but at that moment.

Coach Bryant believed in feeding his boys at least one good meal a day. To ensure this, he brought the cooks from A&M's Sbisa Hall with him and put them up in a hotel in downtown

Junction. He had one of his assistants drive them to and from the hotel every day.

At their first dinner that evening, Coach Bryant made the boys stand up and give a personal introduction, which included their name and hometown and what year of school they would be starting. Coach Bryant followed this by introducing his assistant coaches and trainers. The players quickly found out that Coach Bryant was a man of few words; he wasn't a fiery speaker, but when he spoke they'd better listen, or they'd be gone.

And gone they were, leaving in mass exodus. If a player was disruptive or wouldn't follow the directions of the coaching staff, life for them would come down hard. Coach Bryant didn't need to kick players off the team, the trouble makers or the chaff left on their own accord. The team was losing players each day by attrition; to avoid embarrassment, several were leaving in the middle of the night, hitchhiking their way back to College Station.

After an uncomfortable, sleepless night in the miserable swelter of the metal barracks, the boys were driven from their bunks at the break of dawn. An assistant coach lined them up and marched them like prisoners to the makeshift mess hall where they were fed vitamins, salt tablets, and juice. The coaches knew that whatever would go in their bellies for breakfast would ultimately end up being vomited all over the football field. The extreme heat was unbearable; it was 100 degrees before noon every day. That element, factored in with the constant wind sprints, punishing repetitive blocking and tackling drills, and relentless strength and endurance exercises made this camp nothing less than torture. The football field—*a loose interpretation at best*—was nothing more than a pasture of sandspurs, rock, and mowed-down cactus. There was no bigger sin than to ask for water, and breaks of any kind were few and far between. Even after injuries or heat stroke, Coach Bryant kept the practice moving forward while the trainers attended to the injured. And a player had damn well better be injured, too, because if he were faking it just to get a rest, he'd be running while the rest of the team ate lunch and dinner. Fights broke out as often as rashes beneath their jock straps, usually during the limited water cooler breaks or during one of the meals.

If it were only between two boys, the coaches rarely intervened, letting the boys finish their squabble. Due to pure exhaustion most of the fights were over in a matter of seconds. After the first week the fights were rare, but the misery wasn't.

Indeed the chaff was separating from the wheat and what remained at the end of the ten days was a good crop of dedicated and hardworking men. Oh, yes, and most importantly with regards to winning, there was also a fair amount of athletic talent.

Despite the miserable training camp in Junction, A&M's first football season with Bryant at the helm could only muster one win. Amidst the growing impatience of the local media and the fans, Bear Bryant was building a strong foundation for future success. Eventually things did change and all the hard work began to pay dividends. The football program started getting respect, and more importantly, they started winning. Two years after Bryant arrived at College Station, he led his team to a Southwest Conference Championship with a 34 to 21 victory over A&M's

rivals the University of Texas. In 1957, the Aggies were in title contention again and Bryant's squad was able to earn for one of his *million dollar boys.* John David Crow received the prestigious Heisman Trophy.

Eugene loved football and the camaraderie of the team. He was having the time of his life, both on and off the field. There was no longer an adversarial climate of local boys versus Bryant recruits; they were now one family and one team. They were all "Bryant's boys," a headline coined often in the sports sections of the Texas papers. However, this headline was not always found in the sports section. On more than one occasion this phrase was borrowed for the front page and followed with a less than flattering article. On the football field, the team acquired a persona of being fearless, rough, and wild. That image was acceptable on Saturday; however, away from the gridiron those warrior-like traits were expected to be toned down a bit. But it was not just an image; it was real, the boys were fearless, rough and wild and there was no switch to turn off after the game.

While Bryant did nothing publically to condone that image, he did little to change it. As a result, some less than flattering episodes occurred off campus. One of these extracurricular incidents happened in Houston at a drive-in called, "The Dixie Pig."

One Saturday night after a home game five of Bryant's boys, including Gene and Stan, decided to jump in a car and cruise over to Houston. Their mission was the same as most young, red-blooded American boys: to find young, red-blooded American girls. With a case of beer, the testosterone-charged males were on the prowl. They cruised all the popular hangouts, which got them stares from the girls, but glares from the guys. They were not on their turf and the girls here were off limits. That was the decree that was levied by a small crowd of greasers smoking cigarettes on the street corner in front of the Dixie Pig. So when they stopped at this popular local hangout to purge their bladders of beer, this didn't sit well with the leather-jacketed males.

When Gene, Stanley, and the boys walked into the restaurant, you could have heard a mosquito hiccup. Every head in the house turned to the five boys sporting A&M letter jackets strutting down the checker-tiled aisle. Curiosity in the joint quickly changed to tension as the greasers followed the boys in from outside.

"Who gave you jocks permission to enter this establishment?" The loud voice echoed off the walls of the restaurant, but Eugene and the boys kept right on walking toward the restrooms as if they heard nothing.

"Hey, assholes, I'm talking to you!" This time Stanley grabbed Eugene's shoulder, which made him stop and turn around, halting the rest of the precession as well.

"Briggs, is that dirt bag hood talking to us?" asked Stanley

The five Aggies now stared back from the opposite side of the room at the four antagonistic greasers.

Eugene stepped around and a few steps away from his buddies. He wanted to make sure he had a clear vision of his adversaries and they had a clear vision of him.

"Unless your name is Dixie or Pig, I don't think that my buddies or I need to ask your permission for anything. Now I'm going to go to the restroom to pee and when I come out I'm going to walk over to that table there and give one of those pretty girls a long kiss on the lips. Then when I'm done with that and your ugly face is still here, I'm going to walk over, pick you up, drag your scrawny ass outside, and teach you a lesson in manners." Gene wheeled around and walked away, leaving the greasers speechless, the table of girls blushing, and his football buddies laughing.

Eugene, being a man of his word, returned in five minutes with his buddies trailing behind. Act two of Eugene's theater was about to begin and everyone in the restaurant, including the short order cooks and wait staff, ceased what they were doing to see how the next scene would play out. He walked directly over to the table of girls—who were all smiling up at him—and boldly reached out and clasped the hand of a blond, pulling her to her feet and, as prophesized, planted a long kiss on her lips. Cheers erupted from the patrons when Gene finally released his weak-kneed prey and she swooned back into the booth with her girlfriends. A chair slamming against a table quieted the room again and recaptured the attention of Gene and the boys. The greasers didn't heed Eugene's warning but instead rounded up a few more of their friends from outside.

The greaser who had been doing all the talking before spoke up again. "Why don't you come down here now, football boy, and teach me some manners?" The thug picked up a Coke bottle and broke it over the back of a chair, turning it into a jagged glass weapon, which he waved in the air.

Well, that was an invitation that Bryant's boys could not turn down. Their letter jackets flew off and with a rebel yell from Stanley, Eugene charged across the room like General Lee at Bull Run.

Most of the greasers were all looks and no show; they wanted no part of that rumble and were out the door lickety-split. Within minutes, the remaining greasers that stood with their Coke bottle-wielding leader wished they had retreated too.

As the fists flew, the by-standing patrons poured out of the exits, emptying the establishment. The scene resembled a saloon fight in the Wild West but lasted only a few minutes. The greasers were no match for the battle-hardened football players. After two broken tables, three busted chairs, and numerous shattered dishes, the local Houston police showed up and they were not impressed. Eugene, Stanley, and the other three teammates, along with four of the bloodied local hoods and their Coke bottle leader were hauled downtown to jail. Officials from the school were notified and they, in turn, notified Coach Bryant who sent his assistant coach to bail them out Sunday morning. The next day the headlines in the Houston paper read, "Bryant's Boys in Trouble."

A long-standing student tradition at Texas A&M—symbolizing their burning desire to beat their number one rival, the University of Texas—was a huge bonfire. But it seemed as if the Aggies' losing football season was over before the embers of the ceremonial bonfire went cold.

CHAPTER 26

As disappointing as the record was for Gene, the ten-game freshman season didn't coincide with Katrina's weekend passes from Lackland, so she was unable to make it to any of Eugene's games. In fact, they were not able to get together much at all. Initially, Gene and Stanley would borrow a car and drive down to Lackland about twice a month to see Kat and Gail, sometimes driving all that way just for ten or fifteen minutes of visiting. Like the embers of the bonfire growing cold, so was the romance between Stanley and Gail. Eventually, Eugene was going to Lackland by himself, but that was becoming more and more infrequent because commuting was becoming more difficult. Borrowing a car or talking someone with a car into driving him to San Antonio became increasingly more difficult.

No matter how often or for how long they were able to get together, Kat's letters never stopped. They did have one more communication tool at their disposal: the telephone. Hearing each other's voices did wonders to tide them over until she could get leave.

For Thanksgiving the Brownes drove to Texas, picked Gene up, and the three of them spent the holiday with Kat near the base. Katrina was now property of the United States Air Force and they were very stingy about sharing her—and it would only get worse.

Eugene and Jimmy came home for Christmas break, Easter break, and then for the summer, but not Katrina. Eugene and Jimmy spent the summer working, Jimmy bagging groceries and Gene on Mendel's farm. Any free time they could muster, they were at the rock or fishing Cheat. There was, however, a hollow feeling; something was amiss. Not a moment went by in the woods, on the rock, or on the river that they were not thinking or talking about their absent comrade. One day Jimmy brought a few of Kat's letters to the rock and read them out loud.

When Jimmy finished, Eugene ran home and retrieved a couple of the letters he had, returned, and took his turn at reading. This started a ritual for the boys that helped fill the void left by Kat's physical presence. The readings continued weekly when they returned to the rock and it lasted the rest of the summer. They never ran out of Kat's letters; she was always replenishing the supply. They even collectively wrote a few letters back to her. The funny thing was, during their get-togethers there was a strange sense that Kat was sitting right alongside them, enjoying their companionship. Neither boy dared tell the other that they felt her presence, or admit they could hear her faint laughter even when it wasn't so faint.

CHAPTER 27

Things were changing at the Briggs'. Delbert moved to Pittsburg after taking a bookkeeping job with a steel mill there. Mr. Briggs' contractual obligations in Korea had been met and he was now home. His new position with the U.S. Bureau of Mines required him to work from an office in Washington D.C., but commuting over two hundred miles every day from Point Marion was not an attractive option. Fred really didn't want to uproot his family yet, either. Even though Delbert was gone, Eugene was in college and they still had Mary Lou at home.

It took a few debates with his wife Ertta before Fred was able to conclude that he really didn't want to take Mary from her friends and the sanctuary of this wholesome sleepy community to expose her to the malevolence of the big city. So the best solution was for Fred to get an apartment in Washington, at least for time being. He would work Monday through Friday, stay at his apartment, and then drive home on the weekends. This living arrangement was really no different than most congressmen.

The days turned to weeks, and then months, and the cycle was starting over. Eugene was back on the bus to College Station and Jimmy was off to Durham.

Things were getting easier and more fun for all three of the Point Marion kids. With his first year behind him, Jimmy had settled in at Duke. He was carrying a 4.0 grade average, had joined a fraternity, and was active in several on-campus clubs.

For Eugene, the Aggie football team was beginning to experience winning. They finally had a swagger in their step. Their practices were bearable and there was no animosity amongst the team.

CHAPTER 28

Life was good for the boys, but it was even better for Katrina. She was living her dream; she was flying! Well, at least as a passenger sitting alongside her instructors; but she was advancing and advancing fast.

Kat had breezed through the initial phase of flight school, which consisted of classroom training and simulators. While the boys were sunning themselves on Cheat during the summer, a thousand miles away, Katrina was knocking off the required training hours in hopes of being accepted into Phase Two. She was testing at the top of her class and ahead of many of her male counterparts. But despite her accomplishments, her ranking male instructors were not so pleased. It was very apparent she was ready to take to the air with the first group of airmen, but she went unselected. Then, when it was time for the second tier of males, she went unselected again. Regardless, she took it all in stride and, as always, remained cheerful and optimistic. That's when fate took over.

Maybe it was a glitch in the U.S. military paperwork, or maybe it was the fact that her trainer did her a favor by leaving off a crucial point in his letter of recommendation. He failed to mention that K. Garretson was female. Whatever the reason, she finally got the orders she was longing for.

The recommendation letter came back approved: *Airman First Class K. Garretson advanced to Phase II and III flight training.* Finally it was her time; a Lockheed T-34 light, fixed-winged training aircraft was beckoning her call.

The advanced phases of pilot training continued a few miles to the west at Hondo Air Base; this meant a new home for Kat. So she cleaned out her locker, ran to the other side of the base to give Gail a hug, and then jumped on the bus with her fellow male trainees.

Katrina's arrival at Hondo did not go unnoticed. Immediately off the bus, she was questioned repeatedly and her orders were read and reread by the base staff sergeant that was processing the group.

"K. Garretson," he read. "It seems someone mistook you for a male." He gave her the once-over with his eyes. "Apparently the command over at Lackland needs to have their vision checked. I ain't never seen a more female-looking female than you. Nevertheless, we'll get to the bottom of this, girlie."

While the rest of the men were unpacking their gear, Kat was waiting on a bench outside of the base colonel's office. Finally, the door opened and a uniform walked through; it wasn't just a uniform, though, it was a US Air Force standard issued skirt and blouse that were similar to the ones that Kat was wearing. The only difference was this woman had different-colored bars on her blouse. Kat jumped to her feet and saluted her superior.

"At ease, Airman. My name is Lieutenant Hussey. Colonel Klein will see you now." She turned around and opened the door, motioning Kat to enter the room. As Katrina passed in front of the lieutenant, Hussey quietly voiced, "Very impressive Phase l test scores!" Kat turned to thank her, but the lieutenant didn't give her the chance. She stared Kat in the eye and shook her head as if to request her silence, then barked out their arrival to the back of a tall leather chair.

"Colonel Klein, K. Garretson is here at your request!" The leather chair which had been facing the window spun around, revealing a balding, middle-aged man sitting and waiting to address Katrina, who was now standing at attention in front of his desk.

In a gravelly voice, the colonel growled, "That will be all, Lieutenant." Kat remained at attention, while the Colonel dismissed his lieutenant.

"Sir," Lieutenant Hussey spoke, "may I respectfully remind you that military rules state that a female officer must accompany a male officer during any interrogations or meetings with a lesser-ranked female while that meeting is taking place."

"What! I don't know about any damn rule like that." The colonel shook his head in disgust, but rescinded his order. "Oh, what the hell, you can stay. Just take a seat and keep quiet." Turning his attention back to Kat, he picked up a file that was sitting in the middle of his desk, slipped on his reading glasses, and began to scan its contents.

"Missy, there seems to be some confusion here."

"Airman First Class Garretson, sir!" Lieutenant Hussey spoke out from a chair in the back of the room.

"What?"

"This US Air Force trainee's name is Garretson, not Missy, sir! And could she be at ease, sir?"

The colonel let out a sigh of disgust. "Very well, at ease AIRMAN GARRETSON!" The agitated base commander jerked his glasses off and tossed them and the file back on the desk. "Listen up. I don't know what kind of joke the commanders over at Lackland are trying to pull, but they're pulling the chain of the wrong man. The air force doesn't train women pilots. Everyone knows that women are inferior and have no place in the military other than clerical jobs. Hondo Air Base ain't training no hussies for flying! No disrespect, Lieutenant." The colonel glanced at his subordinate sharing the same name, she stared forward, biting her tongue to restrain all the pent-up rage.

"Lieutenant, has Lackland called me back yet?"

"No, sir!" The disgruntled lieutenant failed to tell him that she had not made his inquiry phone call yet.

"Well, fire off a letter and copy General Helton at the Pentagon."

"Maybe it was the Pentagon's idea in the first place," Lieutenant Hussey opined, while Katrina just sat and listened.

"What do you mean the Pentagon's idea?" Colonel Klein asked.

"You know, Cold War secrets and all." The colonel listened intently to the lieutenant as she laid it on thick. "Those Commie Russians, they have female pilots, so maybe the U.S. wants to counter that. They can't just announce that kind of stuff. We probably should not be discussing that in front of. . ." The lieutenant nodded toward Kat and then continued, "Who else would the Pentagon trust with such an important assignment but you? Sir, this is just what you've been waiting for to get that bump to general. Someone at the Pentagon is watching!" Lieutenant Hussey had the colonel buying everything she was selling. "Well, sir, I guess I better get to writing that letter."

"Wait, hold up a minute. Maybe we shouldn't alert Lackland to this. Those bastards would only screw this up for me." The colonel scratched his bald head, starring out the window, deep in thought.

"Good thinking, sir!"

"But where will Garretson bunk? We have limited space available for women. I'm not sure we have any bunks available."

"She can bunk with me. I have an extra room at my quarters. Oh, yes, I will draft up a letter for you to sign that immediately gets her into officer's school. She can't be flying bombers over the USSR with just an airman rank, now, can she?" Before he had a chance to snap out of his daydream and respond, Lieutenant Hussey snatched Katrina from the chair and they were out the door.

When they were outside of the building, the lieutenant stopped Kat, turned her around, put her hands on her shoulders, and looked her right in the eyes.

"Listen, Mrs. Garretson, I just stuck my neck out for you, so don't let me down." They resumed walking toward the living quarters.

"I don't know how you ended up here at Hondo and I don't care. I read over your evaluation and test scores and even called someone I know over at Lackland to confirm them. Apparently the instructors there thought you were really something special. The only knock against you was your sex." She turned her head away and muttered, "Lord knows I've heard that bullshit before. Not always do high scores in the initial phase equate to being an ace, but dammit, you should have an opportunely to prove yourself. I'm going to do my part to get you trained flying those birds; you do your part by making me proud.

"You are representing all the women who got shafted before you and all the young women that will follow you." They arrived at Lieutenant Hussey's house and went inside. "Since we're living under the same roof, and mind you, only while we're under that roof, you can call me Ann. If you call me Ann outside of the house, I'll have you court-martialed!" Lieutenant Hussey smiled at Kat, and at that moment, their friendship was conceived.

Lieutenant Hussey did do her part by keeping Colonel Klein at bay. She knew exactly what buttons to push to control his ultra-ego. Katrina also lived up to her end of the bargain by making the lieutenant proud, very proud.

Katrina was euphoric, yet very composed and confident. Her first experience taking the controls of the T-34 training plane from the instructor went uncommonly smoothly and even drew a compliment from the surprised instructor. She was truly in control; it seemed as if the aircraft was merely an extension of her. She flew nearly twice the allotted time given to her male teammates, but they didn't mind. Unlike her superiors, most of her counterpart trainees all respected and supported her. It took a while, but once the males got past her female attractiveness, warm personality, and realized she was just as dedicated they were, they were on her side.

Katrina couldn't wait to share her first time flying experiences with her friends and family.

The news of her first flight was way too urgent for conventionally-written letters, so just as soon as she could that evening, she was dialing the telephone. Her first call was to the Brownes, then Eugene, and finally Jimmy. She cried with joy during all three phone conversations.

Kat indeed caught the attention of her flight instructors, who, in turn, passed their acclamations along to their superiors.

Kat accelerated through the ninety hours of Phase 2 and was now ready to advance into Phase 3 and cut her teeth at flying the B-29 and B-52 bombers.

She took to flying the huge fortresses just as smoothly as she did flying the smaller T-34 planes. In fact, her progression seemed to be accelerating, and once again she was at the top of her class. Kat exemplified quick-study abilities that lent to accurate tactical decisions. No matter what situations the instructors threw at her during flight to confuse and create duress, she remained undaunted. This baffled her trainers. Pilots with her lack of flying experience were not supposed to have tough mental skills or instinctive flying abilities, but she did.

Her piloting skills always put the plane exactly in the right position to deliver ordnances accurately to their targets. Her plane and crew won every competition.

Kat would show up every morning to her B-52 or B-29 carrying a pillow to elevate her in her seat and her worn clipping of Jackie Cochran that she wedged between the altimeter and the fuel gage. She greeted her fifty-eight-year-old co-pilot instructor, Major Elliott, with a respectful salute followed by a flirtatious smile. On the ground, she referred to the major as her "old, growly bear" flying coach, but once they were airborne, things were all air force. She responded to him only as, "sir." The crew was made up of one navigator and two gunners, a bombardier, and, of course, an equal amount of trainers for each position.

CHAPTER 29

Katrina had a very demanding schedule as set up by her new mentor, Lieutenant Hussey. During her twelve hours, seven days a week, she balanced both flight and officer's school and all the individual rigor associated with each. Weekend passes, or any days or hours of leave, were not an option. Long days didn't bother Katrina. She was living her dream and, of course, she was 100 percent on board with Lieutenant Hussey's strategic plan of expediting her training before someone up the chain of command caught on. Her only regret with this schedule was that she would miss all of Eugene's home games. She really wanted to be in the stands for at least one of his games. But Kat didn't let this little inconvenience stop her. Just because she couldn't physically sit in the grandstand didn't keep her from attending, at least briefly.

Major Elliott was a huge football fan and an even bigger Texas A&M fan. He was always up for any inside news about the team he could interrogate away from Kat. Every Saturday during football season he'd bring his portable radio onboard and set up the flight plan as to circle the major cities to keep him within signal range of the game. He would sit back, prop his feet up while Kat piloted, and they would both listen intensely to hear the game through the static. Frequently, their exuberant hoots and hollers left the cockpit and could be heard over the loud buzz of the engines, even as far back as the tail wing.

It was the big game of the year: the Aggies' archrival, the University of Texas, had come to College Station.

Everyone in Texas was bursting with excitement, and Kat and the Major were no exception. Katrina had called Eugene the night before and wished him luck, but her encouraging call increased her sadness at the fact that she would not be able attend.

Katrina's head hung low as she approached the giant silver fortress, perched and ready to go on the tarmac in front of the mammoth hangar.

Her partner, Major Elliott, was waiting as he did every morning for his "Angel Kat," his endearing name for her when no others were around.

"Hey, where's my morning smile?" asked the major.

"Sorry, sir." Kat looked up and flashed a smile while she saluted.

"Wishin' you were on your way to the game, huh?" Kat nodded. "Yeah, me too!"

"I always think he's going to get hurt if I'm not there. I know it's silly. Shoot, he's played a lot of football without my butt sitting in the bleachers and nothing's happened to him yet. I'm okay and he'll be okay!" They finished their routine walk-around inspection, then climbed up the ladder and into the plane. The major handed

Kat the flight plan as she strapped herself into the pilot's seat. She studied it for a couple of minutes, and then pulled out a map, looked up, and smiled.

"Are these coordinates at 11:58 a.m. for College Station?" Kat laughed. "You are a crafty old growly bear!" Kat laughed. "I guess we are going to the game after all!" They fired up the props and went down their preflight list while the ground crew pulled the tire chucks. Within minutes they were taxiing down the runway awaiting final approval for takeoff.

It was a crisp, fall day, perfect for football. The Aggies were rolling through the season, discarding their opponents one by one, but there was one barrier standing between them and the Southwest Conference championship: the University of Texas Longhorns.

The time was 11:56 and both teams had taken the field. Texas had won the coin toss and began to line up at their opposition's thirty yard line.

At that moment, Katrina turned to her superior seated to the right. "We are five miles from our target, sir, what altitude should I achieve?"

"You ever see a crop duster work?" Kat's mouth dropped open as she gave a quick look to the major, then turned back at her instruments.

"Affirmative! What are you orders, sir?" Kat asked.

"They should be done with the National Anthem. Let's buzz the damn field!" Kat took another look at him to confirm his intent. He nodded toward the stadium which was beginning to show itself on the horizon. Kat screamed out a war cry that would rival any of the boys from Point Marion, made an announcement to the crew, and dropped the nose. The plane dove almost vertically to one hundred fifty feet before she pulled back on the wheel and the engines roared, then whined as the bird leveled out.

As the biggest game of the year in Texas was getting ready to start, every eye in the stadium should have been on the field, but they were not. They were looking off to the West trying to locate the source of the fast approaching buzz. The ball was on the tee, the referee had blown the whistle, and the kicker was jogging toward the ball. He reared his leg back and delivered a powerful kick to the ball that sent a beautiful end-over-end ball propelling down the center of the field. But no one saw it, not even the return back, as it hit the ground and rolled into the end zone, because Kat's B-52 Stratofortress had just arrived! It was the only time that day that all forty thousand or so fans were cheering for the same thing at the same time.

Eugene was standing on the sidelines next to one of the coaches with his helmet in his hand, grinning from ear to ear. He leaned over and yelled in the coach's ear, "THERE GOES MY GIRLFRIEND!" The entire flyover took only about three seconds, then Kat pulled back the rudder and poured on the fuel, and the plane quickly climbed as vertically as it had dove earlier.

When it got to two hundred feet or so, she banked back hard to the west, then corrected her heading back home. Once again the crowd erupted with cheers and applause!

Major Elliot and the entire crew were all looking out the windows and celebrating too.

"Mission complete, let's head for the barn!" announced the Major over the intercom.

He looked at Kat, winked, and exhaled a big sigh of relief. "Man, does that feel good! My little Angel Kat; you don't know how long I've wanted to do that."

As one might predict, there was a reception waiting for them when they arrived back at base. A not so festive looking group was standing outside of the hangar as they taxied in.

"Oh shit, here we go." The Major laughed. "It looks like someone complained about us going to the game."

Kat killed the fuel and the engines went quiet. The ground crew chalked the tires and the door swung open. With the propellers still twirling, the crew climbed out one by one with Kat and the major bringing up the rear. The reception crowd had dissipated to only one by the time Kat and the major's feet touched the concrete, and that one was Lieutenant Hussey. She saluted the major, then announced her orders.

"Sir, Colonel Klein requests your presence in his office a.s.a.p.! And bring your flight plan." The major finished snapping off his parachute and tossed it to Kat.

"Check this for me while I go meet with Colonel *Cornball.*" Kat snickered, but immediately stopped when the lieutenant glared back. When the major was out of earshot, she snipped back at her subordinate.

"What the hell were you two doing? Were you at the controls?"

"Yes, ma'am, I mean, yes, lieutenant!" Lieutenant Hussey rolled her eyes.

"You are supposed to be flying under the radar, Airman. Blending in, not drawing attention to yourself, graduate flight school, get your rank, and move on. Now everyone in the state is calling the base wanting to know who was flying the bomber that buzzed the football game."

"Is Major Elliott in trouble?" asked Katrina.

"Off the record and behind closed doors, he'll get his ass chewed. But on the record, he'll get praised, probably a promotion. I had, I mean, the colonel had to do some fancy side stepping. Actually, we all got pretty lucky.

"Within minutes of your little stunt we got calls from both universities and the state police to confirm it was our plane. At halftime we got a call from the governor and just before you landed we got a call from Senator Lyndon Johnson. The damn thing was, they loved it! They want us to send a plane every year now. The senator said it was a great display of patriotism. He thanked Colonel Klein for his special gift to the folks attending the game."

"That's wonderful!" Kat excitedly responded.

"That's not so wonderful if they find out the pilot was a female! The governor and senator would view this as a big embarrassment, and we'll all get our court-martials. For the record, you were not flying that plane; you were not even on that plane, understand?"

"Yes, Lieutenant!"

In regards to the big game in Texas, the referees teed the ball again and play resumed. At the end of the day Eugene and the Aggies were victorious. But at Hondo, an altitude moratorium was put in place that day—no buzzing without direct orders from the colonel.

CHAPTER 30

The days flew by and so did Kat. Before she knew it, it was another year and she was an officer—first lieutenant—and only days away from graduating flight school. After flight school graduation, Kat received another bump and was now an equal in rank to Lieutenant Hussey. This bothered Katrina; it wasn't that she felt she didn't deserve it; she'd worked hard and met all the required curriculum. She was embarrassed. Kat felt it was a gross injustice that Lieutenant Hussey, who had served through WWII and the Korean War, and was now basically running Hondo, should be anything less than a colonel. But it was the reality. Katrina was a pilot and Ann Hussey was not. Right or wrong, that was the way it was. Of course, Lieutenant Hussey had no qualms with Katrina. After all, it wasn't Kat's archaic, chauvinistic policy—it was the military's. With the help of her protégé, Katrina, Lieutenant Hussey was just embellishing a loophole in the system. It was not a female that was advancing in rank, it was pilot: K. Garretson. Lieutenant Hussey was simply doing her job, but she had never enjoyed it so much as she did now.

The momentum of the procedural protocol pulled Katrina right along and right through flight school. By now, Colonel Klein was convinced that the Pentagon was behind this Katrina experiment and that he would be decorated with colors for his success in flawlessly carrying out this assignment. But the events which followed were not exactly what the colonel had in mind.

At Hondo, Katrina was not only very well liked, she was very well respected. No one had misperceptions about her sex. She was a pilot and she was an officer. But outside of their base it was a whole different situation. Even in the air force rumors spread like wildfire—and a rumor that was as big this, there would be no way to keep it contained on base. News of Hondo Air Base graduating the first female pilot ever into the United States Air Force traveled at light speed.

The rumors first made their way to close bases like Lackland and Kelly, but then they began spilling over into other states and bases in other countries.

Colonel Klein's phone was ringing off the hook, with his counterparts wanting to confirm this rumor. And of course the colonel was more than happy to boast of his achievement. But the attention didn't just stop with his counterparts.

Katrina was flying a routine training mission across the Gulf of Mexico into the Florida Keys, then West to Mexico and up the Baja Peninsula before returning to Texas. She was gone and didn't witness the caravan of air force cars arrive at the base to relieve Colonel Klein of his command. But she didn't miss everything. After all, she was the reason the air force brass were there in the first place. When she touched down back at Hondo, Kat was immediately escorted into an office and interviewed by a battery of individuals ranging in rank. They announced that they were conducting an investigation of improper use of air force code and conduct, some of which might lead to court martial proceedings of one or more individuals. They were all business, and most of the questions required only a yes or a no. They asked a lot of questions that dealt with her association with Lieutenant Hussey. They also asked if she were aware of or had any conversation with Lieutenant Hussey regarding filing of documents which omitting her sex, as well as her full and proper name. They also asked her if she understood the regulation of the United States Air Force that stated that women were not to be accepted into flight school. All of the questions Katrina answered honestly, but the barrage of questions kept coming and kept increasing in intensity. The only bit of incriminating information that Kat offered was that Lieutenant Hussey said she stuck her neck out for Kat and that she would do everything within her power to get her through flight school. Kat repeatedly interjected comments about her friend Lieutenant Hussey, but was not allowed to finish her sentences. When the officers were finished, they informed Kat that she was immediately grounded and would most likely be reassigned to another base with other duties.

As devastating as the news was for Katrina, her immediate concern was for her friend Lieutenant Hussey.

Katrina immediately knew that the lieutenant had sacrificed her career for her and Kat was mortified. As soon as she was dismissed,

Kat ran home just as fast as she could, but the house was empty. There was no lieutenant, nor were there any of her belongings. Kat burst back out the screen door and ran toward the colonel's office, but changed her direction toward the tarmac as she followed her senses. A C-47 was just starting to roll towards the runway. Kat spotted Lieutenant Hussey in one of the port side windows, so she darted out onto the tarmac and began flailing her arms. From the corner of her eye, the lieutenant spotted Katrina, and when Kat noticed, she gave the lieutenant a long salute. It wasn't the way Katrina wanted to show her gratitude to Lieutenant Ann Hussey, but she knew she may never have another opportunity. It was all she could think of at that moment. From the small window, the lieutenant saluted her back, lowered the same hand to her heart, and then pointed back at Kat. Katrina stood crying on the tarmac as the plane raced down the runway, then disappeared into the horizon.

Still in her flight suit, Katrina walked back to her house. Emotions that were foreign to her were now racing though her head and slicing a gash deep into her heart. How could she have not foreseen this? How could she have allowed this to happen? Was she so selfish about her quest to be a pilot that it had blinded her to what the lieutenant was risking? Had she ignored her parents' voices and even ignored her own telepathy? She needed to hear from her parents, but there were no voices. She needed to be held by Eugene, but he was a thousand miles away. For the first time she seemed so isolated and far away from the people she loved. The boys were home for the summer and the base had never been a good place to communicate with her parents. She even tried to call Gail, but couldn't make contact. Kat really didn't want to burden her anyway, because she knew she was very busy, so she decided not to leave a message. How Kat wished that she were physically back at Point Marion, sitting on the rock overlooking Cheat with Eugene and Jimmy.

Katrina was on the phone for hours with Eugene, followed by the Brownes, but the most comforting voices came later that night while she lay in bed—the voices that assured her that all would be well.

Kat was up early the next morning to report to the new base commander for her new orders, but she never made it past her door stoop. When she opened the door, she was met by an airman preparing to knock. Standing behind him were two men in black suits and sunglasses. Idling behind them in the drive was a black Lincoln. The airman saluted Katrina, then turned around and asked the men if there would be anything further. They responded "no" and he walked away.

"Lieutenant Garretson, may we speak with you?" inquired the men.

"I suppose so," Kat reluctantly responded. Her first assumption was that they were there to ask more questions and gather more evidence in order to court martial someone. They asked her to get in the car. She looked at them funny and asked if they were air force.

"No, Miss. For today's conversation, I'm Agent Smith and this is Agent Wesson. We are from the Central Intelligence Agency."

They opened up their suit jackets and pulled out identification, but there was white tape over the names. Kat reached out and took their IDs.

"CIA, huh?" Kat spoke while still looking over the ID cards and then looked up at the two men. "You want me to fly something; something very secret and something at very high altitude." Smith looked at Wesson, then back at Kat in disbelief. "We'd like you to get in the car and take a ride with us." The men looked around to see if anyone was paying attention to their little meeting.

"Okay, guys, let's go!" Kat handed the cards back to the men and walked toward the car. Wesson scurried around her and opened the back door, but Kat walked on by and around to the driver's side.

"I'm driving, boys!" She opened the driver's door and jumped inside the Lincoln.

"Ah, Miss Garretson, that's a government issue vehicle," Wesson nervously said.

Kat yelled her response as she slammed the door behind her.

"I'm government issued as well!"

The agents did not know what to think. Kat had seized the situation and was now in charge and they were along for the ride. The man calling himself Smith nodded to his accomplice to get in the back. Smith opened the passenger door and climbed in beside Katrina. Smith braced his arm against the dash and Wesson fell back in the seat as Kat floored the accelerator. The long black car fishtailed, spinning its tires and throwing gravel and dirt into the air. She took the car through a maze of streets within the base, then past the main hangar and onto the taxiway.

"Oh I better slow down or we'll have every MP on the base chasing us." She laughed, but still took another lap around the hangar, weaving around parked planes before barreling down a service road to the main radar tower. Kat pulled into the vacant parking lot and put the car in park and shut off the engine.

"Thanks, guys, I hope you don't mind me having a little fun with you this morning, I just needed to let off some steam. So gentlemen, let's hear your proposition!" Katrina turned sideways so that she could see the men's faces while they talked. Smith regained his composure by taking a deep breath and slowly exhaling. He then reached inside his jacket, pulled out a kerchief, wiped his forehead, and straightened his tie.

"I must say, Lieutenant Garretson, you are quite unconventional. Along with your many aeronautical skills, you also have uncanny insight," Agent Wesson blurted from the back seat. "How did you know we were here to talk to you about flying aircraft for the agency?" Kat looked at him and smiled, but didn't reply.

"Women's intuition, right, Miss Garretson?" Smith answered for her and smiled back.

"I am embarrassed to say that our file on you doesn't do you justice. If you would allow me to continue, I'll quickly get to the point of why we came to visit.

"What we talk about in this car is not just extremely confidential, it never happened. We are just three strangers having a completely irrelevant conversation about something that doesn't exist.

"In case you were not aware, Lieutenant Garretson, we—the United States of America, protector of the free world—are at war. Unlike the previous conflicts, this Cold War has no specific battle fronts or zones, yet. There are no missiles being launched or bombs being dropped, or boots on the ground, yet. However, we do know who our enemy is and they have made it pretty clear that they don't like us; they especially don't like our freedom or democracy. But that's common knowledge anyone can ascertain by reading the paper. The newspapers can only speculate on the Soviets' immediate capabilities, while our glorious politicians can only guess at their objectives. Lieutenant, I can tell you for certain, the CIA does know their capabilities and we're pretty damn sure of their objectives. World domination! They are rapidly building up their military and their military assets, including their nuclear arsenal.

"The main duty of the Central Intelligence Agency is to gather, process, and disseminate information. We have assets on the ground and in the air. Believe it or not, we gathered most of our information in Russia by simply flying over and taking pictures. And for all intentional purposes, they have no idea that we were even there. By the time they heard the sonic boom, we were gone. Flying an invisible plane. How does that sound, Garretson?" Katrina turned back forward and stared through the front windshield, digesting what he'd said, then spoke.

"Invisible unless you know what you're looking for. A spy plane, huh? You want me to fly your spy plane."

Smith was amazed that Kat kept one step ahead, but continued. "Now we come to the part where we explain why we came to see you. We have been discreetly searching for a handful of exceptional pilots to fly our camera in the sky.

"Lieutenant, I must confess, we have been studying a K. Garretson on paper; we did background checks, searches of not only you, but all your family. We know that your parents are deceased. All of this is important information, but we had no idea until a few days ago that you were a female. But unlike the air force, we don't give a damn; because most of what we do is secret, we have the ability to make up the rules as we go along. The thing is, Lieutenant, the more we find out about you, you just keep getting better. You're a damn good pilot; you have no traceable immediate family to explain sensitive matters to in case you get shot down. And most importantly, you have no other option. That is, if you want to be an aviator." Kat immediately turned back and looked directly at Smith.

"That's right, Garretson, the choice is yours. You can continue on and finish out your commitment with the air force, filing papers for some asshole colonel on some lowly base in the middle of nowhere, like your friend Lieutenant Hussey. Or you can accept our invitation to be part of the Central Intelligence Agency and fly the fastest aircraft ever built and at the highest altitudes ever piloted." Agent Smith paused.

Katrina shook her head, looked away, and sighed. "I belong to the United States Air Force; I can't just quit and come to work for the CIA. Besides, I'm probably going to get court-martialed. I know at least I'll be tied up testifying in the Colonel or Lieutenant Hussey's court-martial."

Agent Smith continued. "You will still be in the air force until your obligation has been met. Your orders will be to serve your remaining time out under the command of the CIA. The thing is, I can't make you; it's totally volunteer. But once we have your consent, it's a done deal." Agent Smith reached in his pocket and pulled out an envelope.

"I've already got this worked out. I have got your orders right here.

"And by the way, nobody's getting court-martialed." Smith and Wesson laughed. "This little adventure that you were involved with has been very embarrassing for the air force. The last thing they want to deal with is the publicity of a court-martial. No, the colonel will take his early retirement and the lieutenant will probably finish her career running some other base for some other incompetent base commander somewhere else in the world." Smith paused, then opened his door and walked around to the driver's side, opening the door for Katrina. She obliged by getting out and stood toe to toe with him.

"Well, Lieutenant, I'm done talking. This envelope in my hand is your future. What's going to be your choice?" Kat looked at the envelope he was holding.

"Can I wear a dress while flying your spy plane?"

Smith laughed.

"You can fly buck naked if you want!" Agent Wesson gasped in disbelief to what his superior said. Katrina, with a big smile, grabbed the envelope from his hands and asked, "Where do I sign?"

CHAPTER 31

The deal was done; Katrina was now under the command of the Central Intelligence Agency. Within a few hours she was packed and signed out and put on an air force plane to be transported to a discrete air base in Southern Nevada. With their mission complete, Smith and Wesson were back in the car and on to their next assignment, never to be seen again by Kat.

The airbase was dead center of nowhere, about eighty miles or so northwest of Las Vegas, situated in a dry lake bed and shrouded by a mountain range. From her copilot seat flying into the base, Kat thought it looked like a rundown, abandoned airport. No government markings, no markings of any kind—hell there was not even any vehicles or other aircraft. The landscaping around the huge hangar and surrounding buildings was ragged and unkempt. To the contrary, though, the runway was extremely long. There were lots of black rubber marks over the first eight hundred feet or so, indicating a lot of traffic. Kat's pilot had never flown to this destination before; this coordinate grid was known as "The Box" and was a highly restricted airspace.

He had never heard of an airfield within "The Box" in the seven years of his military career. His orders were to land, drop her off, and immediately take off and return to Hondo. He was told that he would not have any tower clearance or ground control.

So his orders were carried out. He taxied over to the large hangar and stopped just long enough for Kat to toss her bags out the door and hop off. He asked her if she'd brought her survival gear, to which she gave a thumbs-up sign and departed the plane onto what seemed to be a deserted airfield. The plane spun around, taxied to the runway, and within seconds, was in the air and gone.

Was this a hoax or some sort of dramatic punishment? she wondered, standing alone on the barren plain of white concrete.

Lugging her bags over her shoulder, Kat began to walk toward the massive steel structure. The buzz of the Douglas C-47 that had brought her to the base faded away and the noise was replaced by the howl of the hot, dry wind careening in and around the above-ground structures. Just as she was within steps of the massive doors a deafening buzzer sounded and the doors began to part. Her attention was to the opening giant doors and not to the jeep that seemingly appeared from nowhere. It came to an abrupt stop beside her and out jumped two machine gun toting solders. They brusquely convinced her to get aboard and the vehicle drove on through the parted doors and into the mega hangar. The jeep drove past the doors into a makeshift tunnel of camouflage-netted partitions that prevented any visibility past the narrow path it created.

The jeep finally came to a stop and from there she was briskly walked to a room where she was transferred to two different uniformed individuals who were less armed. Once inside the room, a third individual joined them. It was a female and she was wearing a white nurse's uniform. She politely asked Kat to hand over her papers and disrobe. The men picked up her bags and papers, then left the room. Once undressed, the nurse did a complete body search and a quick examination, including drawing a blood sample.

Kat dressed and moved on to the next room where they took her photo and fingerprints. From there she was reunited with her paperwork and belongings and taken to a small conference room where she was told to wait.

A few minutes later the door opened and in marched an assortment of individuals. Katrina jumped to her feet in attention. The group filed in front of Kat, looking her over as they passed. Some were dressed in white shirts and ties, some in lab coats, and one in a flight jumpsuit. The last man in closed the door and invited the room to take their seats. Once the group had taken their places, either at the main table or in the rows of chairs, they got started with Kat's orientation. They were cordial, but all business. The introductions at the head table were brief.

The man in charge introduced himself as CIA Chief Agent MacDougall, head of all operations at Area 51. He began by telling Katrina that starting today, her life would never be the same ever again. She would see and have knowledge of information that only a very few in the world have. There would never be a dull day for her, but she could never discuss her job with anyone, including family or friends. Much of the intricacies of her career would be a top secret. She was now a spy for the United States of America. His speech started getting more dramatic.

"Lieutenant Katrina Garretson, welcome to the headquarters of Skunkworks!" Agent McDougall announced and the room respectfully applauded. He turned to the gentleman beside him and introduced him as his civilian counterpart: Kenneth Johnson, head of operations for Lockheed Corporation.

MacDougall continued saying that the Skunkworks bureau was actually the brain child of Mr. Johnson. "His futuristic vision of combining clandestine imagery with super hi-tech aircraft motivated Lockheed to design and ultimately build a high altitude spy plane called the U-2."

Johnson smiled and interrupted. "What he means, Garretson, is that we can now fly high enough over these commie sons of bitches to take their pictures and be out of the airspace before they can say cheese." Johnson gestured to MacDougall to continue and he did.

"Lockheed is under a top secret contract with the government of the United States to build and manage these spy planes in partnership with the CIA.

"Even though the individuals on this base from Lockheed are civilians, they are held to the same scrutiny and the same secrecy as anyone from the CIA or air force. They are allowed to leave the base at the end of their work shift and conduct a normal civilian life outside of the base if they choose. Same goes for most of my agents. However, there are underground barrack accommodations here at their disposal, as well as for military personnel like you to use."

MacDougall went on to explain the layout of the base and its operations. He talked about the layers of security, starting with a select unit of the US Army that was in charge of the outermost sector of the airbase, even though they had no idea what they were protecting. He talked about the multiple gates with daily changing codes. Everyone who left the base and returned was subject to re-fingerprinting as well as random lie detector tests.

"This facility is like an iceberg. Eighty percent of it is hidden beneath the surface. This huge hangar we're in is pretty impressive, but there is an equal-sized hangar right below us. In fact below us about one hundred fifty feet is an entire self-contained city. Operations never cease below ground even though the base above looks like an abandoned airport. There is very limited air traffic, military, or CIA during daylight hours and never do any of the U-2 planes or the U-2-T trainer ever see the light of day." MacDougall closed by informing Katrina that she would start training immediately and wished her luck.

Katrina moved into her room and then was given a tour of the base by a Lockheed engineer who was assigned the task of being her liaison. She was able to make outgoing calls from certain "safe phones" that would scramble signals, making them untraceable. She was coached on saying that she had been transferred to a base somewhere in the western part of the United States, but could not give out the actual coordinates. Of course, she could not receive visitors, but that was no issue for Kat. In a few months she would receive limited access to a small military prop plane that she could use on her days off, to fly home or wherever she desired. This freedom she loved! Actually, she loved nearly everything about her new, exciting career. Her dreams and aspirations were coming to fruition. There were only two things in her mind that kept this job from being perfect. First, she couldn't actually wear a dress as Smith had promised; quite the opposite.

Because she would be flying at the outer layer of the atmosphere, where the air was thin and the temperatures were well below freezing, U-2 pilots needed to wear a special flight suit that kept them from losing consciousness and prevented hypothermia. The Lockheed scientists had designed a bulky space-like suit and helmet that would insulate and feed oxygen while she soared at 70,000 feet. The thing she would fret about the most was that she couldn't share any of the specifics of her exciting experiences with Eugene or Jimmy or the Brownes. All she could say was that she loved to fly and she was flying very, very high.

Just like air force pilot school, her initial days were long and hard, and were spent mostly on the simulators. Within weeks, she moved to spotter jets. Because of the design of the U-2, the cockpit offered the pilot less than stellar visibility, so to counter this handicap, another airborne pilot would guide the spy plane safely to the ground. The U-2 was a very complicated jet to fly. That's one of the reasons Kat's skills were highly sought after.

Besides poor visibility for the pilot, the sixty-three foot long fuselage and the one hundred five foot wide wingspan, the bird-like plane had tandem landing gear like a bicycle. This made for touchy landings. The wings were so wide they required wheels, but they were too thin to permanently attach fixed gears. To offset this, they designed temporary wheels, one under each wing that would fall off at takeoff. To keep the temporary wheels in place while taxiing, two jeeps would drive alongside with a crew member standing up and holding the wingtips to keep it from lifting and dropping the pogo wheels.

But just like the bombers that preceded the U-2, Katrina mastered the aircraft in record time. Within a few months she was flying solo. She had also mastered the photographic imaging equipment.

Unlike the B-29s or the B-52s, the U-2 was a single seat aircraft with no crew, so all activities and responsibilities like photographing fell to the pilot. It involved a whole lot more than just pushing a button.

Because of the altitude, the pilot had to be dead-on with his navigation and weather tracking. The most difficult technique was timing breaks in the clouds. It usually would take multiple trips for a first-time pilot to get usable footage, but that wasn't the case with Kat. Starting with her first flight across the Eastern Bloc European countries, she came back with crisp and valuable images. This blew the minds of the intelligence agents, who teased her of somehow cheating.

Kat loved her new freedom too. It wasn't absolute, but it was a whole lot better than the regular air force. Life at Area 51 was so different from what she was accustomed to at Hondo and

Lackland. She actually had privacy; she didn't have to share with a multitude of other air force personnel. There were no roll calls, no running or group exercises, no boring speeches or protocol to follow. Not even an air force uniform was required. Other than her flight suit that was only worn while strapped in the cockpit, she could wear anything around base. She even had her own room with her very own bathroom. This was something she had never had in her life.

Katrina's career was under way.

Just as soon as she could, Kat was flying to see Eugene. She would normally get two days off after working ten straight—*most of them from the cockpit at the edge of the atmosphere.* As soon as she would get home from a mission, she would shower, get a few hours of sleep, then jump in one of the inconspicuous government planes and fly off to rendezvous with Eugene. She also would love to pop home unannounced and show up at the Brownes, surprising them. With Jimmy, Kat knew her anonymity would be at risk. She also knew if she spent any length of time with him, he'd drill her with a hundred questions for which he wouldn't accept her answers. So she limited her visits with him only to telephone conversations that she kept brief.

CHAPTER 32

The 1957 A&M football season concluded with one of Eugene's teammates, a fellow Million Dollar Boy, John David Crow, winning the Heisman Trophy, but they lost the title game to Rice. After the game, Coach Bryant announced to the team that he would be leaving Texas A&M for the University of Alabama. The coach said there was never a good time to announce these types of things, especially after a loss, but just as they all would be moving on someday, so must he. He did indicate to the underclassmen that they would have an option to come with him to Alabama, but would have to sit out a season before they would be eligible to play.

Eugene was not an underclassman, so just like the coach, he elected to move on immediately. The only reason he was in college to begin with was to play football. But now football was over and so was he. To the disappointment—and against the urging of—his parents and even Coach Bryant, Eugene dropped out of school a week after the season without obtaining his degree. Katrina flew down, picked him up, and flew him home.

Eugene didn't quit school without a plan. He was looking for three things. He wanted to play football, he wanted to live in a warm climate near the ocean, and he wanted to stay fairly close to Katrina, even though she didn't divulge her exact western base location. As a result of his research, Los Angeles was the destination for him. It had everything he was looking for and more. He had heard that L.A. was booming and that the construction industry was hiring and paying high wages. L.A. was also the home for the Rams, an up-and-coming professional football team at the time. Eugene knew if he put his name in and made himself eligible for the NFL draft, he would lose control of where he would play.

Even though there were only a few roster spots open after the draft, he was confident that he could tryout and make the team.

So right after New Year, January 1958, Kat flew to Morgantown picked up Eugene and delivered him to Los Angeles.

Eugene slept on the couch of a former college friend while he looked for a job, which didn't take long. On his second day of looking, he was successful, getting a job as a laborer for a residential contractor. He enjoyed the physical labor and working outside, but most importantly the pay was good. After two paychecks he could afford to get off his buddy's couch and out on his own. He bought an old rusty truck for three hundred dollars and found a one room efficiency apartment to rent over a hardware store. His apartment wasn't much, but it was only a couple of blocks from the beach. In his letters to Jimmy and Stanley, he commented that the sand wasn't nearly as pretty as in Corpus Christi, but the girls were.

Eugene found a gym conveniently located on the beach, where he could work out daily preparing for the Ram's tryout in March.

Eugene's hard work in the gym along with running everyday on the beach did pay dividends. When March rolled around he was ready and did make the L.A. football roster. Eugene signed for a whopping eight thousand dollars, or one thousand dollars a game. But the money was not the main incentive, it was a bonus. He got a chance to play football with a great team, and he felt pretty lucky and blessed.

Eugene moved his workouts from the local gym to the Ram's facility and worked out voluntarily with other teammates until camp started in July. Practices began in August, with the first game of their eight-game season starting in mid-September. The coach, Sid Gillman, had a whole different philosophy of coaching than Paul Bryant. Coach Gillman was very unconventional and ran a wide-open, high-powered offense, which was the antithesis of Coach Bryant's conventional and disciplined style.

Gillman was all about speed, and that's what he loved about Eugene, especially his speed at his size. He wanted to move Eugene from playing fullback to playing guard. Gillman now had a weapon he could use with a set of plays he'd designed. Eugene was as fast as many running backs, but was built like a lineman. Gillman's new offense would pull the guard out from his normal blocking assignment and have him run to the opposite side ahead of the running back. The theory was that overloading a side of the line of scrimmage would devastate defenses. And it did. The Rams' innovative, pulling-guard offense played havoc on opposing teams, and that fall they ran roughshod over the NFL.

During Eugene's first season with L.A., they reeled off an 8 and 4 record. Things were good and they were winning. Eugene was used like a work horse, and the constant wear and tear was taking a toll on his body, especially his knees. At the end of the season, he could hardly walk because of the pain. Shots of Novocain were administered before the later games of the season to numb the pain and allow him to play. At the end of the season he had to have his first surgery. There was no repair or rebuilding of the knee; the only remedy at the time was to remove the cartilage. But he quickly realized the game he loved was somebody else's business. Every player on his team and every player on the opposing teams were all-start caliber. He dared not complain about an injury or question what the team coaches or doctors recommended.

Gene never told his parents of his injury and subsequent surgery for fear of how his mother would react. Ertta had yet to see him play or even listen to him on the radio because of fear he'd get hurt. He knew she would be better off not knowing about his injury. In fact, he mentioned it to no one, including Katrina. That was a mistake, of course, because she knew and called him from the air base as soon as she got back from her mission and gave him hell for not telling her. She didn't remain mad for very long. In fact, within a few hours of her call, she was ringing his doorbell. The closeness of the base to Los Angeles meant she could fly there in about thirty-five minutes. After that visit, she was given a key.

While Eugene and Katrina's careers were underway, Jimmy

was still learning his craft. He was accepted into Duke's School of Medicine, and it was as if he had disappeared from existence. Jimmy was burning the candle at both ends. To support himself, in other words, *to eat,* he had taken a job waiting tables at a popular steakhouse at night. With a full load of classes during the day, it left very little time for studying, let alone writing or phoning his friends.

It had been nearly two years since Jimmy and Katrina were last together. During her first months as a pilot for the CIA, Kat purposely avoided Jimmy, but now that he was in med school, she had no choice in the matter. His busy schedule allowed no time for her or Eugene, and it would continue like that for some time.

Eugene's knees mended and he was back to construction work. Kat was flying more and more missions with very little time off. The CIA opened another secret base in Puerto Rico so they would have her fly in and out of that base depending on her mission's logistics.

Kat fell in love with Puerto Rico and didn't mind when her orders sent her there. She said it was the prettiest place on earth. The base wasn't nearly as elaborate as Area 51, but it was just as covert and secure. It shared the island with Ramey Air Force Base, a traditional air base. Katrina would routinely pack a picnic and walk to the beach to spend the afternoons after her flight shift. Some days Kat would find a secluded area where she could be alone with her thoughts. Other days she would seek a busier section of the beach if she were feeling a bit lonely. She would throw her blanket down next to a family and usually within minutes was playing games with the children. This particular beach wasn't just a popular spot for the locals; it was also a favorite of Ramey's airmen. On any given day there would be hundreds of servicemen and women scattered along the half mile of sprawling sand. And on one particular day, Kat would be surprised by someone she wasn't expecting to see.

CHAPTER 33

"Is that my Kitty Kat?" The familiar shout was followed by an exuberant scream from Kat, who dropping her stuff, spun around, and threw open her arms to a tall female running down the beach.

"Gail!" Kat screamed back. The girls hugged and then clasped hands, jumping up and down and spinning around like a merry go round. Their silly, spontaneous celebration amused everyone within eyeshot.

"Girl, what are you doing here?" Gail asked.

"I'm just doing a little flying for the air force; my orders take me through here occasionally," Kat said.

"You are flying! I'm so proud of you!" Gail responded.

"What are you doing here, lady?" Kat asked.

"This is where my orders took me." Gail opened her arms wide and looked around at the beautiful seascape. "I'm one lucky broad! Believe it or not, I'm the third highest ranking nurse at the base hospital here."

"Look at you! I'm so proud!" Kat jumped up and gave her a

congratulatory kiss on the cheek. Gail looked down and grabbed Kat's hand.

"I don't see no wedding band. How's that man of yours?"

"Eugene's doing great! He lives now in Los Angeles, California. He works construction up until August, then he plays professional football for a few months. Our careers right now make it awfully hard for us to settle down. I do see him often, though. Come on let's find a spot on the sand and we'll get caught up."

It was great for both girls to rekindle their friendship, but for Katrina it was a godsend. Even for Kat, the solitude of spending hours on end in a lonely cockpit practically in outer space without social contact, then returning to a base on an island where she knew no one, was making her somewhat of a recluse. Even though she would constantly converse with her parents at 70,000 vertical feet, she was isolating herself from society.

Telephoning was virtually impossible from the CIA base in Puerto Rico and it was becoming harder from Area 51, too, because of heightened security screening and monitoring. Many of her words were ridiculously bleeped out. Kat still wrote regularly to everyone; she even figured out how to do it while in flight, but that still didn't quench her thirst for social activity.

Spending time and physical contact with Eugene was crucial, but for some things, like conversation, *girl talk* was extremely therapeutic. Even though Kat only made it to the island once or twice a month, she always looked forward to her beach rendezvous with Gail.

CHAPTER 34

The Rams were an offensive juggernaut and Eugene was a big part of the reason. He continued to deliver devastating blocks to linebackers while being pulled that would allow the sweeping back to gobble up huge chunks of yardage. But about five games into his second season, his left knee began giving him problems again. It would take almost three days after their Sunday game before he could walk without a crutch. The pain was more excruciating than a winning season could soothe. He finished the second season with a salvo of Novocain shots, and at the conclusion, awaited the surgeon's scalpel, again.

With very little cartilage left, especially in his left knee, Eugene was faced with a tough decision. Keep playing football and heighten the risk of permanent damage that might prevent him from walking later in life, or retire. The decision was tough and not without a plethora of advice from teammates, coaches, doctors, family, and friends. But the words of wisdom he listened to were from Kat. She told him that the ones advising him to quit were the ones most concerned for him. The coaches telling him he should ignore the doctors and play would almost certainly not be there later in life to push him around in his wheelchair.

Eugene figured that two years in L.A. was enough, and as much as he loved the sun and the fun, it wasn't home. He talked it over with Kat and she felt the same way as he; it was time to move back east. Her philosophy was, as long as she could fly, it really didn't matter much where he lived. So he moved back home again to Point Marion, assuring his father that it was only until he could find a job.

Eugene had his sights set on or near Washington D.C. Perhaps it was his dad's persuasion that had him focusing that direction. Fred, who had an apartment and an office there, had been lobbying Gene for some time to look for work either in Virginia or Maryland, near the capital city.

Everything within fifty miles of the District of Columbia was thriving, and just like in L.A., it was easy for Gene to find a job. In fact, he had several companies bidding for his services and even creating positions just to accommodate him. Having a robust economy was helpful, but the fact that he was a retired football star made his resume jump out and companies wanted him.

For whatever reason, successful people like millionaires, singers, and celebrities seem to gravitate toward athletes. With Eugene, it started back in high school, followed him through college, and on into the pros. Even though he was only with the Rams for two short years, he had a significant fan base. He even had offers for business partnerships, even though he had no capitol or collateral to invest, just the publicity of his name.

Gene stayed in the construction field and took a job with another home builder, only this time with a title of general superintendent in charge of new home construction. The intriguing catch for Eugene was that his new boss, Hank Robinson, was also interested in opening a music hall saloon, and he wanted Eugene to be a partner and manager. He shrewdly recognized Eugene as an asset because of his connections. He knew Gene had a celebrity following that could draw in the high profile country and western acts.

Eugene found a house to rent in Fairfax County, Virginia. It was actually a historical cabin rumored to have been built by George Washington's half-brother. It was old and needed fixing up, but it did have indoor plumbing and electricity and the rent was cheap. Katrina loved the place and it was fairly close to either Bolling or Andrews Air Force Base, so it wasn't a long drive to and from landing or takeoff. Quiet and secluded, it was a total opposite from the hustle and bustle of the City of Angels.

For the next few years, Gene was very busy. During the day, he was overseeing and organizing the building of new homes, and at night he was booking singers and bands to play on the weekend.

The Fairfax County Roadhouse was quite the undertaking. Hank had a parcel of property along Route 66 that was paid for, so he was able to use it for collateral to secure construction loans to begin building his vision. They got the needed permits, broke ground, and built a large, acoustically suitable building in the middle of a massive, twelve-acre stone parking lot. Building this one-of-a-kind establishment to this region of the country was the easy part; the challenge was to fill the place with people and keep it filled in order to pay for it. Another challenge to overcome was that Fairfax County was a dry county; no liquor could be sold. To overcome the booze issue, they encouraged their patrons to lawfully bring in their own alcohol. The Roadhouse would sell ice and mixers. The biggest challenge was that when they were done with the construction, they had no money left to hire the talent or help. That's when Eugene turned to an old friend for help as an investor.

Uncle Gregg to the rescue! After a barrage of colorful language and doling out a wrath of grief for a dose of humility, Gregg was on board. It wasn't his style and would have been too easy for him just to say yes without putting Eugene through hell first. He even surprised Gene by hopping on a plane and flying out to see for himself his investment. The fact was that the Fairfax County Roadhouse would have probably not come into existence were it not for Uncle Gregg.

Everything was coming together. Singing talent was being booked, wait staff hired, and advertising underway. A grand opening party was planned with several of Eugene's celebrity singing pals donating their time to perform. Everything was perfect, except for the absence of Katrina. When home, she worked right alongside of Eugene and every bit as hard, but her trips home became fewer and farther between. Regardless of whether she was there or not, Eugene's plans always included of her. They were a partnership and he was very exuberant about that.

CHAPTER 35

The frequency of Katrina's missions were increasing as tensions mounted between the United States and the Soviet Union. She was the best and the CIA knew it, so they kept her in the air as much as they could. She was dubbed the Dragon Lady by one of the Lockheed engineers because of her mysterious and domineering demeanor. The term stuck and before long the CIA was using it. When critical reconnaissance was needed immediately and there was no margin for error, they would make one request, "Get the Dragon Lady!" Lockheed was so enamored with her flying skills that they promised to name the next U-2 prototype "The Dragon Lady" in honor of her.

Kat needed to talk to Gail and had been waiting for weeks to do so. She found it difficult when she was in Puerto Rico to get a couple of free hours to the leave base. Finally she got her chance after a long tiring series of flights over the Kamchatka Peninsula photographing Soviet ships. She was told that she only had seven hours before she needed to report back, and even though she was exhausted and should have used that time for sleep, she elected to contact Gail. Kat found a pay phone, called her close friend, and was lucky to catch her home. Gail was excited and couldn't wait to get together, but was surprised when Kat declined to meet at their normal spot at the beach. She instead picked a quiet park bench overlooking the ocean that she had found on past walks. Gail knew exactly where it was and left immediately.

When Katrina showed up in a loose-fitting, button-up shirt, Gail knew something was up.

"Look at you, wearing one of your men's shirts!" Gail said. Poised with a weary smile but still a sparkle in her eye, Kat gave Gail a hug.

Gail gently pushed her back and began looking her over from top to bottom, then she reached out and lifted her loose shirt exposing her tummy.

"Oh my Lord, my Kitty Kat's pregnant!" Gail screamed, which in turn coaxed an endearing giggle from Kat. Katrina was warmed by her dear friend's excited response. "So you did marry that Eugene, didn't you?" Gail cautiously asked.

"Yes, well, kinda." Kat grabbed Gail's hand and walked her over to a bench. "The first time we ran into each other here, on the beach, you asked if Eugene and I were married. That got me doing a lot of thinking. It concerned me that Gene and I weren't even talking about it. So the next time I was home, I confronted him the minute I had his full and undivided attention. You do know when I'm talking about, girl?" Gail nodded and grinned.

"At breakfast I asked him if he loved me enough to spend the rest of his life with me tagging along. Of course, he didn't get it. He looked up from his stack of pancakes and said, 'Sure thing, baby!' So I pushed my chair back, stood up, used it to step up on the table, strutted right across, and then jumped into his lap. That got his attention! Then I grabbed a fistful of his hair, snapped back his head, and intensely stared into his surprised eyes. My moist, hot breath pulsated off his skin as I point blank asked, 'Do you want to marry me?' He swallowed hard and said, 'Yes!' After we consecrated the deal in the middle of the kitchen floor, we decided to jump in the plane, fly to Las Vegas, and now we're Mr. and Mrs. Briggs. You, my friend, are the only one who knows we are married. It would devastate the Brownes as well as the Briggs to know we eloped instead of having a traditional Christian wedding. Believe me, I want nothing more than to have a beautiful ceremony, married in our church by Mr. Browne, and we will, just as soon as I finish my dutiful responsibilities." Kat momentarily shut up as she sensed Gail needed a second to digest everything she'd said so far.

"I'm not sure what the people I work for will do if they find out I'm in the motherly way. They don't seem to care much about my personal life as long as I keep performing."

"What does Eugene say about that? And what do you mean *the people you work for*?" Gail asked.

"Eugene doesn't know I'm pregnant and I'm a secret pilot for the CIA." Gail was speechless, her jaw fell open in shock.

"The father of your baby, your husband, doesn't know you are pregnant?" Gail's shock quickly changed to disgust by what she'd just heard.

"You don't understand, Gail. This has been tearing me up for months, but I can't tell him or he would insist I take a maternity discharge. I can't quit! My entire life for the past few years has been one big deceiving lie. Eugene, the love of my life, has no idea that his wife is a spy. I know you are totally ashamed of me now and I don't blame you for thinking that way. I know you think I'm some sort of selfish bitch only concerned with my career, but that's not the case. It's way more complicated than that." Gail looked around to make sure that no one else was near.

"I was sworn to secrecy and could be shot for treason just for the little bit of information that I'm going to tell you. As a United States Air Force officer, you must realize and obey my wishes that these things I tell you remain secret.

"I fly a high altitude spy plane for the CIA; we have a secret base just north of the air force base. You've probably seen it and disregarded it as a private airport.

For weeks I have been photographing the Soviets moving what we believe to be nuclear warheads and long to medium range missiles toward their naval bases. So far, none have made it aboard their ships in dock. Gail, we can't lose track of this operation. It's my duty to this great nation, as well as my family and friends, not to lose track of these doomsday weapons. This enormous commitment and responsibility is the only thing that's more important than my honesty to the love of my life. I hope someday he will understand this and forgive me."

"They must have other pilots?" Gail responded.

"None with my God-given skills. We all have the same

equipment and we all have radar that lets us know when we are over our approximate target, but I know when I'm over the exact target. The bottom line is I come back with the best surveillance pictures. Gail, they've nicknamed me the Dragon Lady. Isn't that funny? Gail laughed

"I can't explain how I know, but I do. I also do something the other pilots don't. When I know I'm almost over top, I dive down from my high altitude comfort zone to around thirty-five thousand feet, level off for a couple of minutes, shoot my close-ups, then climb back up, and go on my way. I only show up on their radar for a brief moment, then disappear." Kat laughs. "Those bastard commies have no idea what to think! I'm their flying saucer!"

Gail looked and listened in disbelief, then changed the subject back. "Look at you. I understand how you could avoid your coworkers, but how are you able to conceal this from your husband?"

"It's easy when I don't see him. I haven't been home for two months. I told him that I'm on a temporary mission and stationed out of the country. We do talk all the time and I know every minute of the day what he's doing. It's hard!"

"Kat, have you had a doctor examine you? Do you know how far along you are?" Gail asked with a concerned tone in her voice.

"I think I'm going on seven months. And to answer your first question, no. That's where I was hoping for your help."

Gail shook her head. "Why didn't you come to me earlier?

Oh, never mind! Yes, hell, yes, of course I'll help." Gail thought a minute. "Come on, girl, I have a doctor friend that I volunteer with once a month at the orphanage. He will look at you. It's his day off and he's probably out fishing, but we'll wait for him on his front porch."

They made there their way to his house and sat on his porch swing, but didn't wait long. The doctor's face lit up when he saw Gail, but it was a more familiar than surprised look. It was apparent that this wasn't the first time Gail had waited on his swing for his return.

She jumped up and met him halfway up the walk, gave him a kiss on the lips, and collected his fishing gear, including a stringer full of snappers.

Gail knew Kat was pressed for time, so she had a quick chat with the doctor before introducing him to Kat. Katrina and the doctor had a brief conversation, then went inside. Gail took the doctor's catch to the backyard to clean while he examined Katrina. When Gail finished her chore she let herself into the house, put away the fish, made coffee, and waited for her two friends to emerge. They soon did and the doctor proclaimed her and the baby to be in good health, but had a stern warning for the young mother as well. He was concerned over Kat's lack of proper rest and warned of the consequences to her health, including the possibility of a premature birth. He purposely announced his warning in front of Gail, hoping that she could have some influence. Gail sensed that Katrina seemed oblivious to his advice. Gail invited her to sit and have some coffee, but Kat declined, giving her friend a farewell kiss instead. The doctor refused to take her money, so she thanked him with a hug and kiss too.

Out the door and down the walk Kat scampered, leaving her concerned friend standing with folded arms looking though the screen door, observing her departure.

Within two hours the Dragon Lady was strapped back in the cockpit of her U-2 preparing for her takeoff one minute after dusk. Katrina's mind was eased and she was again focused on her job and routine.

Several weeks would pass before her orders would allow her to see her friend Gail and revisit the good doctor.

CHAPTER 36

After months of work and planning, the moment of truth had arrived. It was grand opening time for the Roadhouse. Eugene and his partner, Hank, were a nervous wreck. They had verbal commitments from several bands, singers, and celebrities, for whom they had spent tons of cash promoting. The kitchen and bar was stocked with food and nonalcoholic drinks, and all the help had shown up and were ready to go. Jimmy had even driven up from North Carolina to give support to his best friend. They were all set except for the last important ingredient. The patrons! Nothing to do but wait.

Eugene, Jimmy, and Hank sat quietly around a table near the entrance and waited. The deafening silence was broken occasionally by an anxious comment or two from Eugene. "What if the bands don't show? Jimmy, can you check the neon sign again to make sure it's on?" Gene and Hank would alternate getting up and pacing. Finally, it happened. They came! First there was an old truck, then a station wagon, and gradually lines of vehicles appeared, pouring into the entrance like a trail of ants entering their anthill. Slowly

Gene's anxiety eased, especially when he spotted the first bus in line. Gene shouted at Jimmy, pointing to the big silver cylinder on wheels. "Relax, James; it looks like you won't have to sing after all! Our first band has arrived!"

All night long the cars filed in, more buses and limousines than that county had ever seen. It was a who's who of country western superstars that would rival even the Grand Ole Opry. Many surprises, too, even for Eugene; the unannounced arrival of Stanley and few of his football buddies were one highlight. The joint was booming and the cash was rolling in. People were dancing and singing, and to say it got wild and chaotic, well, that would be a definite understatement.

Sometime around two-thirty a.m., a group of party crashers came calling. A motorcycle gang called the Angels of Hades rolled in with no other agenda but to cause trouble.

There were five of them and after they parked their Indian bikes practically blocking the front entrance, they strutted down in front of the stage and took a table. More accurately, they took someone else's table, along with someone else's drinks. In fact they were helping themselves to anything and everything, including the women. Eugene at that time was in the back helping wash glasses, when Jimmy came rushing through the door to the kitchen.

"We've got problems, Gene!" Jimmy's excited voice cried out. Gene now realized there was no music coming from out front and didn't wait for an explanation from Jimmy. Instead Gene followed him right back through the door. Standing in front of the stage were two of the leather wearing weirdoes; one was forcing a young lady to dance against her will, while two others held back her date. Onstage the other two thugs were harassing the band. Folks were beginning to head for the exit. Gene's face turned an immediate shade of red from anger as he pulled off his apron, threw it on the floor, and marched toward the stage. From his peripheral vision he spotted Stanley and his boys heading for the same location. Gene yelled to Stan, "I've got this, buddy!" Stanley halted to Gene's request and watched his friend at work.

Eugene's first stop was at the thug forcing the girl to dance. He tapped the jerk on the shoulder and when he turned around Gene connected with a punch that immediately turned off the biker's lights, sending his limp body crashing to the floor. Without hesitation he went right after the other two. One took a swing and missed, but missing Gene would be a big mistake, because Eugene didn't miss back. One more punch and one less biker. The next biker danced around a bit with a knife he'd pulled from his boot, but he didn't last long either.

Gene discarded him right alongside the other pieces of crap. Watching from stage, the other hooligan was not amused at Eugene's dismantling of his little pretend, tough guy gang. He foolishly began taunting Gene from his high perch, apparently thinking he was safe.

Gene said nothing, just calmly walked over to the edge of the raised staged floor and with one quick swipe of this hand, knocked the loudmouth hood on his ass. He then pulled him forward and lugged him right up across his shoulders like a sack of flour. Gene walked right past Stanley and the boys, past the stunned patrons, past Hank at the front—who was on the phone to the police—to the large plate glass window. There he stopped and tossed old leather boy right on through. The thunderous noise of breaking glass seemed to last forever and still resonated even after the thud of the biker hitting the concrete. Gene, sensing he wasn't quite through taking out the trash, turned around to go after the last one standing, but was spared the labor. The last guy had managed to escape. Sometime during the finale he ran out and climbed aboard his cycle and was now fleeing the scene. Cheers from the crowd erupted, signaling the show was over. The band starting playing again, and Stan and the boys drug the three semiconscious thugs outside to await the police. The last customer left around six, but Eugene, Hank, Jimmy, and some of the help didn't make it out of there until noon. Exhausted, but jubilant, Hank was heard telling Eugene that all in all, the first night was a huge success. "That's an understatement!" Gene responded.

CHAPTER 37

Almost six weeks to the day after Katrina met with the doctor, two Soviet frigates began receiving their ominous cargo: a cache of nuclear weapons and delivery ordinance. They steamed away from the dock with a small escort of just one battleship, as not to draw attention. They cruised out to the open Bering Sea with a southern heading for a destination unknown. But they were not alone. Thousands of feet above them, charting their every move, were the U-2 reconnaissance planes. But the U.S. didn't totally own the sky either. The Soviets had heavy jet fighter patrols armed with intercept missiles at around thirty thousand feet, as their front line of defense against the U.S. bombers.

It was a sleepless marathon for all the people involved, but the Skunkworks program was beginning to pay dividends. Five years earlier, the United States would not have had the aeronautical or photographical technology to collect this detailed information—nor would they have been able to track down their enemies' doomsday devices.

Two U-2 planes and four pilots were involved with this mission, and they were exclusively flying in and out of Puerto Rico. The remaining planes were still flying the normal missions out of Area 51. There was never a moment when the Soviet ships were without spy planes above them. This particular mission was like none before. Instead of flying over a fixed target, snapping a few pictures on a high-tech camera, then heading back to base, the pilots circled their moving target, taking new photos every thirty minutes. Precise timing of these flights was paramount to the success of the mission. Key elements were now more important than ever. Because of the changed conditions—basically hovering over the target until the next plane was in position and still taking off and landing under the cloak of darkness, —fuel management was critical.

With normal missions there was enough allotted fuel left to circle over friendly skies until it was dark enough to descend and land. During Katrina's last two flights, she had to circle until dusk, which resulted in her engine burning out before gliding powerless to a landing.

Katrina and the other three pilots had been basically sleep-flying their missions. Their superiors at the CIA had been feeding them bennies and coffee, and the Lockheed engineers increased the flow of oxygen to the flight suits to help keep them awake. But there was only so much they could do. They were zombies and dangerously close to making a huge error because of it. Kat, most certainly was the worst of the three. She had not been taking the pills for fear of the damaging effects to her fetus. And just dealing with the normal energy-draining effects of pregnancy was beginning to take its toll.

Three hours was all Katrina had on the ground before climbing back in the seat and resuming her flights. She had been so exhausted that all she felt like doing was collapsing on her bed until receiving her wake-up call.

As she glided into base on the third of her particular sorties, she was thinking how wonderful it would be if tonight she had enough energy to take a hot bath and wash her hair. Just then something happened that broke her from her daydream. Somewhere around ten thousand feet she felt something warm fill her panties. "Oh no, not now!" she thought. With her heart racing, she quickly refocused and landed the plane. The thought of giving birth, especially to a premature child, shot adrenalin through her system. She was now in a survival mode and concerned exclusively for the health of her baby.

Just as soon as the ground crew had intercepted her jet, she began unplugging her survival tubes and harnesses. And just as the hangar doors closed behind her plane, she popped the canopy. Within seconds the ladder to the cockpit was connected and she was climbing down to the ground. Her deliberate urgency caught the attention of the handler at the bottom, prompting him to ask if she had to pee. Without delay she responded by tossing him her helmet and stating that *she just did*!

It was eleven o'clock at night, her water had broken, and she needed to get to the doctor. Seeing the base medic was not an option for her, nor was walking almost five miles to the doctor's house.

She couldn't have Gail come get her because she didn't have clearance and wouldn't be able to get six hundred feet from base without being arrested. She stopped in her tracks about ten feet from the jet, now in a total quandary for what her next move would be. From behind her came a delayed response of, "So what did you want me to do with this?" from the handler holding her helmet. Kat turned around to reply to the brash sergeant when she noticed a familiarity to his face. It was apparent he now recognized her too.

"Hey, Sergeant, do I know you?" she asked the now bashful subordinate, who stared down at the concrete floor.

"Yes, now I remember. You're the jackleg that was sent to pick me up at the bus stop and deliver me to Maxwell; instead all you wanted to do is look at my ass. By the way, where's your salute for a commanding officer, schmuck?" The sergeant knew she had him dead to right and she meant business. He quickly jumped to attention and gave her the requested salute. Kat started to walk away, then stopped again to ask him another question.

"Do you have clearance for a land vehicle, Sergeant?"

"Sure do," he responded.

"Then get it and get it now! You are going to take me for a little ride." He stood for a second longer than she liked, so she raised her voice. "WHAT PART OF THAT ORDER DON'T YOU UNDERSTAND, LIMP DICK!" His eyes flew open in surprise, then he bolted off and returned in minutes with a jeep. It was an effort, but Kat crawled in beside him and they were off. The sergeant didn't say a word; he just drove, responding only to her directions. They pulled up in front of the doctor's house. It was apparent by the lack of light that the doctor had retired for the evening. Kat instructed the chauffeur to run ahead and knock on his door. The sergeant didn't question her orders or hesitate, and did just that. It was a struggle for Kat to climb out of the jeep and up the walk to the doctor's door, but she did.

The sergeant's knocks were able to raise the good doctor and he met Kat before she got to the first step.

"I was expecting you, but not for a couple of weeks yet!" the doctor said. Katrina grimaced, then responded.

"I guess you were right, Doc, no sleep equals early delivery."

"Oh my God, are you going to have a baby?" The sergeant's first words since inside the hangar were laced with panic.

"Listen to me, son." The doctor spoke in a calm voice as he helped Kat up the steps of his porch. I want you to drive over to Ramey, to the base hospital, and ask for the nurse in charge. Her name is Gail; tell her that Doc Thomas needs her right away. It's regarding Katrina. Bring her back quickly, son!" The door was about to shut when Kat reached out to stop it momentarily, allowing her to yell out one more order.

"After you return with her, you are ordered to stay put and wait here for me. Understand, Sergeant?" He responded in a subservient manner with, "yes ma'am," and the door shut.

It couldn't have been twenty minutes before the jeep returned delivering Gail. Before it came to a complete stop, she jumped out and ran up the steps and into the house. Better than an hour passed for the sergeant as he sat waiting in the jeep, stretched out listening to the chirping tree frogs. Suddenly, the sound of the tiny chirping reptiles was replaced with the sound of a crying baby. The sergeant sat up in his seat trying to hear more detail, but would have to wait another thirty minutes to hear anything further. A shadowy figure appeared, slowly walking from the side of the house to his vehicle. It was Katrina, still zipping up her flight suit and looking like she had just been run over by a truck. Before he could speak, she told him to start up the jeep and hurry back to the base. He was concerned, but quickly obliged and they drove away. The sergeant broke from his egotistical, ignorant persona momentarily to actually show some concern for his commanding officer.

"Should you be doing this, so soon after giving birth?" Kat said nothing and stared forward.

He continued, but only after shifting back to his old character. "When I saw you back at the hangar, I thought to myself, *Man she's put on quite a few pounds since basic training.* I had no idea you had a bun in the oven." He chuckled and she had no response.

With no time to spare, the jeep arrived back at the hangar after clearing the multiple security check points. He rolled up about thirty feet from the U-2 plane and stood on the brakes, screeching the tires on the concrete floor. He jumped out and grabbed her helmet from the back seat and handed it to her. She took a deep breath and stepped out of the jeep. Using it to support herself, she slowly walked alongside, and then steadied her balance before letting go. Looking up at her intimidating black jet, she realized that in her condition there would be no way for her to negotiate the ladder. She looked over at the sergeant who must have been thinking the same thing. He laughed, walked over to the steel ladder, and helped her get her foot into the first rung. It took nearly ten minutes for both of them to get her into the cockpit, but they did. Tears were streaming down her cheeks as a result of the excruciatingly painful climb. The motion of moving her legs in such a fashion caused tremendous strain and tension to her female area—an area recently traumatized by giving birth and the ensuing stitched episiotomy.

Curious onlookers watched as the sergeant unconventionally helped Katrina access the spy plane. Kat thanked the sergeant for all his help and he climbed back down to let others deliver her orders, coordinates, and reconnect her to the aircraft. Soon, she was ready for flight, the canopy dropped, the giant hanger doors opened, the massive jet engine fired up, and she rolled out onto the tarmac. Within moments, she was airborne and vertical. As the fiery glow of her afterburner faded into the dark night sky, a small group of Skunkworks employees gathered on the tarmac to witness its departure. A voice was heard from one of the curious onlookers asking the sergeant what was wrong with Dragon Lady.

"Oh, nothing much, she just had a baby!" he cavalierly responded.

Lightning filled the sky below her as she flew above the North Pacific Ocean, heading toward the Bering Sea. According to her instruments and onboard radar she was very near the location of her counterpart flying an identical U-2 plane. The procedure would entail a Morse code signal being transmitted from her craft that would be intercepted by his. Once this interception was made the other plane would break from his mission and head home. Kat had just received his confirmation signal, so she knew it was time to start shooting footage. However, she was very well aware of the problem: there were heavy storms. Even their high tech sensitive imaging cameras would have a hard time picking up the naval convoy through the thick clouds.

Kat was very ill, nauseous and dizzy. She was extremely drained of energy and felt something running down her leg; she feared it was blood from loosened stitches caused when boarding the plane. More importantly, she was missing something. Not something tangible, something much more vital. She was suddenly experiencing a disability, her sixth sense that she had all her life, was gone. No visualizing of images in her mind, no voices, nothing. Was she not thinking straight because she was ill or had her brain somehow changed since giving birth? For the first time in her life she was lost. She had no idea what kind of pictures her counterpart had gotten during his so-called shift, but she knew what she must do to get hers. She also realized that this would be her last flight and she wanted to get the best reconnaissance she could. She needed to dive down into the clouds, but she didn't know when and for how long.

She took a deep breath, trying to bring in as much oxygen as she could to help her think straight. Finally, she constructed her plan. She knew that the Soviet radar systems would give her a window of about three minutes before detecting her. So she decided to do a series of dives down to just inside the radar detection zone that would last around two minutes, then climb back up. Her roller coaster plan, following the coordinates given by the CIA, surely would result in valuable images of the Soviet fleet.

She descended down twenty thousand feet, closer but still safe from detection. Then she dove another ten thousand feet, leveled for two minutes, squeezed off some shots, and climbed. No tracers below; she was safe and still undetected. This plan would work, she thought to herself. Fifteen minutes later she repeated the procedure with no detection. But this time, there was one problem: when she'd pulled hard for a steep climb, she must have blacked out. When she'd regained consciousness, she was at nearly seventy-five thousand feet, only a few thousand feet from a sure death. She would try it again, only this time she wouldn't climb so vertically, which meant pushing the detection limit. So she executed the different procedure, and after her descent she climbed up at a lesser degree of ascent. This exposed her for over three minutes, but there was still no tracer fire or missile trails. She must have found the right formula, she thought. She repeated the same plan over and over. Other than feeling deathly sick, she was having a successful night. Her worries, however, began to change; she felt at bigger risk of flying through the storm clouds—perhaps being struck by lightning and knocking out all her electronics—than being shot down by Commie missiles. She surely had enough close-ups, and if she hadn't photographed the ships at that altitude, they weren't there at all.

So it was one more descent for good measure, then back up at a safe altitude to wait for her relief signal.

LOUD NOISE!

WHITE!

CHAPTER 38

It was two a.m. in the morning and the phone was ringing. Pastor Browne was used to receiving phone calls in the middle of the night and they were never good. Point Marian only had two churches and two preachers, so he bore the responsibility of being there for his community whenever they needed him. The needs were usually weddings, funerals, or tragedies. Calls at that time of night were usually tragedies. He turned on the lamp by the phone and took a deep breath, preparing himself for what he was about to hear, lifting the receiver to his ear. "Hello."

"Mr. Browne." Blood shot to his head, as he wasn't ready to hear a familiar voice.

"Eugene? Is that you?"

"Sorry, sir, I know it's late, but have you talked to Katrina? I mean yesterday or today?" Gene had a clear concerning tone.

"No, son, it's actually been a few days. What's wrong?"

"I don't know, probably nothing and I'm sorry to wake you. It's just that I had this awful dream, and she usually calls every day, but it's been nearly two. I don't know how to get a hold of her. Ever since she left Hondo…" Gene never finished his sentence.

"Nonsense, son, we appreciate you for calling." By now Mrs. Browne had joined her husband.

"What's wrong, Mike? Is there something wrong with Katrina?" Mr. Browne put his hand on her shoulder.

"It's Eugene, dear," he said. "Eugene, Lisa and I had been very concerned about her too. We haven't heard from her in days. It's like she was slowly disappearing from our lives." Lisa Browne sighed, responding to her husband's comment over the phone. "She has not been home for months; her letters stopped coming and now her calls," Mr. Browne said.

"I haven't seen her in months either, sir. I don't even know where she is or what she is doing."

"You'd mentioned a bad dream, Eugene. Can you share?

"It was Katrina telling me she loved me." Gene hesitated before continuing. "Then she told me goodbye."

They agreed to resume their conversation again in the morning. Both decided to make some calls, starting with one to the air force.

Needless to say, neither the Brownes nor Eugene could sleep and dawn seemed slow to arrive. Eugene's first call was not to Hondo Air Base, but to Jimmy. He was surprised when Jimmy actually answered the phone on the first ring. Jimmy resided in a house with three other guys and Gene assumed all would still be sleeping.

"Oh, Gene, it's just you!" replied Jimmy. "Sorry, I was hoping it was Kat. I had this weird dream last night!"

"Jimmy, you weren't the only one to have a weird dream. I'm really worried; I've got this horrible feeling in my gut." The boys talked for almost an hour, comparing ideas regarding her whereabouts and where to start tracking her down.

Eugene, as well as the Brownes, made calls to Hondo, and then backtracked to Lackland, but the answer was the same: her whereabouts was classified. Gene even asked for Gail, but they refused to give him any information other than she was no longer stationed at Lackland.

The Brownes, Eugene, and Jimmy were all conducting their own investigations, then calling each other to compare notes. They were helplessly waiting by the phone, anticipating the call that would answer their prayers. But the voice on the other end was never Kat's. The days came and went and nothing. The only smidgen of reassurance that they clung to was the fact that they knew her missions were top secret and perhaps she was not permitted to contact anyone. For that reason they held out hope.

By the end of the second week, the entire community of Point Marion knew that Katrina was potentially missing and were praying for her to call.

The third week brought the most disturbing development to date. Suddenly the response from the air force changed from not knowing where Kat was, to not having a record of Katrina Garretson ever being in the air force.

That's when Fred Briggs got more involved. It was now time

to use his influence. Working for the Bureau of Mines, he had a lot of political contacts in Congress as well as high within the Eisenhower administration. After several more weeks of prodding and pleading, he was finally able to find the right congressman with a connection in the Pentagon. Finally some internal investigations and a special intimate meeting were set up.

The Brownes drove to Fairfax, Virginia, where they met Eugene and Fred, and from there they all drove over to the Pentagon.

The congressman met them at the main gate and escorted them into the building where they received credentials that allowed them deep into the corridors of the massive building. Finally, after trekking down a long hall, they arrived at a large, double glass door. The name of the office, indicated with large block lettering, was the Central Intelligence Agency. The congressman opened the door but remained in the hallway. He told them that this was the end of the line for him, wished them luck, and invited them to go on in, that they were expected. Mr. Briggs shook his hand and thanked him, as did Mr. and Mrs. Browne, and then they all walked through the door.

A prim but cordial woman approached them with a smile as soon as they stepped into the room. She confirmed their names, asked if she could get them something to drink, and then escorted them into a plush conference room, where they sat in front of a large table. Within a couple of minutes, a distinguished gentleman wearing a black suit entered. He was carrying a large cardboard box which he sat on the table in front of them. Behind him followed the woman, who was also carrying a large box. She sat it beside the other, turned, and let herself out of the room, closing the door behind her. The man approached the table and momentarily smiled before introducing himself.

He had a long title that preceded his name that meant absolutely nothing to the worried eyes that stared back. It was apparent that he was uncomfortable with what he was about to say, and his demeanor spoke a thousand words.

Mrs. Browne, who had been holding up until now, began to unravel and shrank into her husband's arms.

"Our Katrina's gone, isn't she, sir?" Mr. Browne's voice cracked as he put his arms around his sobbing wife. Eugene pushed his chair back, stood up, and walked over to the corner of the room, bracing himself for what he was about to hear.

"I'm so very sorry." The man stood at attention as if to deliver a well-rehearsed speech. "On behalf of the Central Intelligence Agency, the United States Air Force, and the Federal Government of the United States of America, I am deeply saddened to announce the death of Lieutenant Katrina Garretson. She passed away as a hero serving her country honorably and courageously."

Eugene furiously pounded the wall with his fist screaming, "No, no!" Emotions erupted in the room.

Even though they were prepared to hear the worst, the unbearable words coming from the man's mouth were like cold, steel daggers driving deep into their hearts.

"That was the official and prepared condolence speech which I never get used to delivering," the man said. "But off the record, I am terribly sorry that this dire news has taken over two months to convey. Please let me explain the situation. Katrina was honorably discharged from the air force and transitioned into the CIA. I cannot go into any detail, but she was involved in highly top secret and convert operations for which she performed at the highest standards. Trust me when I say you should be very proud.

"Upon confirmation of her passing it took several weeks to filter that information back through several layers of military and governmental bureaucracy. In other words, each layer had to confirm her death.

"As per regulation, because of her particular clandestine status with the agency, upon death, all her records were removed from the general file system.

"The other problem was her records. She was shown to be an orphan and all the emergency notification information lines were left blank. That was very odd! If you had not came forward, her records would have been archived and her memories probably lost forever."

The man then left them alone, giving them plenty of time to compose themselves before leaving. They huddled around Pastor Browne and he led them in prayer, reminding them that their faith and trust in God would get them through this, just as it had in the past. He also pointed out, as painful as this was for them; it was a joyous time for Katrina. She would now be joining her mother and father and grandmother in heaven. He asked them to try and reflect on that; it would help get them through this.

CHAPTER 39

Katrina's memorial service was held a week later in Point Marion. Red ribbons were tied around the trees in front of almost every house in town. A World War II veteran from Pittsburg played taps and Kat was given a military gun salute by the local VFW. The actual service lasted only forty minutes and was very emotional. Jimmy and Eugene struggled through the eulogy, recalling scenes from their youth. Pastor Browne had a difficult time as well, but found the strength he needed to recite the following.

"Flesh and blood is only temporary but one's soul remains eternal. Our memories of the wonderful times we shared on earth with Katrina will remain with us until all our souls are together again in the kingdom of heaven."

Everyone was invited back to the Browne's after the ceremony, but Eugene and Jimmy had a different agenda; they elected to visit the rock instead. On the walk over, they both recalled the times they'd read her silly letters and how they always felt her presence, even when she wasn't there. Almost simultaneously, they pulled from their pockets her most recent literary correspondence and felt that reading them on this day was by far the most appropriate thing they could do. They climbed up and took their normal spots, leaving an empty space in between, where Kat used to sit. Jimmy pulled out an old six penny nail he had brought with him and carved, *WE LOVE YOU, KAT!* Eugene had no idea what his friend was scratching out until it was completed, but when he read it, he broke down. Eugene was planning on telling his friend of his secret marriage to Katrina, but when he saw what Jimmy had carved, he couldn't bring himself to do it. He always felt that Jimmy loved her just as deeply as he did and telling him this information now would serve no positive purpose. After several minute of silence, Jimmy decided to continue their tradition, in hopes of lightening up the mood. He unfolded his letter.

"I'll go first," Jimmy said.

Just as he was about to start, they were interrupted by Eugene's kid sister, Mary Lou, yelling at the top of her lungs.

"Eugene, come home quick, there's someone here waiting to see you!"

Mary Lou arrived at the rock out of breath, but was still able to get out her message.

"Come on, she's waiting and she's got a baby!" Gene turned to Jimmy and they both jumped up.

"Who's got a baby?" Mary never replied; she'd done her job by delivering the message and now was running back. Gene and Jimmy pursued, following her back home.

Mary arrived back at the Briggs' home a good two or three

minutes ahead of her brother and Jimmy. Sitting on the sofa was Gail, and beside her sat Ertta, holding a tiny baby. Gene was so surprised, he yelled out her name. Gail jumped up and met Gene in the middle of the room. They hugged, then she began to cry. She felt awful about missing the memorial service and asked Eugene if he could take her and the baby over to meet the Brownes. Eugene was so involved with Gail that he'd completely forgotten about the baby. So he walked over to Ertta to get a better view.

"Okay, Gail, when are you going to introduce us to your little friend?" Gail walked over to Gene and put her hand on his shoulder.

"Would you like to hold her while I introduce her?" Both Eugene and Ertta looked at Gail with a puzzled look, because her voice quivered and now a tear was rolling down her cheek.

"Are you alright, dear?" Ertta asked.

"I knew this would be hard," Gail said. With tears now streaming from her eyes, Gail looked up at the ceiling and said, "Can you help me out a little with this, Kat?" With that statement, everyone in the room including Mary, Fred, and Jimmy were all suddenly fixated on what Gail was going to say next.

Gail held out her arms and Ertta handed her the baby. She kissed it on the forehead, then looked up at Eugene and said, "Eugene, meet your daughter, Chloe!

For a moment, everyone in the room stopped breathing. Eugene immediately sat down and Ertta nearly fainted in her chair. Everyone else was paralyzed.

Nervous and emotional, Gail continued.

"This beautiful little baby girl is Katrina's final gift to you, Eugene." Eugene's eyes began to water as he reached out and received his daughter. An immediate glow radiated from his face and a smile took shape.

"Kat loved the name Chloe," Gene said in a subdued voice. "She always said if she ever had a little girl, that's what she would name her." Gene's eyes were fixated on the sleeping baby. Gail sat down beside him on the sofa, followed by Jimmy and Mary. Fred took a spot next to Ertta.

"How? I had no idea," Gene stammered.

"I know you didn't. She told me she couldn't tell you. Kat was so devoted and dedicated to her country, she felt it was her duty to finish her mission. She was afraid you would have tried to stop her. The guilt was tearing her up inside too." Gail stood up and walked over to her purse, sitting on the end table. She reached in and pulled out an envelope, then walked back.

"She gave me this letter to give to you just in case she didn't get the chance to tell you in person." Gail looked down at the floor and shook her head. "She told me she tried to explain in the letter her motives. She wasn't sorry for her decisions, but she asked for your understanding and prayed someday that you'd forgive her." Gail began sobbing. Ertta directed Mary to bring Gail a box of tissues, than she moved over beside the young woman. She put her arm around Gail and Fred brought her a glass of water. After Gail recomposed herself, she told the entire story from when she first ran into Kat on the beach in Puerto Rico, to the events of the late night delivery. She explained how Kat had snuck out and left after pretending she was asleep. That was the last time Gail ever saw Kat.

"I didn't know what to think. She never came back. I feared the worst, but no one could help us. My doctor friend and I drove over to where she said her secret base was, but were met with armed marines telling us to leave immediately. I went to my superiors at the base; they had no information whatsoever about a Katrina Garretson." We even called the police and filled out a missing person's report. I had all my friends searching the islands, but nothing.

"I knew I had to notify the Brownes that she was missing, and more importantly, I had to get Chloe to you. It took me weeks to get any information. Finally some good soul from records called me back after they'd received a notice of her passing and of the memorial. The card had an attached address. So I took my leave, packed up Chloe, hitched a ride on a transport, rented a car, and here we are." Gail took a drink of water and continued. "All she wanted was to complete her mission for her country, then retire with her husband—who she loved with all her heart—and raise their new baby."

Gail's collective audience immediately looked at Eugene and said in unison, "Husband!" Gene nervously responded, "We planned on re-marrying in a church once she retired."

"That's what she said!" Gail laughed, then changed subjects and reminisced about the special night. "I was so lucky to be there to help in the delivery. You should have seen her face. She was so happy. We both started crying!" Gail paused momentarily to gather her thoughts. "After Doc slapped the baby to life, I handed it to Kat. I wish I'd had a camera. Doc asked what name she wanted on the birth certificate, and without hesitation she replied, 'Chloe Marie Briggs.'" Gene stood up with Chloe and extended his free hand to Gail.

"Come on, Gail, let's take my baby daughter down to the Brownes to meet her other grandparents."

"God indeed has sent us a miracle!" Pastor Mike Browne said with a smile when he met Chloe. "God took our daughter, but gave us a granddaughter!"

And there was another new addition to the Browne and Briggs families: her name was Gail. She stayed for two more weeks, splitting her time staying at both homes. Everyone fell in love with her; she was treated just like a daughter and was made godmother of Chloe. Gail remained close to both families and for years after would fly to Point Marion to be a part of all of Chloe's special childhood events.

Gail finished her career as a nurse in the air force and retired with the rank of captain. She married the good doctor and remained in Puerto Rico until dying of cancer in 1975.

With the help of kid sister Mary Lou and Ertta, Eugene and Chloe moved back to the cabin in Fairfax. The Briggs women and Lisa Browne would alternate staying with them and helping.

Eugene ended up buying out Hank's shares in the Roadhouse and paid back Uncle Gregg within a year. The club was a goldmine and quickly developed a renowned status as being the place to perform; they sold out every weekend. However, it became a strain on the new dad, running a nightclub and raising a child. So he sold it three years later to a famous country and western star, and father and daughter moved back to Point Marion.

Eugene bought and restored the old Garretson place (Katrina's old home), and he and Chloe made that their residence. He started a small construction company and remarried two years later to a retired actress that he'd met during his short NFL career.

Fred and Ertta end up moving to Saint Petersburg, Florida, after he retired. Delbert became a CPA, married his childhood sweetheart, and moved back in his childhood home.

Mary Lou attended a small college in Northern Pennsylvania, graduated, and joined the Peace Corps. She spent most of her young life volunteering or as a missionary before she finally married and settled down near her folks in St. Petersburg.

After eight years of formal education, Jimmy took a job at a hospital in Pittsburg. He became a prominent surgeon and was married and divorced four times.

More than a decade after Kat's heroic service, Eugene received a conduct medal and plaque given by the director of the CIA. Accompanying the hardware was a letter drafted and signed by the director of the CIA and the president of the United States. The letter recognized Katrina's contribution in the Cold War. A handwritten note at the bottom from the director stated that Lieutenant Garrison played a large role in the reconnaissance that contributed to the United States being able to defuse the Cuban missile threat.

CHAPTER 40

The morning sunlight flickered through the leaves of the trees, creating a natural kaleidoscope. It was enhanced ever so slightly by the southern Pennsylvanian breeze moving the porous canopies of green; just enough to provide access for the solar rays to meet the ground below. The beauty of this spring morning would not be upstaged by the symphonic sounds of chirping birds, along with the muffled roar of the Monongahela River as it introduced itself to the mouth of the Cheat River.

The year was 1963 and three figures were walking through the woods carrying a picnic basket and heading for a large rock.

"I'm glad you're coming with us today, Uncle Jimmy," a sweet little voice said.

"I wouldn't think of being anywhere else in the world today, Punkin'!" Jimmy leaned over, picking up Chloe and placing her on his shoulders. When they arrived at the rock, Chloe asked if she could go play while they were getting ready.

"Okay, sweetheart," Gene said, "but don't wander away too far. Your uncle Jimmy and I will spread out the tablecloth on the rock, unload the picnic basket, and we'll be ready to eat." She agreed and ran off, singing and skipping. Gene and Jimmy crawled up on the rock, sat, and gazed out over the river valley.

"Thanks, Jimmy, for taking a little time out of your day to go on our Mother's Day picnic."

Jimmy laughed. "You make a great mom, Gene! You know I was always jealous that Kat chose you over me, but now I know she made the right decision."

"You know, I think that's the nicest thing you ever said to me, Jimmy."

"I was way too smart for her anyway." Jimmy looked over at Gene and winked.

Gene laughed. "Now that's the Jimmy I know! Let's get this picnic underway." Gene stood up and yelled for Chloe. After the third call, she responded,

"Coming, Daddy." Chloe came into sight, still singing and skipping, but this time she was swirling something over her head.

"What is that red thing she's got?" Jimmy asked.

"It looks like a ribbon. It looks like one of her mother's, but how did she. . . ?"

"What's that, Punkin?" Jimmy asked as she arrived at the rock.

"It's a red ribbon, silly head." Chloe giggled. Eugene was waiting for her on the ground and lifted her up onto the rock.

"May I see it, sweetheart?" Gene asked.

"Sure, Daddy."

"Where did you get this?"

"I got it out there." Chloe pointed.

"That's odd. Was it lying on the ground or something?" Eugene asked.

"No, Daddy, Mommy gave it to me!"

THE END

-At least for now

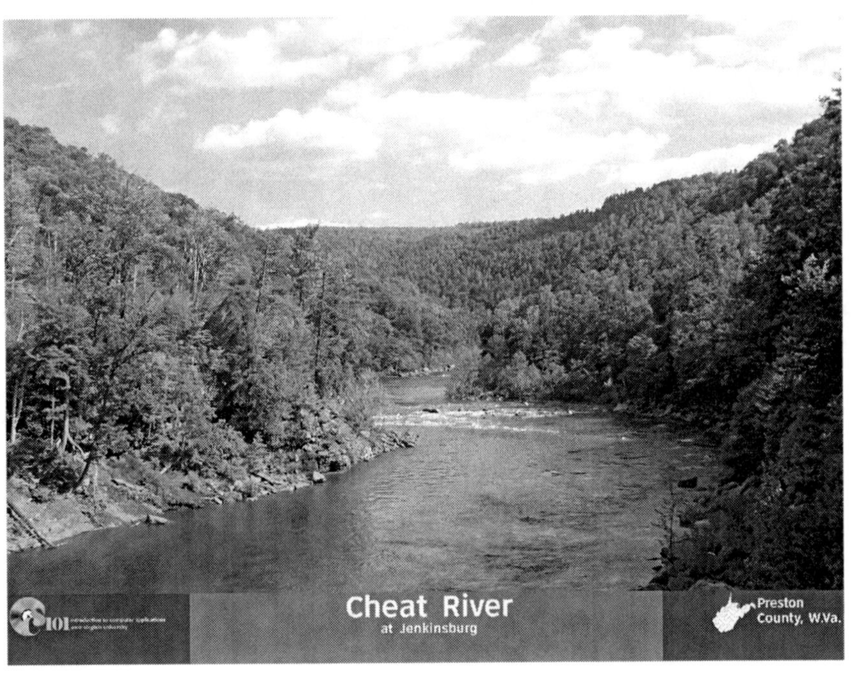
101
Cheat River
at Jenkinsburg
Preston
County, W.Va.

Photographs by Nannette Russel

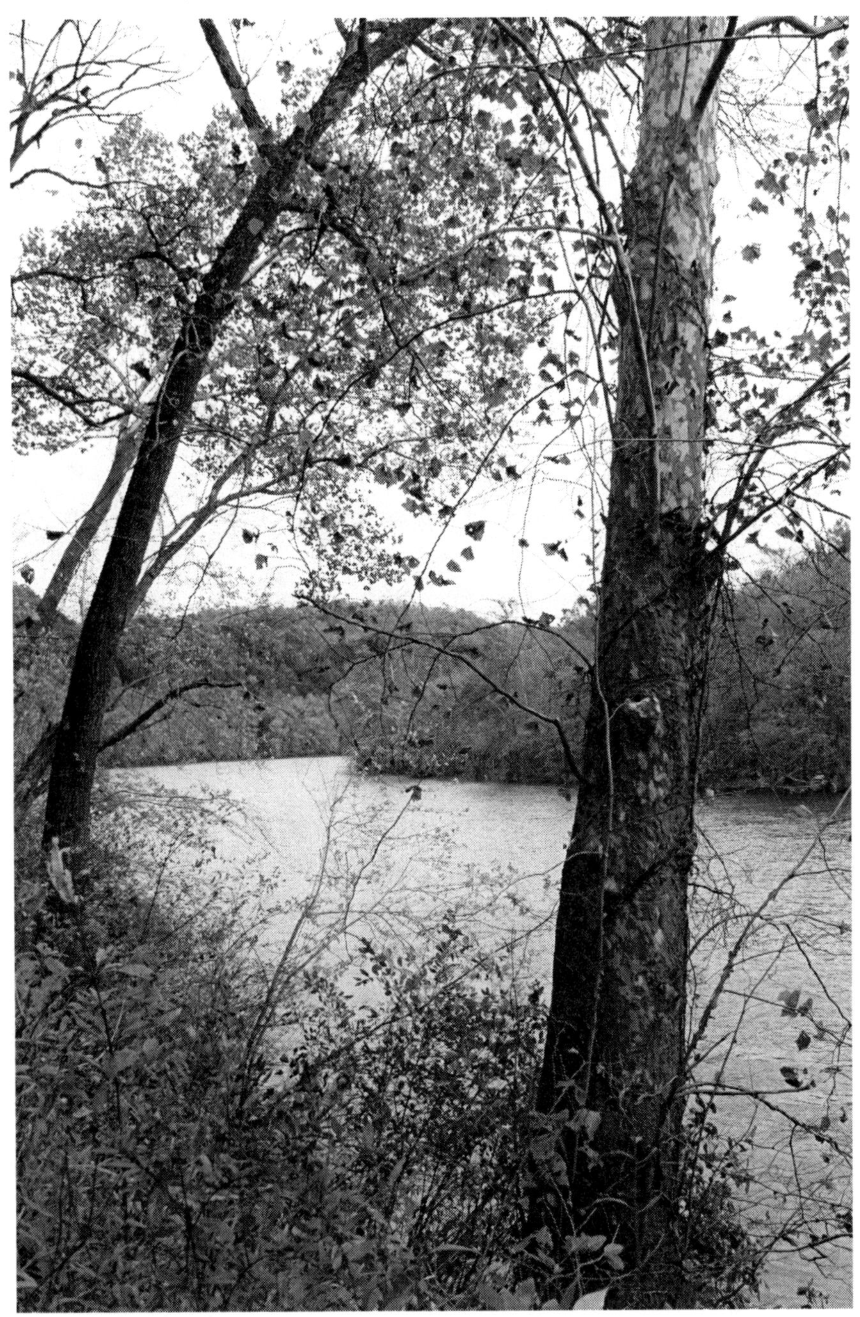

CPSIA information can be obtained at www.ICGtesting.com
Printed in the USA
LVOW081410150212

268836LV00001BA/2/P